W9-BZE-113

It was very peaceful to be lost inside the maze. The tall hedges made the enclosure into a green, leafy room, with a grass carpet and bright blue ceiling of sky. Kate tilted her head back and watched a bird wing its way swiftly through the air.

"Do you think the others are still lost?" Kate asked. "Or did they find their way out and then leave us here?"

"It doesn't really matter, does it?" he replied. "After all, we're not lost."

She leaned over to look into his face, her eyebrows raised. "Actually," she said, "we are."

"Speak for yourself." He smiled up at her. "I'm just where I want to be."

THE
Juliet Club

SUZANNE HARPER

Greenwillow Books
An Imprint of HarperCollins*Publishers*

I would like to gratefully acknowledge and thank Giulio Tamassia, who was delegated president of Il Club di Giulietta (the Juliet Club) by the mayor of Verona, and Juliet's secretaries (especially Elena Marchi). They welcomed me to Verona, answered dozens of questions, shared letters from their files, and in many other ways gave generously of their time as I was researching this book. I would also like to thank Lois Adams, Deborah Barnes, Bill Boedeker, Laaren Brown, Chris Ceraso, Sarah Cloots, Virginia Duncan, Steve Geck, Bretta Lundell, Martha Mihalick, Anneclaire Nelson, Dan Renkin, Barbara Trueson, Mitchell Waters, and Paul Zakris for their support and help.

This book is a work of fiction. References to real people, events, establishments, organizations, or locales are intended only to provide a sense of authenticity, and are used to advance the fictional narrative. All other characters, and all incidents and dialogue, are drawn from the author's imagination and are not to be construed as real.

The Juliet Club
Copyright © 2008 by Suzanne Harper

All rights reserved. No part of this book may be used or reproduced in any manner whatsoever without written permission except in the case of brief quotations embodied in critical articles and reviews. Printed in the United States of America. For information address HarperCollins Children's Books, a division of HarperCollins Publishers, 10 East 53rd Street, New York, NY 10022.
www.harperteen.com

The text of this book is set in 12-point Cochin.
Book design by Paul Zakris

Library of Congress Cataloging-in-Publication Data

Harper, Suzanne.
The Juliet club / by Suzanne Harper.
p. cm.
"Greenwillow Books."
Summary: When high school junior Kate wins an essay contest that sends her to Verona, Italy, to study Shakespeare's "Romeo and Juliet" over the summer, she meets both American and Italian students and learns not just about Shakespeare, but also about star-crossed lovers—and herself.
ISBN 978-0-06-136691-8 (trade bdg.) — ISBN 978-0-06-136692-5 (lib. bdg.) — ISBN 978-0-06-136693-2 (pbk.)
[1. Interpersonal relations—Fiction. 2. Shakespeare, William, 1564–1616 Romeo and Juliet—Fiction. 3. Letters—Fiction. 4. Verona (Italy)—Fiction.
5. Italy—Fiction.] I. Title.
PZ7.H23197Ju 2008 [Fic]—dc22 2007041315

   12 13 14 CG/RRDH 10 9 8 7 6 5 4

First Greenwillow paperback edition, 2010.

For Mitchell Waters

THE
Juliet Club

Prologue

"Which one of Johnny Burwell's eyebrows do you think is cuter?" Sarah asked. Her light brown bangs fell into her eyes as she tilted her head meaningfully at a boy sitting two tables away in the school cafeteria. "Don't look!"

"Don't be ridiculous," her friend Annie snapped, right before she swiveled around to take a long, hard, deliberate look. She narrowed her eyes, then said, "Hmm. That's actually a *very* difficult question."

"At least you have a fifty-fifty chance of getting it right," Kate murmured, refusing to even glance over. She gave a deep, rather pointed sigh, which was completely ignored.

"The right," Annie finally decided. "I like the way

it goes up when he says something sarcastic."

"Oh, I hadn't thought about that," Sarah said, interested. "Now, *I* would have said the left, because it has that funny little tilt to it, but you do have a point—"

"Oh, *please*." Kate took an annoyed bite of her sandwich. Sarah, Annie, and Kate had become fast friends on the first day of second grade and then spent the next nine years talking about everything from the meaning of life to the meaning of mascara. But today Kate was most definitely not in the mood to discuss eyebrows, or the relative cuteness factor thereof.

"Can we talk about something else, please?" she said. "*Anything* else?"

"Like what?" Annie asked innocently. She was of the opinion—often stated and never successfully refuted—that Kate was only slightly less serious than a Supreme Court judge. "Emily Dickinson's poetry? Quantum mechanics? The Constitutional Convention of 1787?"

"Come on," Kate protested. "Just because I don't want to write sonnets in praise of Johnny Burwell's left eyebrow—"

"I don't want to write a sonnet about it." Sarah sighed dreamily. "I just want to sit in silent contemplation of it."

"I know. I saw you contemplating it all through algebra class."

"You have to admit, Kate, that it *is* a very nice eyebrow."

"And you have to admit, Sarah, that you *are* failing algebra."

"I've never met anyone as practical as you, Kate," Annie said. "It's really rather terrifying."

Sarah nodded in agreement. "And *that* is all your mother's fault." After a moment, she added, in the spirit of fairness, "And your father's, too, of course, but in a completely different way."

"Absolutely," Annie agreed. She had recently developed a unifying theory of the universe that boiled down to one indisputable fact: Everything that was wrong in her life could be traced back to her parents. This theory had proved so satisfactory that she was now attempting to apply it to everyone else's lives as well. "And, of course, when you factor in what *Jerome* did to you—"

Kate shot her a look that stopped her in midsentence. She wasn't ready to talk about Jerome, think about Jerome, or even accept the fact that Jerome was still alive and breathing on the same planet as she was.

"Well. Anyway." Annie quickly went back to her

first point. "With parents like yours, it's no wonder that you're so . . . *unromantic*."

And when Kate thought about this, she found she couldn't disagree.

When Kate was eleven years old, her parents had divorced. She was sad, of course, but hardly surprised. The only puzzle was what had taken them so long.

After all, her mother and father disagreed about everything: whether to squeeze the toothpaste in the middle of the tube or from the end, whether to let dishes soak overnight or wash them immediately, whether to pay bills as soon as they arrived or designate one day of the month to write out checks.

And they were polar opposites in the one area that really counts: love.

Her father was a heart-on-his-sleeve Romantic (with a capital R), while her mother was a cool and controlled Rationalist (also with a capital R; neither of them did anything by halves).

Her father was a Shakespeare scholar with a tendency to launch into sudden long orations on the genius of The Bard; her mother was a law professor whose precisely reasoned arguments could reduce law students, opposing counsel, and tardy plumbers to tears.

Her father cried at Hallmark commercials and any movie in which True Love Triumphs. Her mother preferred documentaries on the History Channel, which never made her cry, not even when the barbarians conquered all of known civilization.

Her father thought Valentine's Day was the most important holiday of the year. Her mother thought Valentine's Day was a capitalistic ploy to get people to amass major credit card debt on chocolates, champagne, and flowers.

Kate often wondered how they ever got together in the first place. When asked, her father would hum a few bars of "Why Do Fools Fall in Love?" and then change the subject. Her mother would offer a more scientific, but no more helpful, answer. "There is a natural law that states that, given enough time, the impossible becomes possible, the possible probable, and the probable virtually certain," she would say. Then she would peer over the top of her glasses and add, "Thus the dodo bird. And my marriage to your father."

For six years after the divorce, Kate spent weekdays with her mother and weekends with her father. She split summer vacations neatly in two between the second and third weeks of July. She opened presents on Christmas Eve with her mother (who liked sleeping in) and on Christmas morning with her father (who thought that only the dim light of dawn offered the appropriate sense of mystery).

For six years, Kate listened as her mother pointed out the foolishness of people made giddy with romance. If they happened to see a teenaged couple entwined in the park, her mother would shake her head and say something like, "That girl should be studying for her finals." She would usually say it in a voice calculated to be heard by the girl in question. Kate would blush, grab her mom's arm, and drag her away as quickly as possible.

If her father saw that same couple, he would start declaiming, in an embarrassingly loud and enthusiastic voice, "I know a bank whereon the wild thyme blows, Where ox-lips and the nodding violet grows; Quite over-canopied with luscious woodbine, With sweet musk-roses, and with eglantine." People would stare. Some of them would snicker. And Kate would blush, grab her dad's arm, and drag him away as quickly as possible.

For six years, Kate moved back and forth between these two households, alike in dignity but divided by major philosophical differences about whether the heart should rule the head or vice versa.

Her friends hadn't been much help. Sarah always

got crushes on boys who didn't know she existed, and consequently had become quite skilled at Yearning From Afar. Annie, on the other hand, was like Attila the Hun when it came to romance. Pale, stuttering boys were always falling for her and then wilting as she broke their hearts with ruthless abandon.

Neither option seemed appealing to Kate, who held herself apart from the romantic fray in a way that her friends found most irritating.

"Just wait," Sarah had told her. "Just wait until *you* fall in love! It will happen, *boom*, just like that! Like an earthquake or an explosion or a lightning bolt! *Then* you'll see!"

"It sounds dangerous," Kate had said. "And painful."

"The danger is what makes it fun," Annie had said, her blue eyes sparkling.

"Don't listen to her," Sarah had said reassuringly. "True love makes you feel like—well, like every day is spring!"

Annie had pretended to gag.

"Thanks, but no thanks," said Kate, who had been adding a few items to her to-do list during this conversation. She capped her pen with an air of finality.

Sarah and Annie had exchanged a meaningful look.

"Well," Annie had murmured, in a knowing tone that Kate found quite irritating. "We shall see."

"No," Kate had said with great finality. "You won't."

Which was why her friends had been understandably delighted when Kate, most unexpectedly, fell in love.

Of course, Kate being Kate, she managed to fall in love in a clear-sighted, practical, down-to-earth way that Annie and Sarah found less than satisfactory.

It happened in science lab on the very first day of their junior year. The chemistry teacher had handed her a beaker of some mysterious liquid and told her to carry it to her lab table. She had almost reached her seat when Jerome Hollis caught her eye and smiled. She blushed and tripped over her own feet. He plucked the beaker from her hands as she fell, then helped her stand up.

"Thanks," she said breathlessly.

"For what?" He handed the flask back and her heart gave a little flip. He had straight black hair, hazel eyes, and black-framed glasses. He looked cute, in a nerdy-but-hip kind of way.

She tried to collect herself. "For saving me from a horrible, disfiguring scar, of course," she said. "After all, if I had been splashed with this, um—" She gingerly held the flask aloft.

"Saline solution," he said. "Otherwise known as salt water. You would have been fine."

"Oh." She put the flask down and looked away.

"Although," he added thoughtfully, "if you *had* dropped the beaker, the gravitational force and speed of descent would have meant that it would have, in all probability, shattered."

Kate glanced back at him. "The force could have sent a shard of glass into my eye, blinding me," she suggested.

"Or cut a vein, causing a massive loss of blood. When you take all the disastrous possibilities into account—"

"You should be given a medal for heroism," Kate finished.

"I can't believe they're not pinning it on my shirt right now." He smiled, and she was lost.

If Kate had believed in fate (although she didn't; in fact, she believed most emphatically in controlling her own destiny), it would have seemed that higher forces were at work when she discovered that they had been assigned to the same lab table, and that they were both taking Spanish, and that they had the same lunch period. A few weeks later, he asked her to go to the Halloween dance. After that, Kate and Jerome were officially a Couple.

They studied together for hours (neither of them had ever missed making the honor roll; they shared a mutual horror at the very thought). They had long discussions on a number of political and social issues (they were both pro-environment and anti-fur, and had agreed to disagree on whether globalization would turn out to be a good thing or not). Together, they joined the debate team (and found that spirited arguments were quite enjoyable when the subject had no personal meaning whatsoever). And they both agreed that the only way to truly be in a relationship was to commit to being straightforward and honest with each other (at all times, no matter the cost).

When Kate rather complacently reported all this to Sarah and Annie, she was disappointed by their reaction.

"He sounds great," Sarah had said, with little conviction.

"He sounds *worthy*," Annie corrected her. "And sensible," she added, in the most damning tone possible.

"Exactly! That's why we're perfect for each

other." Kate had said that more emphatically than she had meant to, because she had been wondering, just a tiny bit, if this was what romance was supposed to feel like. Especially after Jerome, in a self-congratulatory mood, told her that their relationship was what any chemistry textbook would define as "steady state." (When she looked this up on the Internet, she had not found the definition reassuring.) "Anyway, what's wrong with worthy?" Kate went on. "Or sensible, for that matter?"

"Nothing," Annie had shrugged. "It just doesn't sound like much . . . *fun*."

Kate knew enough not to take this bait. Instead, she changed the subject and reflected complacently that some people just couldn't understand a truly *evolved* relationship.

For Christmas, he gave her a gold ring with a little ruby—actually, more like a ruby chip, but it was the thought that counted. Kate invited him to the Valentine's Day dance; he invited her to the prom. And Kate enjoyed the smug sensation that, unlike her parents, her friends, and apparently everyone else in the known universe, *she* had this love thing all figured out.

But then, on a beautiful spring morning in early May, Jerome called Kate on the phone to tell her three things in rapid succession: He wanted to break up with her, he would like her to return the ring with the little ruby (*definitely* just a chip), and he was going to the prom with Ashley Lawson (also known among Kate, Sarah and Annie as the Practically Perfect Ashley Lawson, thanks to her shining black hair, sparkling blue eyes, and intimidating fashion sense). The fact that the Practically Perfect Ashley Lawson was everything that Jerome had said he didn't want — frivolous, flighty, and shallow — only made matters worse.

"I don't understand," Kate said. "It doesn't make any sense! What could they possibly have to talk about?"

Annie had sighed, a world-weary sigh that said that Kate had so, so much to learn about the ways of men. "Maybe," she pointed out, "he's not interested in *talking* to her."

"Don't worry," Sarah said. "There are plenty of other fish in the sea, so you just have to get right back on the horse and kiss a lot of frogs in order to find your prince!"

But after being betrayed in such a cold, uncaring, thoughtless, treacherous, traitorous, downright cruel manner, Kate had decided that, when it came to love, it was far better to retire from the field of battle altogether.

Kate took a despondent bite of her chicken sandwich. It tasted like sand.

She mournfully nibbled a carrot stick. It tasted like plastic.

She pushed her food away and watched as Annie began rummaging irritably through her own lunch bag, muttering under her breath. "Tofu and eggplant and bean sprouts." (Annie's mother was a committed vegetarian.) "Gross." She opened another Baggie. "And a tuna sandwich! The last time I checked, tuna fish were living creatures! Not only is this lunch tasteless, but it's internally inconsistent! It fails on every count!"

"If you would just pack your own lunch—" Sarah began.

"No, this is more fun," Annie said, calming down. She began picking every bit of celery out of her tuna salad. "I enjoy destruction."

Kate sighed and shifted her gaze to the window. She could see their reflections in the glass, darkened by the gloomy sky and rain outside. The watery images of her friends made them seem both familiar and subtly different. Sarah was opening her lunch bag with a look of delighted anticipation on her round face (her mother was a chef for a catering company, which meant delicious leftovers). Annie had just run an impatient hand through her hair, so it stood up in reddish spikes all over her head, and was wrinkling her nose at an organic apple. Kate, as usual, looked neat as a pin: Her shoulder-length hair, the color of dark honey, was precisely braided, her brown eyes looked smart and serious behind gold-framed glasses, and her white cotton shirt and khaki pants were crisply pressed. She nodded at her image, pleased.

"If you're quite finished admiring yourself, Miss Sanderson—" Annie's acerbic voice broke in on her thoughts. Embarrassed, Kate made a face at her friend. Annie made a face back, then squinted at Kate with a critical eye. "I thought you were going to do something with your hair."

"I did. I braided it."

Annie didn't even bother to respond.

"It would look so nice if you wore it loose," Sarah chimed in. "Maybe you should have some highlights put in? Or try hair extensions? Or get a perm?"

"No, no, and no," Kate said, exasperated. "Too much work, too much money, too much bother." She didn't mention what they all knew—that when she was dating Jerome, she had been quite smug about the fact that he said he loved her just the way she was, and that he had then dumped her for a girl who spent half her life getting beauty treatments.

Men were deceivers ever, Kate thought, choking down another bite of sandwich. Yet another point that William Shakespeare got exactly right—

Then Sarah cried, "Oh no, look who just came in!"

Kate turned.

It was Jerome, laughing as he sat down with a group of friends halfway across the room.

Kate whipped her head back around and stared down at the table, blinking.

"I'm soooo sorry." Sarah's voice oozed with sympathy.

Kate knew she meant well, but still she gritted her teeth with irritation. "That's perfectly all right. It doesn't bother me at all to see Jerome. In fact, I have decided that the entire experience of dating him, even though it turned out to be a waste of time on one level, has actually, on another level, taught me a very valuable lesson."

"The importance of knowing five ways to kill a person without being caught?" Annie suggested.

"It taught me," Kate replied, "that romance is merely an illusion. On one level, it seems real, but on a higher, more evolved level, it is nothing but a projection of our own imaginations."

"Kate, you know that you only start going on about levels when you're upset," Sarah said. "And no one ever understands what you're talking about, either."

"I," Kate said, enunciating as clearly as possible, "am never going to fall in love again."

"Don't be silly, Kate, you're just upset right now." Sarah patted Kate's arm, then unwrapped another packet from her lunch. "Oh yay, chocolate chip. Want some?"

As she offered Kate and Annie the cookies, she added, "He just wasn't worthy of you, that's all."

"Jerome isn't worthy of dating a slug, let alone someone like you!" Annie agreed hotly. "He's a worm, he's slime, he's the lowest of the low! In my opinion, you are well rid of him!" She grabbed a cookie and bit into it so viciously that crumbs sprayed across the table.

"Shh." Kate glanced around the lunchroom. She certainly didn't want Jerome, or anyone else, to hear this conversation. It might make him think that she cared about him breaking up with her, which was so absolutely, completely, emphatically *not true*. "The concept of love is merely a distraction to a calm and ordered mind. From now on, I intend to focus on more important things—"

"Yessss," Annie interrupted, her eyes glittering with evil intent. "Like sweet, sweet revenge. Speaking of which, I've had a few thoughts—"

At that moment, the Practically Perfect Ashley Lawson strolled over to Jerome's table, carrying a cafeteria tray that held only a large salad (no dressing) and a bottle of sparkling water. Her glossy black hair flowed past her shoulders in gentle waves. Her simple T-shirt and blue jeans somehow looked as if they came from the pages of *Vogue*. A little ruby ring glinted on her right hand.

"I don't even want to know what kind of dark, evil pact she's made in order to look like that!" Annie hissed.

Ashley slid into the chair next to Jerome with a demure smile that revealed an adorable dimple. He gazed at her as if she were his last hope of heaven. Kate tried to look away, but she couldn't. She was transfixed. It was like watching one of those reality shows on TV and being too stunned by the sheer awfulness of it all to turn the channel.

Kate saw the Practically Perfect Ashley Lawson feed Jerome a french fry.

"Nauseating," Annie said. "I'll probably have to have my stomach pumped."

Kate watched Jerome brush a stray lock of hair

from Ashley's practically perfect forehead.

"I predict that she dumps him in a month," Sarah said loyally. "Then he'll realize how stupid he was to break up with you!"

Kate saw him lean over to put his arm around Ashley's shoulders.

"Faithless, fickle, and false," Annie muttered darkly. She sounded like a witch trying out a new curse.

Kate forced herself to look away.

"I said, I'm *glad* he broke up with me," she insisted. "Weren't you listening?"

"Listening, yes," Annie said. "Believing, no."

"Look," Sarah said, "I know you miss Jerome—"

"Miss him?" Kate cried bitterly. "On the contrary. O, how mine eyes do loathe his visage now!"

Sarah and Annie were being totally supportive, of course, the way true friends should be when one of their own is trapped in a web of despair. Still, they couldn't resist glancing at each other and rolling their eyes, just a little.

"Let me guess." Annie sighed. "Shakespeare."

"Yes, and it happens to be incredibly appropriate to the present situation," Kate answered.

"Why is that?" Sarah asked helpfully, as Kate knew she would.

"Titania says it in *A Midsummer Night's Dream* when she awakens from a spell and realizes that she's fallen in love with a man who has the head of a donkey." Kate paused meaningfully. Her friends looked at her. She sighed and decided to spell it out. "In other words, she realizes that she's fallen in love with an *ass*."

"Oh." Annie grinned. "Wow. It's almost as if she knew Jerome *personally*."

Sarah snickered, and Kate felt a little grin tug at the corner of her mouth. It was the first time she had come close to smiling in four days.

She felt the black weight of gloom lift just a little bit.

Then she saw Jerome lean forward to kiss Ashley on the cheek, and her heart turned back to ice.

Act I
SCENE I

That afternoon, Kate went home from school and found her parents sitting on opposite sides of the kitchen table. Her father was drinking a cup of strong black coffee and rapidly tapping his foot, a sign of either great excitement, too much caffeine, or (probably) both. Her mother was sipping the herbal tea that she claimed kept her mind sharp and her outlook serene. Despite the tea, she was looking at Kate's father over the rim of her mug with a familiar expression of barely repressed irritation.

Kate stopped in the doorway and looked from one parent to the other with grave suspicion. Although her father only lived ten miles away, her parents had made avoiding each other into an art form.

"What's going on?" she asked. "Is something wrong?"

"Wrong? No! Quite the contrary!" her father cried. "In fact, I have some wonderful news! Fantastic news! Amazing, stupendous, fabulous news!"

Her mother started to roll her eyes, caught herself, and took a calming sip of tea instead. "I never should have encouraged you to get involved in that community theater," she murmured. "Just *tell* her, Tim."

"All right, all right." Kate's father was so happy that he didn't even stop to give his usual lecture about Why Enthusiasm Is the Most Underrated Virtue in Our Modern Age of Cynicism. "You remember the writing contest I suggested you enter last fall?"

"Which one?" she asked. Her father was constantly handing her entry forms that required that she write an essay, a poem, a short story, or, if all else failed, an advertising slogan. "There was that haiku contest. And I remember writing a ten-minute play over winter break —"

"No, no, *no*, the contest sponsored by the University of Verona!" he cried. "Surely you remember? The university that's holding a series of seminars on *Romeo and Juliet*? One of which I was asked to teach? Because I'm considered one of the world's foremost experts on Shakespeare?"

He looked questioningly at his daughter and ex-wife. They looked blankly back.

"I don't know why I bother to tell anyone about my life, I really don't," he said, rather sulkily. "It's quite clear that no one listens to a word I say."

Her mother pursed her lips. "Well, you do say so *many* words, Tim. It's hard to keep up."

He opened his mouth to respond, but—just in time—Kate remembered dashing off ten pages on nature imagery in *A Midsummer Night's Dream*, right before the deadline. "Oh, wait. Got it. I stayed up until three A.M. to finish the essay. I fell asleep the next day in history." She frowned. "*And* I failed a pop quiz in chemistry."

"Petty concerns that will soon recede into the mists of time!" he said, waving a hand dismissively. "Minor problems that will soon be forgotten! Sacrifices that you will soon see were well worth making! And why is that, you ask?"

He waited. Kate obediently gave him his cue. "I don't know, Dad. Why?"

"Because you won!"

"Really? That's great." Kate opened the refrigerator to get a soda. Considering the number of competitions her parents and teachers urged her to enter, it would be strange if she *didn't* win a few here and there.

"Congratulations, honey." Her mother refilled her cup. "A humanities prize will make your college applications a little more well-rounded."

"Zounds, Emily, is that all you can think about?" Her father began pacing around the kitchen. "Her college applications? How prosaic! How pedestrian! How —"

"Practical," her mother pointed out austerely.

"But surely the more important point is that Kate gets to go to Italy!" He stopped in mid-pace to add, rather anticlimatically, "I *told* you it wasn't a waste of time to start reading the sonnets to her when she was eighteen months old!"

"I never said it was a waste of time," her mother said crossly. "I just thought picture books were more age appropriate —"

"Wait, wait, wait . . . I get to go to Italy?" Kate had only left Kansas three times in her life: to visit her grandmother in Chicago, to go to summer camp in Missouri, and to accompany her mother to a constitutional law conference in New Jersey that was, unbelievably, even more boring than it sounded. "Italy. As in Europe."

"Yes!" Her father bounced a couple of times, beaming at her. *"Congraulazioni!* We'll leave the day after school ends! We'll stay in an actual villa! And for four glorious weeks, we will experience the genius of Shakespeare and the splendors of *la bella Italia!*"

"You'll be there for a whole month?" Her mother's cup clattered into its saucer. "But what about that class in advanced rhetoric at the University of Kansas this summer? Remember, Kate? We signed you up ages ago—"

"Emily." Her father stopped bouncing, lowered his head, and frowned ferociously, a theatrical expression that Kate privately called his King Lear look. "This Is a Once In a Lifetime Opportunity." He thundered out the words, dramatically pausing between each one to make sure they heard the capital letters. This technique was invariably effective with his students (especially the freshmen), but Kate and her mother were far too used to it to be cowed.

"But she'll get college credit for the rhetoric class," her mother said.

"Which she will also earn for studying in the Shakespeare seminar," he countered triumphantly.

"Seminar?" Kate had a sinking feeling that she wasn't remembering the details of this contest with perfect clarity. "What seminar?"

"That's the prize: as one of the Shakespeare Scholars, you will have the distinction, the honor, the *privilege* of studying *Romeo and Juliet* in the heart of Verona, where the play is set!" Her father's eyes were shining as if he had just caught sight of Shakespeare himself. "You're going to learn so much, even though your class is going to be taught by"—his face darkened—"*Francesca Marchese.*"

There was a brief, fraught silence.

Then Kate's mother sighed. "Oh, lord." She got up to add hot water to her mug. "Now I know what you'll be obsessing about for the next month."

"I do not *obsess* about that woman," her father said with cold dignity. "She is not important enough to even think about for more than a minute, let alone *obsess* about."

Kate and her mother carefully avoided catching each other's eye. Kate had grown up hearing stories about the infamous Professoressa Marchese, a tenured literature professor at the University of Verona and her father's most bitter rival.

The problem was that, although her father was very well known in Shakespearean circles, his triumphs were constantly trumped by Professoressa Marchese, who seemed to specialize in academic one-upsmanship. If he was asked to lecture at a prestigious conference, she was asked to chair it. If he was interviewed for a national magazine, she was interviewed on prime-time television, and during sweeps week to boot. The year he finally published the book that he had been working on for a decade, Professoressa Marchese came out with a volume that actually hit the bestseller list for one awful month. Her father had stormed around the house, sputtering with outrage, and Kate had developed a recurring nightmare in which Professoressa Marchese turned into an evil witch and chased her through a library.

And then, just last year, the unthinkable had happened: Francesca Marchese had published *The Shakespeare Secret,* an outrageous novel based on the life of Shakespeare (about which almost nothing is known). Given the lack of actual facts, she had felt free to set forth the proposition that Shakespeare had been the leader of a covert group of alchemists who had discovered the key to immortality and that he had, in fact, never died, but still lived among mortals, collecting material for his next play.

It was total nonsense, of course, but that didn't keep it from hitting the bestseller list in seven countries, selling millions of copies, and making Francesca Marchese both an international celebrity and very rich indeed.

The mere memory of that black year made Kate shudder.

"I'm sure she's perfectly nice," her mother said drily, noticing Kate's shiver. "In fact, you'll have to tell me what she's really like. I'd love to hear the truth after listening to your father's paranoid fantasies for twenty years."

Her father made a tetchy sound, but Kate was focused on the most important aspect of what her mother had just said.

"You mean I can go?"

"Oh, of course you can go!" Her mother sighed. "Honestly, what kind of mother do you think I am?"

"*Thank* you!" Kate hugged her mother as her father did a silent victory dance next to the refrigerator.

A month in Italy! Kate sat down and stared dreamily out the window. Golden sunlight on ancient stone buildings. Olive groves and lemon trees and blue, cloudless skies. History and art and music and really good cappuccinos . . . and pasta! Her mouth watered at the thought.

Later that night she called Sarah on her cell phone, patched in Annie, and told them the good news while downloading Italian language lessons onto her iPod.

"You are so lucky." Sarah sighed. "A trip to Italy is the perfect way to get over—" her voice dropped meaningfully. "*You* know."

"I know what?" Kate asked, honestly puzzled.

"You know," Sarah insisted. Then, when it became clear she had to be more explicit, she said, "*Jerome.*"

"Oh, right. I'm already over him," Kate said. "I haven't thought of him in hours." She smiled complacently as she realized this was, in fact, true.

But Sarah wasn't listening. "I know exactly what will happen! You'll meet some incredibly handsome and romantic Italian guy—"

"Now, wait a minute," Kate said.

"—and you'll both fall in love at first sight—"

"Hold on—"

"—and Jerome will become nothing but a distant memory!"

"Not distant enough," snapped Annie, who continued to harbor hopes for revenge. "I still think we should have put itching powder in his jockstrap and reformatted his iPod with Broadway show tunes."

"You have a true genius for retribution, Annie," Kate said.

"Thanks," Annie said, gratified.

"But if I did any of those things," Kate added

firmly, "it would imply that I still care about Jerome, which I *don't*."

"Fine," Annie grumbled. "But I agree with Sarah. An Italian romance is just the thing to put Jerome in his place. Imagine it, Kate," she said in a low, thrilling voice. "You'll come back tanned and glowing and *elegant*. You'll absentmindedly begin speaking Italian in the middle of conversations. Sometimes you'll forget yourself and casually mention Roberto—"

"Roberto?" Kate interrupted.

"Or Enrico or Raffaele, the *name's* not important!" Annie said impatiently. She took a deep, calming breath, then went back to weaving a hypnotic spell. "You will wear a simple gold necklace that he gave you as a symbol of his undying love. You will exude an air of soulful mystery." She finished with the solemn authority of an oracle. "You will be *transformed*."

For a few seconds, the air vibrated with the power of this prophecy.

Then, somewhat spoiling the effect, she added, "And that's when Jerome will realize how completely stupid he was to break up with you!"

"Yes! It will be just like a movie!" Sarah said happily.

"Listen," Kate interrupted. "I am going to Italy to *study Shakespeare*, not to fall in love."

The cell phone thrummed with silent disappointment.

"In fact," she went on, "I consider myself lucky to have dated Jerome—"

"Because you found the state of complete boredom restful?" Annie murmured.

"Ignoring that," Kate said. "No, because it means that I have realized at a young age the folly of love! Now I can renounce romance and focus on doing something better with my life. Something *important*."

"If you say so," Annie said, sounding completely unconvinced.

"Well, I think it's terribly selfish," Sarah said grumpily. "After all, while you're in Italy, we're going to be slaving away at the Burger Barn and spending boring afternoons at the pool, just hoping to live vicariously through you. And I know you, Kate! You're going to send us e-mails about literary analysis and subtext and character notes. It's so unfair!"

So then Kate had to spend fifteen minutes cajoling her friends into a better mood by promising to e-mail them constantly about everything except Shakespeare, take millions of photos, and buy them lavish gifts.

But there was one matter on which she would not budge. No matter how they begged and pleaded, she refused to consider the possibility of romance. After all, she had finally found the cure for crushing heartbreak and bitter betrayal. It was Italy, where she could lose herself in the study of great literature and history and art and music—in everything, she promised herself, except falling in love.

"So, what do you think?" Annie asked Sarah, who had called her cell as soon as they finished talking to Kate. "Will she really insist on rejecting every flirtation, every wink, every smile, every possibility of love and romance just because of"—she spit the name out—"*Jerome?*"

"Oh, you know Kate," Sarah said comfortably. "She just likes taking a *position*, that's all. Once she gets to Verona—Verona! Can you imagine? I would just die if I could go there! You know, maybe I could talk my parents into a trip to Italy for my graduation present—"

"Sarah!" Annie snapped. "We are talking about our friend *Kate*."

"I know that," Sarah said, injured. "That's what I was saying. Once she gets to Verona, she'll forget that she's been tragically hurt by love and get a crush on some cute Italian boy and all will be well."

"I'm not so sure," Annie said darkly. "You know

how she loves to prove a point. She'll spend all her time in some dreary library, her nose stuck in a book."

"Not in Italy," said Sarah with serene confidence. "When she comes home, she'll be in love, I'm sure of it."

"Really?" Even over the phone, Sarah could hear the sudden, sharp interest in Annie's voice. "How sure?"

Even though Sarah knew better, she said confidently, "Absolutely, positively sure. In fact, I'd be willing to bet—"

"—your silver necklace with the four-leaf clover charm?" Annie asked quickly. Sarah swore that wishing on this necklace had helped her pass algebra, won her a place on the drill team, and summoned a blizzard on the day her unwritten history term paper was due. Not that Annie really believed any of that, of course, but she wouldn't mind wearing that necklace herself. . . .

"Fine," Sarah said, "if *you* will wager your black suede boots." She had lusted after those boots ever since Annie had made a major score at an outlet mall and gotten them for seventy-five percent off. The fact that they both wore exactly the same size only made Annie's triumph cut deeper. "The ones with the buckle on the side and the wedge heels," she added, just to be absolutely clear what was at stake.

"Done!" Annie said recklessly.

And so a wager was made; a lucky silver necklace and a pair of black suede boots, size six, were put into play; and the power of love was put to the test. . . .

Act I
SCENE II

Kate stared up at the villa where the Shakespeare Scholars were going to stay. It was eight o'clock in the evening, and she and her father had finally arrived after traveling for almost twenty-four hours straight, thanks to weather delays, missed train connections, and all the other assorted misfortunes that can befall the unlucky traveler. They had entered through a large wooden door that led into a courtyard, an enclosed area where, Kate presumed, carriages used to stand, back in the day before cars. Then they looked through an archway to a small front garden and at the villa itself.

It was built of old stone that had been softened by age: moss crept up the walls, and centuries of use had worn shallow indentations into the front steps. Faded green shutters covered the windows, giving the house a secretive look. A series of ancient terracotta pots were lined up on either side of the front steps, filled with a profusion of blue, yellow, and pink flowers.

"*Villa Marchese*," she murmured, a shiver of excitement running through her. "*Bellisima!*"

But her father glared, first at the villa, then at her. "Indeed," he said coldly. "It's amazing what the wages of sin can buy these days." He finished with a huge yawn.

Kate gave him a look. She knew her father had a chip on his shoulder when it came to Francesca Marchese, but really . . .

"You wouldn't feel so tired if you'd taken that herbal supplement for jet lag like I did," she said. "And sin seems a little strong."

"I'm speaking of academic sin, of course," her father said. "To think that she acquired all this"—he made a wide, sweeping gesture with his arm to encompass fifteen bedrooms, extensive gardens, a ballroom, and an entire floor of servants' quarters—"by writing that ridiculous book!"

"A lot of people loved *The Shakespeare Secret*," Kate offered meekly. Three million people, to be precise.

She herself had purchased a copy in secret and stayed up until two in the morning to finish it. Unfortunately for her father, she had found it enthralling, something that she could never, ever admit. "And the reviews were pretty good." In fact, the reviews were fantastic, which her father knew quite well.

"Yes, yes, yes," he said testily. "She has achieved fame and fortune by cheapening the work of the greatest playwright the English language has ever known. Very impressive." He stood stock-still and glared at the villa as if he were a virtuous David confronting the immoral might of Goliath. "Well, as long as we are forced to reside in this den of iniquity, I suppose we might as well get settled."

He walked up the steps to a massive oak door and swung the heavy brass knocker, one, two, three times.

Each knock echoed in the quiet courtyard with all the force of a magical incantation, then the door swung open, revealing a bent, elderly woman. She was wearing a black dress, black lace-up shoes, and despite the heat, a black cardigan. She had a long black staff topped with a tarnished silver knob, which she seemed to be holding not for support but as a potential weapon should the need arise.

"Buon giorno," her father said. "We're here for the Shakespeare Seminar."

"Ah, *si, si.*" She smiled broadly, revealing a blinding set of dentures, and pulled the door open a little wider, gesturing for them to come in. "Shakespeare, *si!*"

"I'm Professor Tim Sanderson. This is my daughter, Kate," he said, as he hauled his suitcase over the threshold. "And you are . . . ?"

"Si, si!" She nodded her head vigorously and pointed to herself. "Maria!" Then, introductions accomplished, she started up the sweeping staircase at top speed. After a moment's hesitation, Kate and her father looked at each other and realized there was nothing for them to do but follow.

Maria ushered them through a maze of halls with the courtly manner of an old family retainer. They walked past walls lined with enormous oil portraits in heavy gold frames, the faces dim and darkened by age; past dozens of doors, a few open just enough to offer teasing glimpses of grand four-poster beds and vases filled with fresh flowers; and past wall niches that contained plaster statues of saints or more flowers.

"Must cost a fortune to keep this place going," her father said. "She'll probably run through all her money within a year and not even know where it all went." He looked pleased at the thought. "Sad, really."

They had reached another flight of stairs. Her father eyed it with the look of a mountain climber who can see the summit but isn't at all sure he can make it. "Ah, another floor?"

"*Si, si!*" Maria made an energetic gesture toward the heavens, smiling maliciously. She was obviously ready to sprint up four more flights, carrying a suitcase or two if necessary.

"Lovely," he said. "But perhaps we could stop for just a moment . . . jet lag, you know. . . ."

"If you'd set your watch to Italian time as soon as we got on the plane," Kate said, seeing an opening, "and if you'd worn that sleep mask so that you weren't awake all night —"

"Yes, yes, yes," he said testily. "I'm sure that if I had done all that I would now feel fresh as a daisy, but I didn't and I don't!"

They staggered up the stairs to the next landing, where he halted, mopped his brow, and took several deep, shuddering breaths. He spotted a series of old black-and-white photos hung on the wall and pointed to them with feigned interest. "Are these family, then?" he asked Maria. "*La famiglia di Professoressa Marchese?*"

The elderly woman spared the photos one scornful glance, then hit the floor with her cane. *"Morto!"* she cried, pointing to a stiff portrait of a man in a three-piece black suit. Her face lit with glee that seemed to say, *He* is dead and *I* am not!

As she led them down the hall, she lifted her cane and pointed to one photo after the other as she cried triumphantly, *"Morto! Morto! Morto!"* Dead, dead, dead!

Finally, after walking past a half-dozen more rooms, this morbid march ended and they came to a halt. The woman opened two doors, one across the hall from the other, and gestured that they should take their luggage inside.

"Oh, our rooms at last!" her father said with relief. "How delightful."

As her father entered his bedroom, Kate blearily wheeled her suitcase into her own. It was a large room with high ceilings and tall windows covered with green velvet curtains. There was a four-poster bed draped with rich tapestries and an ornate mirror hanging over a marble fireplace. Kate wandered over to peer at her reflection. It wavered in the dim green light so that she seemed to be floating underwater.

There was a knock on the door, and she turned to see her father leaning against the door frame as if only that support could keep him from sliding to the floor from exhaustion. "I think I might need a tiny nap before we go out to see the sights," he said, blinking owlishly at her.

"You know, the latest research shows that it's helpful if you try to stay awake until your normal bedtime."

He just made a noise in his throat, like a discontented bear, and waved one weary hand as he disappeared. Kate went into her bathroom to brush her teeth and wash her face. Apparently, the bathroom was shared with the bedroom next door. Someone had scattered lipsticks, lotions, gels, conditioners, powders, eye shadows, curlers, bobby pins, hand creams, manicure scissors, facial scrubs, and moisturizers next to the sink.

Kate shook her head at the sight as she virtuously unpacked her own bathroom kit: toothbrush, toothpaste, deodorant, one lip gloss (pink), one eye shadow (sand), and one mascara (brown).

She brushed her teeth quickly and wandered back to her bedroom, thinking fuzzy thoughts about how glad she was that she had followed her anti-jet-lag regimen to the letter. That's why she still felt so . . .

She stifled a yawn.

. . . so completely rested and refreshed. Kate

stacked her Italian dictionary, several guidebooks, and a history of Italy neatly on a table, then stretched out on her bed and began flipping through one of the guidebooks. As she found the section on Verona, she couldn't help feeling sorry for her father, who was probably passed out in his bed across the hall. . . .

She yawned again. Her own bed, she couldn't help but notice, was incredibly comfortable.

. . . while *she* was ready to explore the town. . . .

But as her vision blurred and another yawn overtook her, Kate realized that her body had other ideas. A wave of exhaustion swept over her. Her eyes closed, her book fell from her hand, and Kate fell deeply asleep.

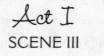

Act I
SCENE III

When Kate woke up on Saturday morning, it took several moments of staring up at the brocade canopy to remember where she was. When she did, she sat up with a start, checked the bedside clock, and was astonished to see that she had slept for almost twelve hours. She felt alert, energetic, and remarkably cheerful.

She jumped out of bed and surveyed her room with great satisfaction. For the past few years, whenever she had fallen subject to a fit of melancholy, she had imagined living in a garret. A charming, light-filled garret, of course, that would comfort her soul by offering her beauty and peace and, most of all, solitude. No one would be allowed in her garret. Absolutely no one —

"Not even us?" Sarah would cry, a note of betrayal in her voice.

Kate had sighed, aware of how foolish she had been to share this fantasy with her two best friends. "You, of course, would be granted visiting privileges," she would say to Sarah. And with a nod to Annie, "You, too. Naturally."

Annie had merely lifted one sardonic eyebrow. "Thank you so much. No heat in winter, I suppose. Cold water all year round. Only a radish for supper. How dull, and how like you, Kate."

But when Kate had imagined her cozy garret, this had been what she had seen. Walls with faded frescoes, bookshelves filled with volumes covered in shades of lemon and ivory, high ceilings with ornate moldings, and warm Mediterranean sunlight slanting through the shutters.

She jumped out of bed, pulled back the window curtains, threw open the shutters, and discovered that her room faced an enormous garden that stretched out behind the villa. Closer to the house, dark green hedges divided the lawn into neat flower beds; borders of purplish gray lavender edged the paths; and a wide avenue, lined by stately rows of cypresses, bisected the lawn with geometric exactitude.

But there were hints of wildness and mystery as well: a shadowy forest beyond the hedges; a rustic bench tucked under a rose-covered arch; glimpses of a high stone wall, crumbling with age. A bird suddenly winged from one tree to another, a swift arrow against the sky. Bees hummed drowsily in the hot sun, and she could smell a spicy, sun-warmed fragrance that seemed both familiar and exotic.

As she was trying to identify it, there was a knock at the door that led to the bathroom. Then a tanned, laughing girl with long blond hair and cornflower blue eyes burst into her room.

"Well, hey there!" the girl said in a Southern drawl. "You must be Kate Sanderson! I'm Lucy Atwell, I'm from Jackson, Mississippi, and I'm real pleased to meet you! My room's just on the other side of the bathroom; we're sharing, but I guess you figured that out. I've already met a few of the other students—there's Winnie, who's super serious, and Jonathan, who's super intellectual, but Tom across the hall is real nice. At least he's still in high school, like us."

As Lucy paused for breath, she glanced at the suitcase Kate had placed neatly at the foot of her bed. "Did the airline lose the rest of your luggage? 'Cause I've heard that happens a lot when you travel overseas and I have to tell you, I was just scared to death it was going to happen to me, but thank the lord all my luggage got here all right —"

"No, that's all I have," Kate interrupted.

"Oh." Lucy looked taken aback but quickly recovered. "Well, aren't you smart to travel so light! Now, I brought six suitcases —"

"Six. Really." Kate tried to imagine how much could be transported in that many suitcases. Probably her entire wardrobe, with room to spare.

"I know that seems like a lot, but let me tell you, that was the *bare minimum,*" Lucy said, somewhat defensively. "In fact, that's what I told the man at the check-in counter, because he was being really sarcastic. I finally had to say, look, I *would* pack less stuff, but then everything would be at home!"

Kate wrinkled her forehead. There must have been some lingering fogginess from the trip, because she didn't seem to be able to track that reasoning. "Quite true," she said at last.

Lucy wandered to the dresser, where Kate's workout clothes were still piled high, waiting to be put away. "You must really like to exercise," she said.

"I run every day, if I can," Kate said. "If you'd like to go with me, I'd love the company."

"Oh, honey, I wouldn't run unless I was being chased by a bear," Lucy said with a flip of her hand.

"I hate getting sweaty. But maybe Tom across the hall would go with you. He looks very athletic."

"So who *is* this Tom-across-the-hall?"

Lucy brightened up immediately. "Oh, he's a super-sweet guy, which is good because we're the only three Americans. Well, the only Americans who are still in high school. There are a bunch of college kids staying here, too, but they're not going to be in our seminar, and I can tell you I am just completely thankful about *that* because I've already met a few of them, and in my opinion, they are *way* too intense."

As they headed across the hall to meet Tom, Kate learned that Lucy's father was a businessman known as the Sofabed King of the South; that her mother was a former Miss Mississippi; that one of her six suitcases was actually empty, ready to be filled with what she bought in Italy; that there were only a hundred and three people in her high school class; and furthermore —

Tom Boone opened his door. "Hey." He had sun-bleached hair, clear green eyes, and a smile that belonged in a toothpaste commercial. "Are you guys hungry?"

As they headed downstairs in search of breakfast, Lucy confided that she simply *adored* Shakespeare, that she harbored a secret hope of playing the part of Juliet in her high school's fall production, and that *Romeo and Juliet* was simply her favorite play of all time.

"I mean," she finished up, "it's so *romantic*."

"Why does everyone always say that?" Kate asked as they walked into the dining room, a note of exasperation in her voice. "Even a superficial reading of the text would indicate that the word 'romantic' doesn't really apply. After all, the story does end with a double suicide."

Too late, Kate realized that they were giving her odd looks, the same kind of looks that she used to get in school when she got too enthusiastic about iambic pentameter or the construction of sonnets.

She could almost hear Annie's voice in her ear, making a point that they had argued many times over the years.

"You're such a nerd," Annie would sigh.

"So? What's wrong with being a nerd?" Kate would snap. "Bill Gates is a nerd, and he's the richest man in the world."

"There's nothing wrong with *being* a nerd," Annie would say patiently, as if she were merely stating the obvious. "What's wrong—or at least monumentally inappropriate—is letting people *know* you're a nerd."

Lucy was saying blithely, "Well, I know the ending is a downer, but I just stop reading before Juliet takes that sleeping pill. After all, before that happened, things were going *so well!*"

Kate opened her mouth to point out that, in fact, by the time Juliet drank the potion, the Capulets and Montagues were well enmeshed in a bitter rivalry, two people had been killed in sword fights, and Romeo had been banished . . . then she remembered Annie's warning and quickly shut her mouth.

But maybe Tom would reveal hidden depths. A deeply held passion for poetry, perhaps, or an interest in the historical context of the plays.

"What about you, Tom?" she asked as they started down the breakfast buffet. "Why did you enter the Shakespeare Scholar competition?"

To her surprise, the question seemed to unnerve him. "Me?" He looked up from a serious contemplation of the yogurt, fruit, and cheese, his expression startled, as if it had never occurred to him that someone might ask him this question. Finally, he muttered, "Um, well, I guess I just, you know . . . like Shakespeare?"

Kate nodded encouragingly and waited.

But he glanced away, his eyes lighting with interest on a plate of prosciutto. He picked up a piece of the thinly sliced ham and took a cautious bite. "Hey, you should try this. It's really good."

"What was your essay about?" Kate persisted.

"Well, I just picked an idea," he muttered. "I didn't think about it too much."

"Did you bring a copy with you?" Kate asked. "I'd love to read it some time."

"Yeah, well . . ." Now he looked positively hunted. "My hard drive crashed a month ago, so I don't know . . ."

He was rescued by Lucy. "Well, I'm just glad I won, I really didn't think I had a chance in the world, to tell you the truth, but here I am in Verona!" she said. "Walking the actual streets where Romeo and Juliet walked! Oh, listen, I have a fabulous idea. Why don't we all go to Juliet's House after we eat? We have hours before we have to get ready for the opening-night party, and I just can't wait to see where all the events of the play took place in real life! Imagine standing on the very spot where Juliet stood when she first met Romeo!"

Her eyes were shining with enthusiasm, so Kate decided not to mention that no one could confirm that a Capulet family had ever lived in the house, that Juliet's existence had never been proven, or that the famous balcony had been added to the house in 1928.

Instead, she shrugged and said, "Why not?"

Act I
SCENE IV

When it came to romance, Kate knew that people preferred illusion to reality. Even when they *knew* it was illusion, they would always rather be diverted by the magician's sleight-of-hand than discover how the trick was done.

Case in point: the courtyard of Juliet's House, where she and Lucy and Tom were now standing.

They had walked across an ancient bridge to get to the part of town where Juliet's House stood. Sunlight glinted off the water, which ran swiftly beneath the stone arches. Tall, dark green cypresses stood along the riverbanks like arrows, black as shadows against the cloudless blue sky. When they reached the other side of the river, they had wended their way through narrow streets lined with old buildings. They had to inch along behind the tourists who stopped every few feet to consult their maps, but Kate, usually so impatient to get where she was going, didn't mind. Everywhere she looked, she saw a view that could have been transported directly from a Renaissance painting; everywhere she walked, she felt the mysterious presence of centuries of people walking the same path; every breath she took seemed to smell of dark coffee and fresh-baked bread. A feeling of absolute contentment filled her up and carried her all the way to number 23 Via Capelli, where, at last, they arrived at Juliet's House.

When they turned down the street and found the right address, they discovered large iron gates that opened into a stone tunnel, which led in turn into a small courtyard. The courtyard was crowded with people taking photos of each other, the famous balcony, and a bronze statue of Juliet. Not one person, Kate noted, was reading the informational signs helpfully posted nearby, or even thumbing through a guidebook. A bustling gift shop was located directly across the courtyard from the entrance to Juliet's House, and that was what attracted Lucy's attention first.

"Oh, look!" Lucy said, pointing at a row of tiny corked bottles in the window. Each one was filled with a different colored liquid—amber, ruby, emerald, bright blue—and had a handwritten label that said *elisir d'amore*. "How cute! But what does"—she frowned slightly as she sounded out the Italian words—"el-ee-zir dah-moh-ray mean?"

"Love potion," Kate said. She gave a disapproving sniff. "Otherwise known as colored sugar water."

But Lucy was already pulling out her wallet. "Let me see how much I have on me."

"You're just throwing your money away. You could bottle that at home."

Lucy stopped counting her euros long enough to give Kate a long, searching look. "You're a very *sensible* person, aren't you, Kate?"

"It doesn't take much sense," Kate said crisply, "to avoid drinking potions in Verona."

But Lucy just shrugged and said happily, "Well, *I* think it's a great souvenir! I'll be right back."

As she darted into the gift shop and Tom drifted away to look at postcards, a tired-looking woman stood on the steps in front of the entrance and called out, "*Attenzione!* I will begin now my lecture on Juliet's House."

A few people moved closer to the tour guide, and Kate pulled a pen and small notebook from her purse to jot down notes.

"You will notice above me the famous balcony," the tour guide said.

The small group looked up and nodded. It was hard to miss.

"When standing here, one can perhaps imagine Romeo, waiting below, yearning for one single glimpse of his beloved Giulietta—"

Kate shifted from one foot to the other and tried to suppress a yawn.

To her right, a woman was brandishing a camera in the air and yelling, "Sam, Sam! Go stand under that window and let me get a picture of you!"

"—one can perhaps envision Juliet, not quite fourteen years old, waiting breathlessly above us, gazing into her future—"

Kate turned her head slightly to look around the courtyard. Her gaze passed without interest over a stand of postcards, then stopped. In the far corner, a young man was leaning against the wall, one ankle crossed over the other, looking completely at ease. He had dark eyes, tousled brown hair, and the classic profile and self-possessed air of a Renaissance prince. In the midst of the courtyard's hectic atmosphere, he stood still and watchful, only moving to take a bite of the apple he was holding. Even that simple gesture was somehow regal, and Kate suddenly imagined that he might have been transported across time from some earlier, more elegant century. She frowned slightly at this uncharacteristically whimsical thought. Perhaps she had a little jet lag after all.

Then another boy, shorter and with wild black curls, pushed a bike through the crowd with a cheerful *"Permesso!"* and let it crash to the ground. He said something that made the first boy laugh, then picked up his bike and continued to talk, even as the first boy kept surveying the crowd.

His eyes flicked from one person to the other, seeming to assess each one in turn—and then they met Kate's eyes, and she found herself staring directly at him. For a long moment, neither one of them looked away . . . then Tom came up to her and the spell was broken.

"I'm going to head back to the villa," he said, clearly bored. "See you guys later."

He vanished. Kate could feel, on the back of her neck, that the boy was still staring at her, but she refused to turn around and risk meeting his gaze again. Instead, she trained her attention on the tour guide and took dutiful notes that later made no sense to her at all.

❊　❊　❊

"*Ciao,* Giacomo." Benno propped his bike up and leaned against the wall next to the bike with a sigh of relief. It was turning out to be a very hot day, he'd been running errands since eight in the morning, and his day wasn't even half over yet. *"Come stai?"*

"Eh." Giacomo took another bite of his apple, making a face at its tartness, then shrugged. "All right, I suppose."

"Why so glum?" Benno's witchy-black eyes glinted with curiosity. "Has the lovely—I'm sorry, I've forgotten the name of your latest girlfriend—anyway, has she dumped you already?"

Giacomo gave him a sidelong glance, one eyebrow raised expressively. He did not get dumped.

"Yes, that is the only reason I can think of for your sadness today," Benno continued, a little maliciously. "You are pining away for your lost love. . . ."

Giacomo raised both eyebrows at that. He didn't pine away.

Benno couldn't resist. "She has broken your heart!" he finished dramatically.

Finally Giacomo was irritated enough to speak. "My heart," he said loftily, "does not break."

Benno grinned. "Oh, right. You don't have one."

A corner of Giacomo's mouth lifted in an answering glint of humor. "True."

"So if the problem is not your latest girl," Benno persisted, "what is it?"

Giacomo sighed and leaned back against the wall. "Truthfully, I do not know why I am so sad. I know I *should* be happy."

"Yes, you should," Benno agreed. "No work, no responsibilities, no worries, no cares." He considered all the jobs he was juggling this summer—selling trinkets to tourists at his uncle's souvenir stand, working as a waiter for his second cousin's catering company, delivering flowers for the nephew of his aunt's best friend, and running errands all over town for anyone who would pay him. He considered all that, and thought black thoughts about Giacomo.

But he merely added, "*Dolce fare niente*. It is sweet to do nothing."

"You forget that I am going to be held hostage in a dreary seminar room for the next month," Giacomo said.

"Me, too," Benno pointed out.

Giacomo shook his head. "I can't believe you let yourself be talked into taking a class during the summer break. *I* was not offered a choice, but *you* could have said no."

"Someone dropped out and the class has to have an even number of people," Benno said. He decided not to mention the small stipend he had been offered that would more than compensate for the money he wouldn't earn. "And it sounded interesting."

"Interesting!" Giacomo took another bite of apple. "Four weeks of dissecting symbols and metaphors with strangers who didn't have enough wit to think of a better way to spend their summer!"

"Mmm."

Four weeks sitting around a cool, dim room in the Villa Marchese . . .

"Summer is a time to have fun, not study," Giacomo complained.

Four weeks of not running errands all over town or, at least, not running quite as many errands as usual. . . .

"It's not as if I haven't heard every thought that could be uttered about that wretched play," Giacomo went on.

Four weeks of just . . . *talking*. Not standing in the hot sun selling souvenirs, not washing dishes in a steamy restaurant kitchen, and not carrying heavy boxes up three flights of stairs for old Signora Giordano . . .

"It will be unbearable," Giacomo finished.

If Benno hadn't been such a sunny, sweet-tempered, and forgiving friend, he might have punched Giacomo in the nose.

Instead, feeling saintly, he said, "Perhaps you will meet a new girl in this seminar. Perhaps she will be beautiful. Perhaps she will fall in love with you—"

"Undoubtedly she will fall in love with me." Giacomo grinned as he said it, but Benno knew he was only half joking. Girls were always falling in love with Giacomo.

"But as for being beautiful . . . the girls in this class have already been recognized as brilliant scholars, so the odds are against it." Giacomo took a disconsolate bite of his apple and scanned the courtyard again.

"Let's think of happier things," he said. "The future is not here yet, but the present shows remarkable promise." He tilted his head toward the crowd. "After all, it's the start of another summer season and we stand in a courtyard full of starry-eyed, romantic girls from around the world. What do you think, Benno? Do you see any possibilities?"

"I always see possibilities," Benno said, a little disgruntled. "I would rather see probabilities, as you do. Or absolute certainties. That would be even better."

"You need to have more self-assurance, Benno. That is the key. No girl is attracted to someone who lacks confidence."

"Thank you for the advice," Benno said. "I never knew it was that easy. Of course, now that you've pointed that out to me, my troubles have vanished."

Giacomo smiled to himself. "Well, let's see if we can find someone for you." He inclined his head slightly toward a girl with blue-and-magenta streaks in her hair. She was laughing loudly and occasionally giving one of her friends a shove to punctuate a particular comment. "She seems fun."

Benno looked at the girl out of the corner of his eye. "Too jolly."

"Mmm, you're probably right." Giacomo's restless eyes landed next on a girl with thick brown braids and plump, rosy cheeks. She wore stout hiking boots and carried a backpack that looked serious enough for a climb up Mount Everest. "And her?"

"Too hearty."

"Unfortunate," he agreed sadly. "What about that one?"

Benno followed Giacomo's gaze. "Ah, *sì*." This girl looked a little bit more promising. She was tall and slim, with hair the color of dark honey, pulled back in a neat braid. Gold-framed glasses perched on an entirely acceptable nose. She had a rather grave air, as if perhaps she had a secret sorrow that only a warm and witty person such as himself could dispel. . . .

Benno pulled himself up short. He had made the

mistake before of creating an elaborate story about a girl based on nothing more than the way she tilted her head or the kind of shoes she wore. He had learned to his sorrow that appearances could be very deceiving. Teresa, for example, had worn a micro-mini skirt and stiletto heels that had given him *entirely* the wrong impression.

"So, what do you think?" Giacomo asked.

Benno refocused his attention. "She is an American. Without a doubt."

"And how did you make that deduction?" Giacomo found Benno's Sherlock Holmes act quite amusing, and encouraged it whenever possible.

Benno gave a disdainful sniff. "She's wearing *khakis*."

"Ah, yes."

Benno added, his head cocked to one side. "Smart and studious."

"Based on?"

"Three books stuffed in her purse," Benno pointed out. "And she's not just listening to the tour guide, she's taking *notes*." He clucked disapprovingly.

"Mmm." Giacomo glanced at Benno. "But perhaps you would consider asking her out for a gelato, just to practice."

But Benno was already shaking his head. "Her

nose is too pointy," he said hastily. "You know I hate pointy noses."

"What a pity," Giacomo said, trying not to smile. "I guess today is not your day."

"Hmmph." Benno cast one more scowl at the courtyard. Giacomo, he reflected, had it far easier when it came to romance, for he liked all different kinds of girls: tall, short, plump, thin, blondes, brunettes, redheads. Once he had even dated a girl who shaved her head.

But Benno couldn't lose his heart to just anyone. "It's a curse," he muttered.

"What's that?"

He gave Giacomo a meaningful look. "High standards."

Giacomo grinned at him. "Who is this perfect girl you keep waiting for? Describe her to me and when I find her, I'll point her out to you."

"I'm not looking for perfection," Benno protested. "I just want someone who is pretty, smart, kind, and loving. Oh, and fun to talk to. And probably talented in some way." He thought about that for a moment. "Maybe she sings or likes to paint."

"Nice to see you're so easy to please," Giacomo said drily. "Any preference for hair color?"

"Oh, well, when it comes to that . . ." Benno

shrugged carelessly. "That's up to God."

His mobile phone rang. He took one look at the text message and jumped to his feet. "That's my uncle, he's going crazy because I'm not at work yet and I still have to pick up the letters to Juliet—"

"Don't worry, I'll do it for you," Giacomo offered as he tossed the apple core in a trash barrel. "Who knows, I may meet a new friend inside!" He favored Benno with a wicked smile and headed for the door of Juliet's House.

By the time Lucy wandered back to Kate's side, the tour guide was wrapping up her speech by reciting words that she had clearly said many, many times before.

"If you close your eyes, perhaps you can imagine an ardent young man standing here—"

Somewhere behind Kate, a young girl began begging her mother to let her buy a souvenir in the gift shop.

The tour guide's voice became louder. "—he is hoping, yearning, *praying* to see the girl of his dreams—"

Somewhere to her left, a group of teenagers shrieked with joy to see one of their friends appear on the balcony above.

"—he does not know what he will do if he can't catch at least a glimpse of her—"

Somewhere to Kate's right, a baby began to wail.

And just as she was feeling that she had to get out of here *right now* before she was driven insane, she saw the boy again. He was in the sunlight now, strolling around the statue, smiling as his eyes swept carefully over the crowd.

Then, just as the tour guide said, "Imagine him, heartsick and lovelorn, standing beneath this very balcony!" the boy stopped, just so, beneath the balcony.

It was a pose calculated to draw attention to him, and it did.

Lucy whispered in her ear, "Look, it's Romeo come to life!"

Kate rolled her eyes.

After a long pause, the boy began moving toward the crowd. Lucy eased herself to the left, casually placing herself in the perfect position to intercept him on his path. Kate sniffed at this obvious ploy and turned her attention back to the tour guide, who was saying, "Or a balcony very *similar* to this one, at any rate—"

Kate continued listening as the tour guide moved on to talk about Verona's social hierarchy in the

Middle Ages. It was a thorough, comprehensive, and detailed explanation, and the crowd soon began to get restless. Kate trained her gaze on the tour guide, not deigning to look over to see what kind of silly drama was being played out to her left.

Well, just one quick glance. The boy had reached Lucy. Kate heard him say, in a deep, warm voice, *"Buon giorno."*

"Hi there!" Lucy said cheerfully.

"Ah, you are American?" he asked. Even though Kate was concentrating fiercely on listening to the tour guide, she noticed that his English, spoken with a British accent, was quite good.

"Sì, I mean yes," Lucy said. "I'm from Jackson, Mississippi. I'm Lucy."

"Piacere." Pleased to meet you. "My name is Giacomo."

"Giacomo." From the lilt in Lucy's voice, Kate knew, even without glancing over, that Lucy was smiling and blushing. Kate's eyes slid sideways just as Giacomo glanced over at her. Embarrassed, she looked away, but then she couldn't help herself. She looked back.

He winked at her.

She stuck her nose in the air and, as pointedly as she could, turned back to listen to the tour guide.

But at that moment the tour guide was ending her spiel. Her shoulders slumped, her voice listless, she finished by saying, without much hope, "If you would like to continue the tour inside Juliet's House, the admission fee is only four euros."

Despite this warm invitation, the crowd began to disperse. Apparently, most people decided that, having seen the famous balcony for free, they had no need to spend money to see the rooms inside. Kate left Lucy, who was clearly enthralled by her new acquaintance, went inside to pay for her ticket, and climbed the narrow staircase to the first floor.

At least it was much calmer inside and quieter, too. She wandered through surprisingly spare rooms with bare wooden floors and plain walls decorated with an occasional fresco. There was a fireplace with logs neatly stacked, as if ready for Juliet's father (or servant, more likely) to set them ablaze. There was a heavy wooden chair ready for Juliet's mother (or nurse, more likely) to sit down and take up some darning. And there was a door leading out to the balcony, ready for Juliet to step through and address the gentle, loving night.

The rooms looked like an empty stage set, waiting for the actors to appear and bring the world to life. Except that understudies had apparently taken over the scene, and they were obviously ill rehearsed for their roles.

For example, the two teens who were now standing on the balcony. They giggled and waved to their friends below as if they were on a homecoming parade float.

"Romeo, Romeo, wherefore art thou Romeo?" one of the girls called out in a silly, high-pitched voice.

Kate shook her head and turned away just in time to see Lucy and the boy from the courtyard enter the room, their heads bent toward each other, laughing. Quickly, she climbed the stairs to the next floor where more tourists were milling about, taking snapshots of the fireplace andirons and reading the informational placards out loud to one another.

Sighing, Kate ducked into a side room that was blessedly free of other people. And, in fact, there weren't many things to see except two glass cases displaying costumes for Romeo and Juliet, and a bed.

Actually, it was The Bed.

Then Kate read a sign on the wall and discovered that, far from being an antique, it was actually a movie prop from the 1968 film adaptation of *Romeo and Juliet*. Kate made a face at the bed and climbed the stairs to the next floor.

As she was taking a closer look at a fresco on the

landing, she heard Lucy's breathless voice float up from the floor below.

"Oh, look! Is that—?"

"Yes. The very bed where Juliet slept," he assured her.

Honestly. The sign made it quite clear the bed was a fake—

"It's pretty small, isn't it?" asked Lucy, the daughter of the South's Sofabed King. "You'd think Juliet would have had at least a queen."

Kate shook her head at that. It didn't help when she heard him laugh as if Lucy was the soul of wit.

"Well, people were smaller then," he said solemnly. "Juliet was probably quite petite. About your size, I imagine."

Worse and worse! Annoyed, Kate cleared her throat loudly, then coughed, and then, for good measure, pretended to sneeze before stomping down the wooden stairs.

"Oh, hi, Kate!" If Lucy was put out by being interrupted, she didn't show it. "This is Giacomo."

"Piacere," he said, smiling.

"Hi," she said coolly.

Giacomo's smile dimmed a bit.

"And guess what?" Lucy went on. "This bed is the *actual bed*—"

"Actually, it's not." Kate nodded toward the sign. "It's a movie prop."

"Oh." Lucy seemed a bit crestfallen at this news, and Kate wished she hadn't said anything.

She glanced at her watch and then at Lucy. "We should probably go, so we have time to get ready for the party."

"Oh, yes, you're absolutely right," Lucy said, "but I want to take a picture on the balcony first. Stay right here, don't move, I'll be right back."

As she rushed out of the room, Giacomo turned his attention to Kate.

"You look very disapproving," he said lightly.

"That's because I *am* disapproving," she answered.

Not the faintest trace of a smile. Giacomo sighed. Probably not his type.

"Well, Juliet's House does attract such romantic young ladies," he said. "It seems a shame to disappoint them."

"Your work for the tourism board must keep you busy."

Was there a sarcastic edge to her voice? Definitely not his type.

"Got it!" Lucy came rushing back, holding her camera up in triumph. "Thanks for waiting!"

"You're quite welcome," Giacomo said smoothly,

smiling down at her. But as they left Juliet's bedroom, Kate saw him glance toward the balcony, where another gaggle of girls had gathered. "I have a few matters to take care of before I leave, but perhaps we will see each other again."

"Oh, I hope so!" Lucy said. She cast a quick, imploring glance at Kate. "Maybe we could stay just a *tiny* bit longer. . . ."

"We should have left fifteen minutes ago if we wanted to be on time," Kate answered, checking her watch again. "If we leave now, we'll only be fashionably late, instead of embarrassingly late."

Giacomo gave a rueful shrug and took Lucy's hand. "I fear that the fates have conspired against us. But remember, such moments were meant to be short, and being short all the sweeter."

"Oh. Well. Yes. I suppose that's true." Lucy sounded bewildered but pleased.

Kate barely refrained from rolling her eyes at this flowery and ridiculous good-bye. It was like Shakespeare, she thought, without the sense.

Lucy chattered on blithely as they walked downstairs and out the door, not noticing Kate's silence.

Not only was she silent, she was brooding. It was a good thing, really, that she had had her heart broken already, thus inoculating her at an early age from the folly and madness of love. It meant that she was now sensible and clear-eyed and calm, and would never make a fool of herself again, the way Lucy did by swooning over Giacomo.

But as they crossed the courtyard, Kate couldn't resist looking back over her shoulder. Giacomo was now standing on the balcony, smiling down at a girl who was gazing up at him with an expression that, even from this distance, was obviously adoring. As if he felt Kate watching him, he glanced up and, once again, their eyes met. He smiled and winked. Then he deliberately turned his gaze back to the girl's face.

And Kate lifted her chin, spun around, and walked away.

Entr'acte

Sarah and Annie had made a pact: They would read all Kate's e-mails and compose their answers to her in each other's presence. In this way, they reasoned, they wouldn't be tempted to offer the kind of advice and counsel that could result in her either falling in love (and thus resolving their bet in Sarah's favor) or resisting all forms of romance (and thus declaring Annie the winner).

This plan also allowed them plenty of time to comment (constructively and with great affection, of course) on their friend's foibles while consuming an enormous number of snacks. A few days after Kate had left for Italy, they had received the first e-mail.

"About time!" Sarah said indignantly on the phone. "Do you want to come over here? My mom's experimenting with a new version of chocolate cream pie and she needs tasters."

"I'm on my way."

They read the printout of Kate's e-mail while eating several slices of pie, then headed for Sarah's bedroom to discuss it in detail. It was, they agreed, annoying in the extreme: in what should have been the juiciest passages, it was as terse and uninformative as a telegram. . . .

"Read the part about Tom again," Sarah urged. "He sounds cute."

Annie found the requested section and obligingly read it aloud. "'I'm not really sure why Tom wanted to be in this seminar. Every time I bring up an interesting topic, like the historical incident that *Romeo and Juliet* was allegedly based on or the literary precedents that used the same basic plotline, he changes the subject. Usually to soccer, which seems to be his only interest. Or at least it's the only thing he's interested in talking about.'" Annie lowered the paper and peered over it at Sarah, who was shaking her head.

"Historical incident?" Annie asked, incredulous. "Literary precedents?"

"Kate really has no idea how to talk to boys," Sarah said sadly.

❀　❀　❀

. . . or it was cryptic and incomplete as a spy's ciphered message . . .

"And what about Giacomo?" Sarah asked.

Annie flipped over a page and read aloud. "'I did meet a guy named Giacomo who, it turns out, is also one of the Shakespeare Scholars. But before you get too excited (yes, Sarah, I'm talking to you), I have to tell you that he is completely full of himself. He's the kind of guy who's always presenting his profile to its best advantage, if you know what I mean. You can just tell that he thinks he was put on Earth to delight every female within fifty miles.'"

"I can't believe that's all she wrote about Giacomo!" Sarah was scandalized. "She didn't even tell us how they met! Or what he looks like!"

"Kate is a terrible correspondent," Annie agreed.

. . . or it covered, in exhaustive detail, aspects of her trip in which Sarah and Annie had absolutely no interest.

"Why does she keep going on about *Shakespeare*?" Sarah asked impatiently.

"Because he's the greatest playwright in the

English language. Because she's attending a summer conference on Shakespeare," Annie said.

"I know, but still—"

"And because she has a completely ridiculous set of priorities," Annie added, as they read on.

Act I
SCENE V

"Make haste, make haste!" Kate's father cried as he pounded on the door. "The guests are arriving for the reception!"

Kate leaned against the double sink in the bathroom as Lucy peered raptly into the mirror, carefully sweeping blush across one cheek. Kate had finished her own makeup (mascara and lip gloss) in five minutes. Now she watched, fascinated, as Lucy created a new face with the concentrated patience of a portrait painter.

"We should probably go," Kate said.

"Mmm," Lucy said absently, as she engaged in a tiny adjustment to her eyeliner. "Just . . . one . . . more . . . minute . . ."

Kate turned to look uncertainly at her own reflection. She wasn't sure about the dress. When she had bought it for the ill-fated prom, she worried that it would look too fancy. But now that she was in Italy, her dress looked more like something a nun would wear. A nun who lived in the seventeenth century and didn't get out much. Lucy, on the other hand, was wearing a filmy turquoise dress that made her eyes look even bluer, and her gold hair was piled on top of her head in a careless mass of curls.

Another pounding at the door, and the sound of her father's voice. "Anon, anon!"

As Lucy delicately brushed another layer of gloss on her lips, Kate wondered idly how she would cast Lucy in a Shakespeare play. Wearing her ethereal blue dress, she looked perfect for the part of Titania, but Lucy's personality seemed too sweet for the strong-willed Queen of the Fairies. Perhaps Bianca in *The Taming of the Shrew*? Lucy seemed like the kind of girl who would have several suitors dancing attendance on her at once. . . .

Suddenly, Kate didn't care to stand there any longer watching Lucy turn a pretty face into perfection. She muttered an excuse and went to her open bedroom window, where she stood breathing in the soft, scented air and gazing out at the garden. It looked like a landscape from a dream: mysterious and shadowed in the deepening twilight.

And then, between one breath and the next, an unusual sensation swept over her. First, she felt as if she were floating outside of her body. Then she had the absolute conviction that her life back in Kansas — her ordinary, normal, regular life — was the dream world and that she had just awakened to a new, and enchanted, reality.

She had just reached forward to touch the window frame, which was reassuringly solid under her hand, when her thoughts were interrupted by a rapid knock on the door and her father's urgent voice calling out, "Come, let's away!"

With one last look out the window, she left her room to go to the party.

The villa was ablaze with light. The high windows were open to the warm summer night. A river of guests dressed in silks and satins and tuxedos flowed through the rooms on the first floor, onto the terrace that had been strung with twinkling lights, and down into the garden, where carefully placed luminaries glowed softly in the dusk.

Kate and her father walked into the ballroom, with Lucy and Tom right behind them. It was an expansive room, with large arched windows, six sparkling chandeliers, and pale yellow walls decorated with gilt. Lots of gilt.

"Wow," Lucy said.

"This looks like the kind of room you'd sign a treaty in," Tom said, looking a bit intimidated.

Kate's father bounced a couple of times from sheer joy. "Isn't this marvelous?" he said. "Oh, look, there's Sebastian!" He waved both hands exuberantly at someone at the other side of the room. "And Julian!"

Kate followed his gaze and saw a bald man happily clutching a drink in each hand and talking to another man with a remarkably strange toupee. But she knew that they weren't who her father was really looking for.

"Do you see Professoressa Marchese?"

"No." His eyes narrowed dangerously as he glanced from one person to another. "Of course, I'm not sure what she looks like these days. Once she became rich and famous, she stopped attending conferences. Too busy to toil in the groves of academe with the rest of us." He added waspishly, "And she's been using that same author photo for at least twenty years. Too vain to let the years show, I suppose."

"Mmm," Kate murmured noncommittally. Her father had spent two weeks hunched over his computer, learning Photoshop in order to "give a little touch-up, that's all" to his own faculty photo. "I wonder if she's even here."

"Oh, she's here." Her father's eyes darted around the room. "That woman loves being the center of attention. Quite narcissistic, Ollie Jameson says."

His face brightened. "Ah, speak of the devil! There's Ollie over by the buffet table. Which looks absolutely stupendous." His buoyancy restored, he plunged eagerly into the crowd, calling back over his shoulder, "I'll find you later! Have fun!"

In a far corner of the ballroom, Silvia di Napoli was attracting attention. She didn't have to see the shocked sidelong glances directed at her, or hear the appalled comments, or observe the dismayed expressions. She could feel the reaction of the crowd, and she reveled in it.

She leaned against the wall, holding a tall fluted glass of *prosecco* in one hand. Her pose was the picture of nonchalance, but it was, in fact, calculated to achieve exactly the effect she wanted. Silvia had chosen her dress tonight with great care. It was made from a silvery material that clung to her body like molten metal and then flowed to the floor, where it puddled at her feet and made the mere act of walking an adventure in staying upright. As if to make up for all the extra material lying on the floor, the middle had been cut out to reveal an angel-wing tattoo that stretched across her midriff. It was her latest move in a long-running campaign to drive her parents mad. They didn't have to know that it was only a temporary tattoo. At least not right away.

She had styled her dark brown hair so that it stood out around her head in a wild, gravity-defying halo, outlined her large eyes with smoky eyeliner and purplish gray eyeshadow, and coated her lips with a deep red color that bordered on black. In a nod to the formal nature of the evening, she had finally decided to put just one silver hoop in her right ear and three in the left. Still, she was satisfied that she looked threatening and dangerous and rebellious — the exact opposite, in other words, of the insipid hometown heroine, Juliet.

As she glanced casually around the room, Silvia noticed many of her parents' friends, all pillars of the community, all stodgy and conservative, and all secretly thankful that their daughters weren't like her. She saw Benno, who gave her a cheeky wink and was immediately scolded by the head waiter. And then she spotted the mayor of Verona, who was holding court with the town's more influential and wealthy citizens.

Silvia wrinkled her nose in disdain. The mayor was a short man who wore custom-made shoes with two-inch heels. He was a proud man who insisted on adding a silly scarlet sash to his tuxedo for official occasions. And, most damning of all, he was a completely embarrassing man who also happened to be her father.

His gaze locked with hers and his cheerful grin slipped for just a moment. Then, quick as a blink, it was back, and he was tactfully excusing himself from the conversation in order to head in her direction. Silvia braced herself. By the time he got to her side, his normally ruddy face had flushed a deep purple and she could see a vein pulsing in his forehead.

"*Ciao*, papà," she said in as deadpan a voice as she could manage. "You look very well this evening. Quite dashing."

He couldn't help himself; he glanced down and preened for just a moment before he remembered that this was his daughter speaking. She hadn't said anything that wasn't sarcastic since she turned thirteen. He felt a touch of nostalgia for the twelve-year-old Silvia, who had papered her bedroom walls with photos of clean-cut pop stars and cute puppies, who had begged to go to work with him just so they could be together, who had blushed if a neighbor chided her for being too loud. . . .

But that Silvia was gone. In her place was this, this *alien* who said everything with a sneer and eyed him disdainfully and made him feel like the oldest, most ridiculous man on earth.

"More to the point, *I* am dressed appropriately," he said. He realized that he was gritting his teeth. He remembered what his dentist had said about cracked molars, and made a conscious effort to relax his jaw. "You, on the other hand—" He glanced at the tattoo and closed his eyes in pain.

"The invitation said formal," she said, innocently. Her face darkened as she remembered that she had a grievance of her own. "*I* wanted to buy a new dress for this party, but *you* said it would cost too much! *You* said that the babies needed new high chairs! *You* said that our family now had different financial priorities! And this is the only formal dress I have, remember?"

"Yes, and I also remember that there used to be a bit more of it!" her father hissed.

Silvia glanced down complacently. "I know," she said. "I altered it myself. It's an original design."

"Original." Her father glared at her. "You'll be lucky not to be charged with indecent exposure. And if you are"—he gave her a warning look—"don't expect any favors just because you're the mayor's daughter!"

Silvia ignored this comment with the disdain it deserved.

First, she never told *anyone* she was the mayor's daughter.

Second, her father was not, by any stretch of the imagination, an authority on fashion. She curled her lip at his tuxedo (which was vintage, but not in a good way), his high-heeled shoes (which kept making him lose his balance), and that scarlet sash (which made him look like an extra in a second-rate opera company).

"Fine," she said loftily. "If the police arrest me, I will plead guilty to having a unique and inventive fashion sense."

He remembered what his wife had said about keeping his temper and forced himself to smile. "At least try to behave yourself tonight," he said with a passable attempt at sounding conciliatory. "That's all I ask."

She lifted one eyebrow and waited. When her father said that something was "all he asked," more demands invariably followed.

Her father did not disappoint her. "And please, get

to the seminar on time every day," he went on, "not twenty minutes late! And pay strict attention to Signora Marchese, and do all your homework, and don't dispute every single word she says, the way you do with me!"

"I *don't* dispute every single word you say," Silvia snapped. "And if you're so worried about how I will do in this stupid seminar, I don't know why you went to so much trouble to get me in!"

"Shh!" His eyes darted around the room to see if anyone had overheard. "That is between us, Silvia, please, I told you that!"

He pulled a red silk handkerchief from his pocket and mopped his forehead. Silvia winced at the handkerchief but smiled with satisfaction at the sign of guilt. "You wouldn't be suffering from nerves right now if you hadn't decided to do something illegal," she said primly.

"*Illegal?* I pulled a few strings, that's all!" he hissed. "When that girl from Germany had to drop out at the last minute, I saw an opportunity for you to better yourself—"

"And for you to get closer to Francesca Marchese," she said in an insinuating tone.

"Yes! Yes! I admit it!" He was practically dancing on his toes with outrage. "And so? What of it? *I* am the mayor! *She* is one of Verona's most prominent residents and internationally famous, to boot! And you, *you —* "

"People are staring, papà," Silvia said. Her face was pure innocence, but her eyes sparkled with delight.

He opened his mouth to yell, then remembered what his cardiologist had said about high blood pressure and took a few deep breaths instead. He carefully tucked his handkerchief in his pocket, arranging it with great deliberation until it was again a perfect scarlet triangle. When he was more composed, he finished in a strangled whisper, "And *you* are a young girl who should be *grateful!*" He glanced at his watch. "I must go. It's almost time for my speech. Please, *mia cara* . . . just try not to attract more attention than you have to."

He scurried off. As Silvia watched him move through the crowd, her sharp eyes spotted three teenagers standing across the room. The girl in the blue dress looked overawed by their surroundings. The other girl, with the dark blond hair and glasses, wore a simple black dress that was probably supposed to be elegant but managed only to look dreary. And the boy—Silvia clucked her tongue disapprovingly. His shirt didn't fit well, his tie was askew, and he kept glancing suspiciously at his glass of *prosecco* as if he'd never had sparkling wine before. They were, undoubtedly, the Americans.

Her smile broadened. Here, at last, was some new entertainment.

Silvia tilted her glass back to take the last sip of her drink, then headed across the room.

Tom went to a school on the California coast that offered a P.E. elective in surfing. He played soccer and lacrosse. His hair had been lightened by the sun to a pale gold, his tan was perfect year-round, he drove a BMW.

Even at a school where most of the students looked as if they could star in a TV series, Tom's easy grin and amiable manner meant that girls flocked to him. He never had to make the slightest effort to get a date. He walked across campus with an easy, rolling stride, the picture of unthinking confidence and grace. He was living a charmed life.

Of course, he hadn't known that. Not until now.

Now he was here, in Italy, and it wasn't just a different country, it was a different world. He took another sip of his drink and looked around the room, listening to conversations in different languages and realizing with shame that he couldn't figure out what language was being spoken half the time, let alone understand what was being said. The food was odd, too, and he'd never seen so many people dressed so fancily, and he was beginning to wonder just what he was doing here. . . .

And then he saw a vision.

A slim girl was moving toward them, slipping through the elbow-to-elbow crowd as easily as a garter snake slithering through the grass. As she moved around a small knot of partygoers, Tom spotted her bare midriff and what looked like, even at a slight distance, a really amazing tattoo. He blushed and hastily raised his eyes. Despite her wild hair and dark, glittering eyes and that tattoo, she had a heart-shaped face that could have looked sweet, if it weren't for her sardonic expression. Instead, Tom thought that she looked like an angel who had decided that it was far more amusing to be wicked than to be good.

The girl sauntered up to them and coolly surveyed Kate, Tom, and Lucy. "*Ciao*," she said, her voice faintly amused. "You must be the Americans."

Kate defiantly lifted her chin and said the only three sentences of Italian she had learned well enough to say with confidence. "Yes, I'm an American. My name is Kate. What is your name?"

Tom barely heard her. He didn't understand what she was saying, anyway. And the girl didn't look impressed. "Silvia di Napoli," she said.

Tom decided to take this as his cue to join the conversation. "I'm Tom," he blurted out. "Tom Boone. I'm from Laguna Beach. That's in California, well, you probably knew that. . . ." His voice trailed off, then he added, with a touch of desperation, "Great surfing."

He winced as he heard the words come out of his mouth. As if this girl cared about Laguna Beach, about surfing, about him.

She gave him a cool look up and down, then rattled off something he didn't understand. *"Immagino che non parli italiano, vero?"* I don't suppose you speak any Italian, do you?

He could only stare at her, his mouth hanging open. The rapid-fire words sounded like birdsong to him. Beautiful but incomprehensible.

She sighed impatiently. "Just as I thought," she said in English.

He gathered his thoughts with difficulty and managed to say, "Um . . . what?"

"You don't know any Italian."

"Um, well . . ." He couldn't stop staring at her. His mind was blank. He felt like one of those zombies in the horror movies that he loved to watch late at night: unable to move or speak of his own volition, an empty shell, powerless in the presence of a force much greater than himself. "Only a little bit. I mean, I know words like zucchini and fettucine and linguine."

This was terrible. This was awful. This was why zombies weren't allowed to speak.

"Basically, you know, I can say any *ini* word," he said, trying to finish with a display of wit. He had heard somewhere that girls liked it if you could make them laugh.

But Silvia did not laugh. In fact, the look she leveled at him was scorching. It was clear that, when it came to witty conversation, he had fallen far short of the mark. "We can speak English," she said offhandedly. "I've been studying it since I was five."

"Oh, great!" He took a deep breath and forged on. "Anyway! Are you one of the other Shakespeare Scholars?"

"*Sì,*" Silvia said. After a minuscule pause, she added, "I mean, yes."

"We all know what *sì* means," Kate snapped.

Silvia smiled a small, catlike smile. "Oh? Well, it is a beginning."

Kate narrowed her eyes. One of the witches in

Macbeth, she thought. Most definitely. All she needs is a cauldron.

Fortunately they were interrupted at that moment by a young waiter who swooped toward them through the crowd, holding a tray of hors d'oeuvres at a perilous angle. He skidded to a breathless stop and presented the tray to them with a theatrical gesture.

"*Buona sera!*" he said. "May I offer you something this evening? Bruschetta? Stuffed mushrooms?"

"Thanks." Tom's eyes lit up, and he reached for a mushroom.

"Or perhaps the strange dry chips with the mysterious green paste on top? It is a new recipe, created especially for this evening by our cook." He smiled at Kate as if they were sharing a private joke. He had wild black curls, sparkling black eyes, and a crooked grin that made him look like a mischievous and not altogether kindly sprite.

Puck, Kate thought automatically, even as she tried to remember where she had seen him before. He would be perfect as Puck in *A Midsummer Night's Dream.*

"I am told that it is incredibly delicious, but"—he leaned forward to whisper conspiratorially—"the chef sometimes lies."

She couldn't help smiling back; his good spirits

were contagious. "I'll try the strange chips," Kate said.

As she picked up one of the appetizers, the waiter winked at her. "Such bravery! Such daring! I stand in awe of your courageous spirit!"

He gave a little bow. His hair badly needed to be brushed, but his bow was the essence of courtliness.

Kate ate the cracker in one bite. "Very tasty," she said.

"Excellent," the waiter said solemnly. "Our chef now has a reason to live."

"Oh, please." Silvia turned to the others. "Benno always plays the clown with tourists. He says they love it."

"Yes, I get much bigger tips," Benno agreed cheerfully.

Kate's smile vanished. "We're not tourists. We're here to study."

Instantly, his expression turned sober. "Of course not. I apologize most sincerely. And deeply? Yes, sincerely and deeply."

Silvia snorted. "Deeply is fine," she lectured. "Sincerely is fine. But both together? No. That is too much."

Benno smiled and made a comic face. "Silvia is my English tutor. She is an excellent teacher.

She keeps me on the straight and narrow."

"I don't let him talk on and on and *on*, the way he does in Italian," Silvia corrected him. She was trying to sound severe, but Kate could tell that she was pleased by the compliment.

"Benno!" Across the room, a slim man wearing a severe black suit frowned and snapped his fingers.

Benno gave an elaborate shrug of apology in response, then turned and winked at Kate. "*Scusi.* I'm supposed to be working." He stood as tall as he could, lifted his chin, and strolled sedately through the crowd, his tray held perfectly parallel to the floor.

Lucy said, "I hope he doesn't get in trouble for talking to us."

Silvia shrugged one shoulder. "Benno is always in trouble. But Alessandro"—she nodded in the head waiter's direction—"he's Benno's mother's cousin's son, so the most he will do is yell a lot." Her eyes slid sideways to look over Kate's shoulder. "And, of course, Benno is used to that—"

She stopped in midsentence, her expression changing in an instant from amused to disdainful. The shift was so abrupt that Kate, Tom and Lucy automatically turned to see what had caused her reaction.

It was the boy from Juliet's House. Kate watched

him as he descended the grand staircase as assuredly as a prince entering his throne room.

"Oh, look," Lucy said, her eyes shining like stars. "It's Giacomo!"

Silvia's head turned toward her with sudden sharp interest. "You know him?"

"Yes, we met him today," Lucy said. "At Juliet's House."

"Rrrreeeaally." Silvia rolled her *R*s and stretched out the vowels of that word, making it sound more knowing and scornful than Kate would have supposed possible. "How *interrresting*."

"Why is that interesting?" Lucy asked, but before Silvia could answer, Giacomo strolled over to where they were standing.

"*Ciao*, Silvia," he said, a mocking gleam in his eye.

"*Ciao*, Giacomo," she replied, a poisonous glare in hers.

"That dress is very, ah —" He hesitated, smiling, as if sorting through a number of different adjectives. "Nice," he finally said.

"Nice?" she said, sounding cross.

"Did I say nice? I misspoke." He took another long, appreciative look. "Actually, it's scandalous. Shocking. Borderline indecent."

Silvia sniffed, a little mollified by this, but Lucy

said earnestly, "I think it's absolutely amazing, but let me tell you, my mama wouldn't let me out of the house wearing something like that!"

Too late, she felt the atmosphere turn glacial. "Of course, my mother's very conservative," she added lamely. "We're from Mississippi, you know."

"I think it's great," Tom blurted into the silence, then turned red as everyone looked at him. He stared down at his empty glass.

"So! Giacomo! What are you doing here?" Lucy asked brightly.

Before he could answer, Kate's father came bounding up. "Hello again, Shakespeare Scholars!" he cried. "You're all enjoying the party, I hope!"

Kate turned her back on Giacomo. "Of course," she said to her father. "It's great."

"'O wonderful, wonderful, and most wonderful wonderful! and yet again wonderful! and after that, out of all whooping!'" said her father, who had had several glasses of wine. His eyes brightened as Benno swung by with a tray of appetizers.

He motioned for Benno to stop, and started putting together a small plate of food while simultaneously flagging down another waiter for a refill of wine. *"Grazie,"* he said. Before Benno could move on, he added, "May I ask you something?

Who is that man over there, by the portrait?"

Benno looked. "Oh, that's Franco Manzini. Very rich. Made his money in sardines."

"Ah." Her father pursed his lips as if this were of great interest and gestured toward someone on the other side of the room. "And the elderly woman in the purple dress?"

"Signora Ricci," Benno said agreeably. "Her family is very old. They've lived in Verona for centuries."

"Interesting, very interesting," her father said, nodding sagely. "And, er, that woman over there, I wonder who she is?"

There was a real note of interest in his voice this time, Kate thought, so she turned to take a closer look. The woman was tall and regal, both in her posture, which was perfect, and her dress, which was opulent. Her dark brown hair was pulled back in a simple, elegant chignon. She moved in a stately fashion toward them, her mouth curved in a smile of secret amusement, as a small man bobbed eagerly along in her wake.

The man, who was wearing a 1970s-era tuxedo, a bizarre red sash and—could those be platform shoes?—managed to shoot ahead of the mysterious woman at the last moment so that he could handle the introductions.

"Buona sera!" he cried. "Allow me to introduce you

to the driving force behind the conference, the creative genius who has brought international acclaim to the University of Verona and to our town, the author of books that have sold millions of copies worldwide, the brilliant Professoressa Francesca Marchese!"

Kate felt her mouth drop open. *This* was the infamous, the wicked, the nefarious Professoressa Marchese?

Kate snuck a quick look at her dad. He looked the same way he did that time last winter when he had slipped on an icy sidewalk and landed on his backside: too stunned to breathe.

Francesca Marchese smiled and said in a sultry voice, "I am so glad to finally meet you in person, Dr. Sanderson. Although I've obviously known you by reputation for years."

Was it Kate's imagination, or did Professoressa Marchese say the word *reputation* with a lemony touch of irony? She glanced sideways at her father and knew instantly that he suspected the same thing.

He threw his head back in a challenging way and said, "Delighted, delighted," sounding anything but. "I've followed your career with great interest as well. Although I must say I haven't gotten around to reading *The Shakespeare Secret* yet." He chuckled as if to say a fellow scholar would understand that. "You know how it is. One must stay current with the academic journals. Hard to find time for reading . . . hmm. What would you call your book? Popular fiction, I suppose."

"Indeed, I'm happy to say that it's turned out to be quite popular," she said calmly. "And I have always enjoyed your work, too, Dr. Sanderson. Although I don't remember reading anything recently." She took a sip of wine. "Perhaps I somehow missed your latest publication?"

Her father did his best to stare disdainfully down his nose at her (which wasn't easy; Professoressa Marchese was a tall woman and they stood eye-to-eye). "Actually, my next book will be published in the fall," he boasted. "A massive work, the culmination of my career. My editor is very excited about it. In fact, she thinks it could enjoy great popular success as well."

"Ah yes, it's so rewarding to have a best-seller outside academic circles." Professoressa Marchese paused just long enough for everyone to remember that she had already accomplished that feat. Twice. "I wish you the best of luck with it," she added kindly.

He glanced around the room as if looking for the nearest exit, and saw Lucy, Tom, and Silvia standing nearby, listening to this exchange with varying degrees of fascination and puzzlement.

"I'm sorry, we're forgetting our manners!" he cried heartily. "I don't believe everyone's been introduced. Professoressa Marchese, this is Lucy Atwell, Tom Boone, and my daughter, Kate."

The fearsome witch of Kate's childhood smiled warmly at her. "*Piacere*. I am so pleased to meet you." Then she waved one graceful hand at Giacomo and added, "And I am most pleased to present to you Giacomo Marchese. My son."

Entr'acte

"He's the son of her father's sworn enemy!" Sarah said with undisguised glee.

"Sarah," Annie began, a note of warning in her voice.

"Star-crossed lovers!" Sarah snatched the paper from Annie's hands and reread the passage with an air of triumph. "You have to admit, I'm already ahead on points."

"Except that they hate each other," Annie pointed out. "*Loathe* each other. *Despise* each other."

"Exactly! It's perfect!" Sarah cried. "This is the way the greatest loves in the universe always start!"

Annie crossed her arms and stared at her friend. "You are so gullible."

"What?" Sarah happily bit into a cookie. "Don't be a sore loser. "

"Kate is made of sterner stuff than you imagine," Annie said. "She took a vow to never fall in love, and she won't. You'll see."

But Sarah, her eyes gleaming, just took another cookie and didn't bother to answer.

Act I
SCENE VI

"The villa's main building was erected in 1682, with the two additional wings added in 1703." Kate was pacing through the villa's garden on gravel paths with Lucy at her side, reading from a pamphlet she had found in the library. "The intricate design of the garden is typical of the Renaissance, with separate 'rooms' created by box hedges and a high wall surrounding the entire garden, shielding it from public view. Even within the garden, there are many hidden spots that a visitor may stumble upon as he or she wanders through the carefully planned landscape: secret bowers and grottos, sunken pools, a fountain tucked within a small grove of lemon trees. The highlight of the garden is the large and elaborate maze, near the rear of the property, where the manicured garden becomes woodland and the sense of being lost within the labyrinthine hedges feels both delightful and slightly dangerous—"

Kate raised her head and looked around. "I wonder how far we are from the maze. That sounds interesting."

"Well, let's rest for a second before we go looking for it." Lucy sat down on a wooden bench in the shade and fanned herself with her hand. "Lord, and I thought Mississippi was hot!"

Kate stretched out on the grass, flopping on her back and staring up at the sky, so bright and blue that it looked enameled. "We can stop for a few minutes, I guess," she said. "There are acres of grounds to explore, according to this brochure." But she said it in a desultory tone. They had risen late, since it was Sunday, and had eaten a large meal with the other Shakespeare Scholars that served as both breakfast and lunch. As Lucy had said, they were an intense group: The girls tended to have fervent eyes and lank hair, while the boys went in for black-framed glasses and long-winded monologues.

There was Winnie, a solemn Swiss girl with heavy black bangs and hair that hung straight to her shoulder, so that she looked as if she wore a helmet;

Jonathan, who managed to mention that he was going to Oxford five times in five minutes (and wore a brand-new Oxford T-shirt to underscore the point); Frank, from Florida, who carried a heavily underlined copy of *Romeo and Juliet* everywhere he went; Erik, a brooding Danish boy who always sat hunched over, his eyes darting about as if he were expecting an assassination attempt; and Cynthia from Connecticut, who had a supercilious drawl and said things like, "Well, of *course*, everyone knows that Edward de Vere was a *fair* poet, but one only has to look at his *alliteration*, which one might call clumsy if one were being *kind*, and one would realize that the theory that he actually *wrote* Shakespeare's plays is *laughably* ill conceived."

This, despite the fact that no one had even mentioned Edward de Vere.

Kate had tried chatting with them, but every conversational gambit was met with pained smiles and pitying looks. Finally, tired of being snubbed, she gave up. Kate's father immediately began holding court with this little group, discoursing about everything from the accuracy of the history plays to whether Shakespeare favored drinking cider or beer. They listened to him with rapt attention and completely ignored Kate, Lucy, and Tom.

Kate frowned at a cloud drifting by. It looked like a hedgehog. Over lunch, Cynthia had lectured the table for twenty minutes about Shakespeare's usage of the word *hedgehog*. It had been remarkably tedious.

Kate made a face at the cloud and flipped through a few more pages of the pamphlet. "It says here that Professoressa Marchese commissioned statues of Shakespearean characters for the garden after she bought the villa," she remarked idly. "It might be fun to look for them."

"Statues?" Lucy wrinkled her nose. "Maybe later, when it cools off." She slid off the bench to join Kate on the ground. "I wonder where Giacomo is. You'd think he'd be at lunch, since he lives in the villa."

Kate shrugged. "Off doing his own thing, I suppose. He must have lots of friends in Verona." She yawned. Everyone else had trooped upstairs for a siesta after their meal, an Italian tradition which her father had said was one more indication that this was the most civilized country on earth. Both Kate and Lucy had felt too excited to take a nap. But now, Kate felt her eyes closing. The garden was quiet except for the hum of bees going about their business and birds chirping in a nearby tree. In the distance, a church bell rang, and Kate's happiness was complete. Nothing could disturb this sense of peace and well-being and complete contentment. . . .

"You know, I was just thinking," Lucy said. "Wouldn't it be great to have a summer romance in Italy?"

Annoyed, Kate opened her eyes and turned her head to look at Lucy, who was smiling, her eyes closed against the sun. "Rather unoriginal, though," Kate said repressively. "And have you read the syllabus? And the reading list? We won't have time for romance."

Lucy chuckled. "Oh, Kate, you are a *hoot*!"

Kate sat up, no longer drowsy. She pulled up a blade of grass and began shredding it methodically.

"And speaking of romance," Lucy went on dreamily, "he is gorgeous, isn't he?"

Kate pulled up an entire handful of grass and resisted the temptation to throw it in Lucy's face. "Who?"

Lucy turned her head to look at Kate, her blue eyes astonished. "Giacomo, of course!"

"Oh." Kate's tone was dismissive. "Him."

"Yes, *him*! Honestly, Kate!" Lucy said, exasperated.

"Looks aren't everything," Kate said. "After all," she quoted, "'the devil hath power t'assume a pleasing shape.'"

"Oh, he's not the devil!" Lucy protested.

"No, I know, that's not what I—"

"Although if he *was*," Lucy interrupted, "I can tell you that any girl on earth would be tempted to sell her soul."

"Not me!" Kate sniffed.

"But you just admitted that he has a pleasing shape."

"No, no, that was *Shakespeare* who said—"

"And, anyway, I don't care what you think." She turned her face to the sun and closed her eyes with finality. "In my opinion, a little romance is just what this seminar needs to make it abso*lute*ly perfect."

Kate tossed her handful of shredded grass to the ground. Why was everyone going on about love and romance, just when she had forsworn both? Lucy was almost as bad as Sarah and Annie.

That thought reminded her that it was time to send another e-mail. She had already found the one computer in the villa with an Internet connection. It was in the library, a grand, high-ceilinged room on the ground floor, and she had managed to dash off a couple of short notes. But every time she poked her head into the library today, she had found Winnie sitting in front of the computer, scowling with concentration at the screen.

Kate glanced at her watch. Although she would like nothing better than to take a nap in the garden, the library was sure to be empty now that everyone — even stern Winnie — was taking a siesta. It was the perfect time to write a longer, more detailed e-mail. She might even have time to browse through a few of the Shakespeare commentaries she had seen on the shelves.

She glanced at Lucy, who had fallen asleep and was now snoring. A dainty, pretty snore, of course, but still a snore. Kate grinned, jumped to her feet, and headed inside as church bells began once again to ring in the distance.

The last bell rang, the sound fading through the evening air. A long pause. Then, *"Nel nome del Padre e del Figlio e dello Spirito Santo."* The sonorous sound of the priest's voice echoed through the dim church.

"Amen," the congregation replied dutifully.

"La grazia del Signore nostro Gesù Cristo, l'amore di Dio Padre e la comunione dello Spirito Santo sia con tutti voi," the priest went on.

"E con il tuo spirito." Even though there were only two dozen people in attendance, their voices rolled through the cavernous sanctuary like waves breaking on the beach on a hot summer afternoon. It was a sound that Giacomo found soothing. In fact, he loved everything about the atmosphere at Santa

Lorenzo: the dim light, the candles flickering along the walls, the warm summer breeze that floated in when a latecomer opened the door, bringing with it the ordinary sounds of dogs barking or people laughing.

He leaned back, closed his eyes, and drifted off into his own thoughts as his grandmother sat beside him, saying the responses with the ease of decades of practice.

Giacomo had grown up going to this church. Because his father had moved back to England after the divorce and his mother traveled frequently for her work, he was left with his grandmother, who went to church every day. As a small boy, he would trot along behind her into the church and wait as she genuflected, then slid into her favorite pew. He would mimic her actions and sit next to her as she greeted her friends, other small widows dressed in black who were always sitting nearby like a row of friendly crows. They would often trade a bit of whispered gossip before crossing themselves and settling down to the routine business of worship.

Then he would drift off into a daydream, lulled into a hypnotic state by the priest's monotone, often staring vaguely at the church's frescoes and the strange, stiff people painted on the plaster walls.

Over the course of centuries, the paint had faded, the plaster had become worn, and feet, hands, and sometimes even faces were often rubbed out completely. So when Giacomo was nine, he had begun to invent new names and identities for them. The stoop-shouldered man with the anxious expression and round, startled eyes became Saint Mordecai, the patron saint of those who had neglected their homework. The short man with a halo of fluffy white hair and a cheerful face was rechristened Saint Archibald, who helped people pick out the right gifts for special occasions. The stern woman holding up an admonitory finger earned the name Saint Gertrude, the patron saint of substitute teachers put in charge of unruly classrooms.

But his favorite had been the young woman tucked away in a small chapel on one side of the sanctuary. She was surrounded by people clutching their heads and pointing dramatically at the sky, while she gazed calmly out of the painting, as if she couldn't believe how worked up everyone was getting. Giacomo had named her after his friend Giancarlo's older sister, who had been sixteen at the time and much too grand to notice the passionate devotion of a grubby little boy like himself.

Her name, he had decided, was Saint Rosaline.

The patron saint of hopeless crushes.

"Giacomo!" His nonna nudged him in the ribs with a sharp elbow to let him know that it was time to kneel.

He gave her an apologetic shrug and quickly did so, bowing his head over folded hands. When he was nine, he had been convinced that the saints would talk to him if he listened closely enough. Now that he was seventeen, of course, he knew they didn't.

Except for Rosaline, whose voice sometimes seemed to sound inside his mind, like bells chiming underwater.

After a few moments of kneeling with his eyes shut, he decided that he had given a reasonably good impression of piety and risked a quick glance up at Saint Rosaline. She gave him a cool look in return.

I have not seen you for some time, Giacomo. A decade, at least.

He cast his eyes to the ceiling. Saint Rosaline could be worse than his grandmother when it came to chivvying him to church. "It has been two days."

She gave a slight shrug. *Two days, two years, two centuries, when you've been stuck on a church wall for as long as I have, it's all one and the same.*

The prayer was over. Giacomo got up from his kneeling position. Then, filled with a warm, sanctified glow, he reached down to help his grandmother up.

She jerked her arm out of his grasp and glared at him, her black eyes snapping with outrage. "*Basta, basta!* Let go, leave me be!" She swatted at him irritably. "Stop being so holy!"

"I'm just trying to help," he hissed. "And it *is* a church."

"I've survived almost eighty years without your help! Or anyone else's!" she hissed back.

Giacomo gave an expressive shrug and slid back in his seat. "Fine."

"In the darkest of times!" she went on, grabbing the pew in front of her.

"Friends were lost!" She pulled hard on the pew and it rocked back, disturbing the man at the end, who had fallen into a light nap. He woke with a snort and looked around wildly.

"Family was lost!" She pulled again, harder. Giacomo thought he heard the wood crack.

"I alone"—she finally heaved herself up, flashing him a look of grim triumph—"prevailed!"

Satisfied that she had made her point, she fell back into her seat, fanning herself with her hand.

Giacomo glanced up at Saint Rosaline, who was laughing. *It's better than a play*, she said, delighted. *But tell me, Giacomo, what is new in your life?*

"Nothing," he thought.

No new girls? Her voice was teasing. *Come, come, surely there is some sort of tale to be told. What of that seminar you've been complaining about for weeks?*

That seminar. Giacomo felt a prickle of irritation at the thought of it. He didn't want to talk about it, but if he tried to ignore Rosaline, she was likely to get petulant.

Rosaline looked at him expectantly.

"There is one girl." The only real possibility, in fact. He gazed at the candles flickering on the altar and tried to sound enamored. "Um, let's see. Her name is Lucy, she has hair as fine as spun gold, eyes like sapphires, a smile as bright as day—"

Oh, how nice, Rosaline said, clearly bored. *And how amazing to find one girl who manages to embody every cliché.*

He shot her a dark look.

She smiled blandly back. *No one else?*

"Well, Silvia will be there, of course."

She chuckled. She had heard a lot about Silvia over the years. *Ah, that should be fun.*

"Delightful," he said, with a touch of gloom. After a pause, he added reluctantly, "And there is one other girl—"

Oh? There was a spark of interest in Rosaline's

voice. Giacomo hurried to snuff it out.

"But *she* is a disaster."

Really. That sounds much more promising.

He stole a look at the fresco. "What does that mean?"

Only that it's time you fell in love.

Fall in love? Please! He would have laughed out loud if he wasn't sitting in church. "I've fallen in love hundreds of times," he pointed out. "Remember Paola? And Jocelyn? And Marte and Cecelia and Sandra and Gigi . . ."

He could have gone on, *would* have gone on, but she was shaking her head with that infuriatingly patronizing look that only someone who had been around since the fifteenth century could summon.

It's time you experienced true love, she said. Then, as if to make her point clear, she went on. *The kind that brings both rapture and despair, the kind that turns your world upside down, the kind that—*

"Yes, yes, yes." Giacomo was getting testy. "I've read the poetry."

The members of the congregation were shifting in their pews, preparing to kneel as the service neared its end.

You may have read the poetry, she said tartly, *but you haven't lived it. And that's what makes the difference.*

"Hmmph." He didn't realize that he had made that noise out loud until an elderly lady two pews in front of him turned to give him an admonishing look and his grandmother poked him sharply in the ribs.

This is what comes of making up conversations with frescoes, he chided himself, as he dropped to his knees and bowed his head. Nothing but trouble.

Act I
SCENE VII

"What, daydreaming already? Class has not even begun."

Kate spun around to see Giacomo leaning in the doorway of the seminar room, yawning. "I was beginning to wonder if I had the time wrong," she said, making a great show of checking her watch.

She had gone for a run at dawn, showered, dressed, and arrived in the seminar room early, only to find that she was, as usual, the first one there. It was a large room on the second floor, with six windows on one wall, a small fireplace, and bare wooden floors. In the center of the room sat a long table surrounded by seven chairs. Kate had seated herself, pulled out her fresh notebook, favorite pen, and well-thumbed copy of *Romeo and Juliet,* and settled herself in to wait.

After five minutes, she had been bored; after ten minutes, annoyed; and after fifteen, wondering if everyone else had been mysteriously killed in their beds. Indeed, Kate was half hoping that was the case, since it was the only possible excuse for all of them being so late. To calm herself, she had gone to the window to look out at the garden below. Even as she watched birds wing in and out of a tree, however, she had been aware of sounds from the next room that indicated that her father and his students—obviously serious scholars who understood the importance of punctuality—were already getting started.

"Wasn't class supposed to start at nine?" she added with some asperity.

"Or thereabouts." Giacomo dropped into one of the chairs and closed his eyes.

"It's already ten minutes after."

"You Americans," he said. "You always want to get started, get going, get things done!"

And what's wrong with that? Kate thought, feeling nettled by both his comment and the amused look he gave her.

"I'm simply looking forward to this seminar," she

said coolly. "I can't wait to get started."

"Oh, yes," he said solemnly. "Me, too." He pulled a few sheets of folded paper from his back pocket and tossed them on the table. "Do you have a pen I could borrow?"

"Of course," she said, handing him her spare. She glanced down at the paper, which had obviously been torn from a spiral notebook. "You don't have a notebook either?"

He grinned at her. "You sound positively scandalized."

"Well, no, I'm just . . ." Kate stopped, at a loss for words. Coming to class without a pen and notebook was like showing up in her pajamas. She couldn't imagine it. "Here," she blurted out. "I brought extra notebooks, too. Take one of mine. *Please.*"

He laughed, but he nodded his thanks and took the notebook just as Silvia stomped into the room. This morning she was dressed in a short black skirt, a gray T-shirt with a torn hem, ragged fishnet stockings, and heavy black boots. She wore four earrings in each ear and a ferocious frown.

"You're up early, Giacomo," she said.

"Of course," he said. "It is the first morning of class, after all." He gave Kate a smiling glance and added piously, "And punctuality is a virtue."

Kate rolled her eyes a little at that, but she smiled back.

Silvia's sharp eyes flicked suspiciously from Giacomo to Kate, but she just tossed her backpack on the table with perhaps a little more force than necessary. The buckles snapped open and a battered notebook, several chewed pencil stubs, and a handful of crumpled candy wrappers spilled out.

She threw herself into a seat and flung one leg over the arm of her chair. "Well, I am surprised," she said. "Considering what you were up to *last* night."

Her waspish tone implied massive impropriety, a bacchanale that was best left to everyone's imaginations. Giacomo shrugged.

"You should not be fooling around with Anna Tomassi," she went on. "She has five brothers. And they are all much bigger than you."

He simply smiled in a way calculated to annoy her.

"You need to watch out for this one," Silvia said to Kate. "I am warning you as a friend."

Kate lifted her chin an inch as she met Silvia's gaze. "I'd already figured that out, thanks."

"Condemned without a trial!" Giacomo protested mildly. "This hardly seems fair. I should at least be allowed to argue in my own defense, don't you think, Katerina?"

"It's Kate," she said.

"Kate," he repeated. The word sounded clipped and abrupt. He tilted his head, as if considering this. "I think I prefer Katerina."

His British accent disappeared, and *Katerina* rolled off his tongue with a beautiful Italian pronunciation, making the name sound different, foreign, exotic, as if it belonged to another person altogether.

"*I,*" she said firmly, "prefer Kate."

He raised his eyebrows at that, but before he could respond, Tom rushed in through the door. He was breathless and his hair clung to his forehead in damp spikes. "Hey, everybody," he said. "Oh, good, class hasn't started yet."

Lucy strolled in unhurriedly after him and gave them all a sunny smile. "I'm sorry, it's totally my fault we're late," she said. "I saw this cute bakery down a side street yesterday and I wanted to check it out, so Tom came with me and somehow—"

"We got a little turned around," Tom said.

"Aren't you a gentleman," Lucy said, peeping up at him from under her lashes. "I managed to get us completely and totally lost! I'm sure I would still be wandering the streets if he hadn't remembered to bring a map!"

She made it sound as if he had rescued her from a

remote mountain in Tibet, Kate thought. Did this approach really work on guys?

She glanced at Tom. Apparently the answer was yes. He ducked his head in confusion, then actually pulled out a chair for Lucy to sit in. Kate had never seen anyone do that in real life, except for waiters at fancy restaurants. And they were *paid* to pull out chairs.

Lucy sat down as gracefully as a butterfly alighting on a flower. The faint scent of perfume, something light and flowery, drifted through the room. When Kate flipped open her notebook, she noticed that she had somehow broken a nail.

Lucy smiled happily and looked around the table. Her gaze fell on Silvia's skirt, which was a complicated affair involving a ragged hem, a number of large and vicious-looking safety pins, and what could have been bloodstains, although the material was so inky black it was hard to tell.

"What an interesting skirt," she said in a doubtful tone. She spotted a brooch pinned to the skirt's waistband and brightened; it looked like a rose. "Oh, that pin is darling!"

Silvia glanced down at the brooch with some pride. "*Sí*, it is an antique," she said. "See the little hinge? It opens up." She demonstrated. "Two centuries ago, the woman who wore this pin used it to carry a deadly poison with her."

Lucy's eyes widened. "Why?" she breathed.

"To kill her unfaithful lover, of course," Silvia said carelessly. "Or perhaps, to kill the woman who wanted to steal her lover's affection." Her eyes glittered with enthusiasm as she gave this second possibility some serious thought. "Yes," she finally decided. "Kill your rival, keep your lover. That's a much better plan."

"Would she really want to keep him, though?" Lucy sounded dubious. "I mean, if he's cheating on her?"

Before this interesting point could be discussed further, the door was flung open, revealing Professoressa Marchese framed dramatically in the doorway. She was wearing a white silk blouse, a dark skirt cinched with a wide leather belt, and extremely high black heels with extremely pointy toes. Gold earrings and necklace winked with reflected light; even at a distance, they looked genuine and very expensive.

"Welcome," she began in a low, thrilling voice, only to be interrupted by Benno, who staggered in carrying a large box. He dropped it on the table with relief and sank into a chair with a muttered apology for his lateness.

She cleared her throat and began again. "As I was saying. Welcome to the University of Verona's first Summer Shakespeare Seminar.

"The purpose of our seminar is not to learn Shakespeare through the head"—she pointed to her own head as if to illustrate the point—"but to feel him, through our hearts!" She swept her hand through the air until it dramatically landed on her ample bosom.

She paused as if waiting for applause, but when she was met with silence, she plunged on. "You will not be sitting at a desk, poring over dusty books and writing endless essays!"

Tom and Benno looked cheered by this.

"No!" Professoressa Marchese continued. "Instead, you will live and breathe and experience Shakespeare to the core of your souls! How, you may ask?"

Kate glanced at Giacomo. He had tilted his chair onto the back two legs and was rocking dangerously back and forth, staring at the ceiling.

"By embodying the spirit of the plays through physical movement! By exploring the sense of the poetry through acting! By channeling the spirit of Shakespeare's most romantic characters by answering letters that have been sent to the Juliet Club! And what, you may ask, is—"

"The Juliet Club?" Lucy interrupted.

Professoressa Marchese shot her a quelling look and Lucy sank back into her seat. "As I was about to say," the professor went on, "the Juliet Club is a volunteer organization that answers thousands of letters sent to Juliet each year from people around the globe. People who are lost, wandering, desperate for advice about love. I have received permission for all of you to serve as volunteers during this seminar. You will each answer at least two letters a day, although you may discuss your response with your classmates. In fact, I would recommend . . ." She paused as if mentally replaying what she had just said. "No," she corrected herself, "I would *encourage* you to do so. A photocopy machine is available so that you can keep your letters on file." She gestured toward the box. "We selected letters from other teenagers, of course, so the problems you're presented with should be quite familiar."

"I thought we were supposed to be *studying* the play," Kate began.

"Indeed, you will! In fact, you will need to study it extremely closely in order to channel the voice of Juliet," Professoressa Marchese said. "Each line of Shakespeare, when examined closely, reveals worlds within worlds within worlds. The way a character speaks, responds, moves, doesn't move, every tiny detail tells you something important about that character."

A small line appeared between Kate's eyebrows. Professoressa Marchese was making it sound as if they were on the same side here when, actually, they weren't at all. "I agree," Kate said, trying to be polite. "But I don't see how writing letters filled with love advice will teach us about the play itself—"

"Trust me," Professoressa Marchese snapped, clearly losing patience. "When studied properly, my method will teach you more about this great work of art than you would ever learn by studying the play as"—she curled her lip with disdain—"*mere text.*"

The professor did not raise her voice; nevertheless, the last two words rang out as clear as a bell at dawn, just when the voice of Kate's father had stopped for a moment.

There was a long silence that seemed to hum with tension. And then, as if in response, a loud voice boomed from the room next door. Kate had no problem imagining her father in the full throes of his first lecture. He would be striding back and forth, declaiming in a lordly fashion, and waving his arms excitedly in the air. And as for what he would be saying . . .

"As always with the Bard, one must begin by

making sense of the rhythm and words," he was say-ing, his words becoming louder and clearer through the wall. "In other words, the *text*. None of this touchy-feely nonsense that is so fashionable these days! No, we will take a rigorous, classical, *intelligent* approach to *Romeo and Juliet*. We will measure the meters of the verse until our hearts beat in iambic pentameter! We will explore the richness of the lan-guage! We will discuss the historical context. . . ." His voice faded a bit as he apparently turned to stride forcefully in the other direction.

Professoressa Marchese's eyes flickered toward the cloakroom door, then she turned back to her class. "So many people insist on teaching *Romeo and Juliet* as an academic exercise," she said, perhaps a bit more loudly than was strictly necessary, especially since she was addressing six people rather than a crowd of thou-sands. "Count the syllables, analyze the metaphors, note the line breaks! Paagghh! How dry! How dull! How *drearily unimaginative!*"

There was another pause in which the very air seemed to be electrified. Then it was broken by the cloakroom door in the other room slamming shut with a bang that made everyone jump. Professoressa Marchese simply smiled with satisfaction.

"I assure you," she said in a calm voice, "at the end

of our month together, when you present your program at our gala costume ball, you will be amazed at how much you have learned by approaching the play experientially!"

"We're presenting a program?" Tom sounded concerned.

"There's going to be a costume ball?" Lucy's eyes sparkled with delight.

"*Si*, it will be a fantastic celebration and a marvelous opportunity for you all to demonstrate what you've learned," she said. Her eyes became dreamy. "The villa will be gorgeous, filled with light and flowers and music. The guests will arrive. They will be served drinks, they will begin to mingle, they will walk through the rooms and into the garden. And in every room they enter, around every corner they turn, they will come upon a scene from *Romeo and Juliet* being acted out by our wonderful Shakespeare Scholars!"

Giacomo cast his eyes to the ceiling, but Lucy seemed enthralled, Silvia attentive, and Benno and Tom cautiously interested. Kate folded her arms, withholding judgment until she had heard more.

The professor waved her hand slowly through the air, as if she could make the scene appear before their eyes. "They will walk out into the perfumed night and hear Romeo wooing Juliet on the balcony!" she said in a hypnotic tone. "They will enter the ballroom and see an elegant Elizabethan dance! They will pause beside a flower bed and hear the greatest poetry the world has ever known being recited! It will be as if they have stepped into Romeo and Juliet's world! It will be . . . magnificent!"

"Magnificent," Lucy repeated, sighing.

Then Tom said, "But I can't act." He was definite on this point. "Not if there's an audience. Not even if there's *not* an audience." He wondered if he had made his position quite clear. "Not at all," he finished firmly.

It was as if he had awakened Professoressa Marchese from a dream. "Not to worry, Tom," she said briskly. "I have engaged the services of a brilliant theater director, a Signor Renkin, to help you rehearse. And your parts will not be long or difficult. My plan is to focus on a few key scenes from the play and have each one performed several times during the evening's festivities, so each Shakespeare Scholar has a chance to shine."

Tom did not look convinced, but Professoressa Marchese sailed on. "Signor Renkin also will teach you an Elizabethan dance to perform —"

"We're going to *dance*?" Benno asked, horrified. "In *public*?"

"I will take you all to a costume rental shop next week to pick out what you will wear on the gala evening—"

Lucy actually clapped her hands at this news. Even Silvia looked interested before she caught herself and sank back down into her chair with a scowl.

"I'm not wearing tights," Tom said, mutinous.

Professoressa Marchese ignored this. "And finally, Signor Renkin has a great deal of experience in stage sword fighting—"

Tom and Benno perked up.

"We get to fight?" Tom asked. "What kind of swords?"

"Where will we practice? When can we start?" Benno was trying not to get too carried away, but he was already imagining the dashing figure he would cut, bounding across a stage, up and down a staircase, even—why not?—swinging on a rope from a balcony, wildly waving his rapier, and then killing all his dastardly foes.

"And we all get to fight?" Silvia was intent. "Not just the boys?"

Professoressa Marchese laughed. "Of course, Silvia, I would walk in fear if I tried to keep a sword from your hand."

Silvia gave a thin, satisfied smile at that.

"But all that will wait until the morrow! For now . . ." Professoressa Marchese opened the box that Benno had brought in, reached inside, and held up a letter. "I have the first letter for you to answer as official members of the Juliet Club."

Dear Juliet,

I am totally in love with a boy named James. I'm only fifteen, and my parents won't even let me date for another year, so James and I have been meeting in secret. My problem is that it's really making me nervous because I'm afraid we'll get caught. Plus, James used to date this girl Alice and even though he doesn't even like her anymore, he doesn't want to break up with her because he says she's kind of a hysterical personality and he's afraid of what she might do. So he still has to go out with her sometimes, just to keep her stable. Anyway, I'm asking for your advice because you had a very similar situation with Romeo (except for the part about Alice), so you know how it feels! Please write back as soon as you can.

Jill B.

Professoressa Marchese finished reading the letter aloud, then put the paper down and looked around the table. "A most thought-provoking letter, don't you agree? Kate, we will start with you. What advice would you give to Jill?"

"She should forget James," Kate said promptly. "Don't date until she's twenty-one, and then only under strict supervision. And quit writing to fictional characters for advice."

Silvia raised her hand. "Aren't we supposed to answer the way Juliet would?" she asked sweetly. "Excuse me for saying so, but that response doesn't sound very romantic."

"Is our advice supposed to be romantic, or useful?" Kate asked.

"Both, if possible," Professoressa Marchese replied.

"Well, I feel real sorry for her," Lucy said. "And I'm not sure about that James. He sounds kind of sneaky."

Benno couldn't let that go. "He has only been accused of liking two girls at the same time," he offered humbly, and then wished he hadn't.

"Only? *Only* accused of—!" Lucy couldn't even finish her sentence, she was so astounded by this reaction.

Silvia narrowed her eyes dangerously. "If she

loves this James, he is worth fighting for!"

"You're not saying she should hurt Alice," Lucy asked, impressed by her vindictive tone.

"Not Alice, no," Silvia conceded. After a moment, she added darkly, "But as for this James—"

"Silvia doesn't believe love is real unless someone has to go to hospital for at least five stitches," Giacomo said. "'Though she be but little, she is fierce.'"

Silvia managed to both scowl and look gratified at this assessment of her character. She shoved his chair with her dangling foot and said, "Pah! Five stitches is calf love. True passion requires at least ten." The mere thought seemed to put her in a better humor. She added, "*And* a lasting scar."

Lucy gazed at them with round eyes. "I really don't think that violence is ever the answer," she said solemnly.

Silvia bit back a sarcastic remark—why did Americans always take everything so *seriously*?—and asked, "And so what would you suggest?"

"Well, I think she should just sit down with James and have a heart-to-heart talk with him," Lucy said. "Tell him that he has to choose. It's either her or Alice."

"Why should *he* get to choose?" Silvia snapped.

"And why should she trust what he says?" Kate

added. "He's already shown that he has a duplicitous nature."

"We don't know that," Giacomo protested.

"Of course we do." Kate waved the letter in the air. "The evidence is right here."

"Based on what line?" Giacomo took the letter from her and made a great show of frowning at it in puzzlement. "Based on what example?"

Kate crossed her arms and lifted her chin a defiant half-inch, a sure sign to those who knew her that she was about to defend her position with the enthusiasm of a centurion repulsing the barbarians at the gates.

"Not all evidence needs to be explicitly stated," she said. "Especially given that the letter writer, in this case, sounds, well . . . shall we say, less than self-aware. Under the circumstances, I think we should be allowed to consider subtext, to examine what is implied as well as what is declared."

"We should also consider the possibility of an unreliable narrator," Giacomo pointed out as his mother gave a nod of surprised approval. "After all, we've only heard the girl's side of the story."

"Are you saying she's lying?" Silvia asked heatedly.

"Not necessarily," he said. "But perhaps she has misread the situation? Perhaps she's reading more into his declarations of love than are really there?

Perhaps her interpretation is flawed?"

There was a shocked silence. "Well?" Professoressa Marchese asked smoothly. "What does everyone think of that theory?"

Kate, Silvia, and Lucy looked at one another, united in disgust.

"He said he loved her!" Lucy cried. "There's only one way to interpret that!"

"I agree," Silvia said. "And if he has told her that he loves her and is still seeing this other girl—"

"Maybe more than one," Lucy reminded her.

"*Girls,* yes," Silvia amended, with a nod of thanks. "Then he clearly has an evil heart. Jill should exact retribution!"

Giacomo opened his mouth as if to speak, but Benno got there first.

"No, I think Giacamo is right," Benno said. "This girl is clearly crazy."

There was a moment of outraged silence, broken finally by Kate.

"Not really," she said to Benno. "You don't really think that?"

"There are many crazy girls in the world," he said defensively. "Believe me."

"Of course, you are an expert on that subject," Silvia murmured.

"I have had some distasteful experiences," Benno said with dignity, "which I'd rather not discuss."

"I'm merely saying it's one possibility," Giacomo said to Kate, ignoring Benno.

Tom was examining the letter intently. "Don't crazy people usually have really bad penmanship, all scrawly and everything? Her handwriting looks pretty neat." He looked more closely. "She does dot her *I*s with hearts, though."

"She is not crazy," Lucy said. "For heaven's sake."

"Why is it girls are always right and guys are always wrong?" Tom asked the air.

"No one is saying that!" Kate was exasperated. "But you have to admit that in this particular case the evidence seems to indicate that Jill *is* the wronged party."

"By her own account!" Giacomo pointed out, raising his voice to be heard over the others. "By her own hand!"

"Yes!" Kate shot back. "Because *she* is the one who cared enough to write, while this James person is obviously going on his merry way, not giving a thought to the girl he's left behind, the girl he has grievously wronged, the girl he said he loved—"

"Yes, that's *your* interpretation, but where is the evidence? Where are the facts to support it?" asked

Giacomo, becoming even more heated.

"Just look at the letter!" Kate was close to yelling, herself, as she picked up the paper and waved it in the air for emphasis. "It's all right there in the text!"

"Excuse me. Excuse me! *Excuse me!*"

The din of battle was abruptly silenced as everyone turned to see Kate's father, looming in the doorway, his hair standing on end as if he had been running his hands through it.

"Professoressa Marchese," he said in a tight, controlled voice. "If I might have a word?"

"But of *course*, Professore Sanderson," she said, flashing a brilliant smile. "Is there a problem?"

"A problem? A problem?" Kate's father sputtered. "Yes, I would say so. I would indeed say so!"

She arched one elegant eyebrow. "And what, please, is the nature of that problem? Please, do not hold back. I believe in open, honest discussion."

"Yes, I can tell," he said. "Because *your* class's open, honest discussion is becoming so noisy that it is quite impossible for *my* class to think! We can barely hear one another speak!"

"Ah, passion! A wonderful quality, and one that I believe should be *encouraged* in the classroom. And, of course," she purred, "in all other areas of life as well."

"Yes, well, er . . ." That seemed to stop him, but he recovered quickly. "Yes, yes, I would be the last person to quell an interesting discussion, but we have already begun a very intricate textual analysis."

"Oh, indeed. I am sure we would not wish to deprive you or your students of the heady joys of textual analysis," she murmured, making the last two words sound as dusty as a shelf of ancient Latin texts. "I believe I heard you explaining that technique a little earlier, through the wall that we share between our classrooms?"

He flushed. "I apologize if *my*, er, passion for the subject disturbed you," he said stiffly. "But now that we have begun to really delve into the play . . . Well. It requires great concentration."

Professoressa Marchese glanced at her class, then strolled over to put a hand on his arm. "My students are doing so well, I feel quite confident leaving them to continue on their own. Perhaps we should continue this conversation in the hall? In private?"

"Oh, ah, er . . ."

Kate had never seen her father at a loss for words. She found it a rather disturbing sight.

The door closed behind them. The newest members of the Juliet Club looked at one another for a long moment, trying to recall where they had left off.

"It's too limiting to debate whether Jill is crazy or not when, of course, there is another possibility," Kate said, heading back into the fray.

Giacomo gave her a cool look. "And that is?"

"That is, that she's misreading the situation, but she's misreading it in his favor, assuming that he has honorable intentions."

"But just because she *thinks* he has good intentions doesn't mean that he *does*." Lucy picked up the point. "I remember this one time when I was in the third grade? And Jesse Cantu decided that he liked me? But I didn't like him? So he decided that I would fall in love with him if he rescued me from some kind of danger, because that's what always happens in the movies? So one day he told me that there was a surprise waiting for me in the cupboard at the back of the classroom and all I had to do was go in at recess and open the cupboard door—"

"And you believed him?" Benno interrupted, aghast.

"Of course!" Lucy said indignantly. "Because I'm from Mississippi! Where we believe people! So anyway, when I opened the cupboard there was a whole mess of spiders in there and I know people say that spiders scuttle away when they see you coming, but these spiders jumped out at me like they were rabid or something and Jesse ran into the room to save me but I was screaming so much that the principal called 911!" She paused for breath. "And the only good thing that happened was that we all got out of school for the rest of the day."

There was a brief silence as everyone absorbed this. Finally Silvia muttered, "Men are pigs."

Giacomo sighed. "How old was this boy with the spiders?" he asked Lucy in a patient voice, as if they had all gone off the rails but were fortunate that he was there to put them right.

She frowned, as if suspecting a trick, but finally answered, "Eight."

"As I thought! Far too young to realize what a mistake he was making," he said triumphantly. "But I'm sure he learned from this sad experience, yes? He didn't keep trying to attract women with spiders?"

"Well, no, of course not," Lucy said. "Jesse's still real immature, but he's not an idiot."

"There you are, then." Giacomo leaned his chair back, teetering on the back two legs, looking pleased with himself. "Everyone makes mistakes in love. The point is to learn from them. For example, Jesse learned—"

"What?" Kate scoffed. "That attacking a girl with

spiders isn't a good way to say 'I love you'? That should have been obvious from the start."

"Well, yes." He nodded, as if conceding the point, but then added, "Of course, all knowledge is useful."

"But not all knowledge is worth the cost."

"And what cost is that?" Giacomo's deep brown eyes were alight with enjoyment.

"Looking like a fool."

"Oh, *that*." He folded his arms across his chest with the air of one who is about to win an argument. "That's nothing to concern yourself with. After all, love makes fools of everyone, don't you agree?"

"No, I don't." Kate bit off each word. "I don't agree *at all*."

"How astonishing," he muttered.

"In fact," she said meaningfully, "*I* would say that love only makes fools of those who were fools to begin with."

She smiled at him, clearly pleased with her riposte. Giacomo let his chair fall back to the floor with a thump.

"If the world was left to people like you," he said in an accusing tone, "we'd all be computing love's logic on computers and dissecting our hearts in a biology lab."

"If the world were left to people like me," Kate

said with conviction, "it would be a much better place to live."

"Oh, yes," he said sarcastically. "Because it would be orderly. Sensible. And *dull*."

"Love doesn't have to end in riots and disaster and, and, and . . . *spider attacks*!" she said hotly.

He ran his hands roughly through his hair, completely ruining its artfully tousled look. Kate felt a flicker of satisfaction. It was the first time she had seen him make a gesture that didn't look as if it belonged on the stage.

"What's the point of love if you don't risk disaster?" he demanded. He stopped, as if hearing his own voice becoming heated, and took a deep breath. Then he tilted back in his chair again and grinned at her. "Even to the point of spider attacks."

"I think you're taking this argument entirely too lightly," Kate said, trying not to sound cranky, and failing.

"And I think you're taking it entirely too seriously," Giacomo said, trying not to sound rankled, and failing.

That was when Silvia, looking from one to the other, had a very brilliant idea.

Act I
SCENE VIII

"I have an idea about how we can play a joke on Kate and Giacomo."

Silvia had said this in Italian, but it's easy to catch the sound of one's own name being spoken, even in a foreign language. Kate stopped outside the seminar room, her hand on the partially open door.

After class had been dismissed, she had gone all the way to her room only to discover that she had forgotten her favorite pen. Sighing, she had retraced her steps and was now standing very still, her hand on the doorknob. Kate was not a sneaky person by nature. In fact, she prided herself on being upfront and honest and straightforward and direct. But Silvia's voice had sounded gleeful and sly, and Kate was not so honorable that she could resist listening for just a moment.

Casually, she moved down the hall and tried the next door, the door to the room where her father had been teaching his class.

Good, it opened.

And the room was empty. Even better.

She slipped inside and then stepped into the musty darkness of the small cloakroom that connected the two larger rooms, moving gingerly to avoid knocking over an umbrella or rattling wire hangers. She eased the door open a crack and peeked through.

The housekeeper, Maria, was moving creakily around the room with a dust rag. Every few steps, she would stop and dust a piece of furniture with meditative care. Silvia was sitting at the table, glaring at her as if that would make her move faster.

Perhaps it would have, with a more susceptible person. But Maria had the air of a woman who had outlasted wars, famines, pestilence, and a long-term infestation of in-laws. She would not be hurried. She continued pottering around the room, humming slightly under her breath, until Silvia sighed and said, "Let's speak in English, Benno, so she doesn't understand us."

"Very well," Benno said. "But be quick—my uncle wants me at the souvenir stand by three o'clock, and he's in a vile temper today. The shipment of candy hearts has gone missing, the woman who paints the small watercolors of Verona is sick with the flu, and yesterday a tourist knocked over an entire shelf of plaster Madonnas."

"*Basta, basta!* Enough, enough!" Silvia flapped her hand at him. "Why do you talk so much if you are in such a hurry?"

"I'm trying to tell you! Mario will dock my pay if I'm late again."

"Listen to me!" she hissed. "Today I came up with the idea for a most brilliant joke."

Benno stopped rattling around the room and gave her a sharp, interested look. "My uncle can wait," he said. "What kind of joke?"

Through the crack in the door, Kate saw Silvia smile a pointed little smile. "You heard how Giacomo and Kate were arguing during class today."

"*Si,* of course," he said, grinning. "Giacomo is sure to make her insane by the time she goes back to America. "

"Yes, no doubt," Silvia said, clearly indifferent to Kate's mental state. "But what would be even more diverting," she went on, "would be to watch Kate drive *Giacomo* to the brink of madness!"

There was a brief pause as Benno looked at her assessingly. Then he laughed. "Oh, I see!" His eyes were filled with wicked delight as he hopped up to sit cross-legged on the table.

"You see what?" Her voice was wary.

"If I were Giacomo, I would be very worried about my safety right now! I would be checking the lock on my door! I would be thinking of hiring a bodyguard! I would be letting the cat taste my dinner for poison —"

"*Basta!* Stop talking like a fool!" Silvia glared at him.

He shook his head in admiration. "I do admire a girl who can hold a grudge."

Kate's interest quickened. She shifted her position so that she could see Silvia, who had started pacing around the room.

"I don't know what you mean." Silvia tossed her head with disdain. "I never waste a moment's thought on him."

"Now, now," Benno said with false sympathy. "Just because he broke up with you . . ."

"He did not break up with me!" Silvia said, her eyes flashing dangerously. "*I* broke up with *him*!"

"Oh, I'm sorry, you're right, I forgot." Kate could

see Benno watching Sylvia, his face impish. "*You* broke up with Giacomo, and you *never* think about him, and you don't know the *meaning* of the word grudge. Right." He pretended to be puzzled. "So now why, exactly, do you want to play a trick on him?"

Kate strained forward to hear the answer.

Silvia stopped pacing long enough to snap, "Because it will be fun! And if I must sit in that dreary seminar room for the next month, I might as well find a way to amuse myself!"

"Oh, of course," he murmured, with only a hint of disbelief in his voice. "That makes perfect sense."

There was a brief silence. Kate peeped through the crack in the door and saw Silvia, her arms crossed, giving Benno a thoughtful look.

"Also," Silvia went on, "I think it will be good for his character. You know he is so used to getting his own way."

"Very true." Benno still sounded amused.

"And so *arrogant*!" Siliva said, casting a sly side-long glance at Benno. "He thinks he can make any girl in the world fall in love with him."

"Hmmph." Benno's mood shifted. He looked gloomy. "Many of them already have."

"He barely even has to speak," Silvia went on, watching him closely. "They just fall in love with him at first sight. Even after he leaves them, they still adore him."

Benno's face darkened. Silvia was right. It was so unfair. Why was Giacomo blessed with perfectly disheveled brown hair and a classic profile and a warm smile, while Benno had been born with messy black hair and a beaky nose and a lopsided smile? Not to mention *short*.

"*È vero*. It's true." He fell back on the table and crossed his arms, staring blackly at the ceiling. He had dated exactly two girls in his life, and both relationships had ended with screaming recriminations, a series of increasingly violent text messages, and, in one case, a few very scary threats from a protective older brother. Benno wasn't sure why his love life seemed destined to turn into grand opera; he just knew that he always went wrong somewhere. And, he feared, he always would.

"It would be so satisfying," Silvia finished softly, "to see Giacomo play the fool for once."

"More than satisfying," Benno muttered. "It would be cosmic justice."

"And that Kate!" Silvia rolled her eyes.

Kate frowned and pressed her ear to the door.

"She has a very superior attitude, don't you think?"

Kate dug her fingernails into her palms.

"She seems all right," Benno said offhandedly. "A

little too serious, maybe." He turned his head to look at her. "Why? What does Kate have to do with this?"

"That is the trick we play!" Silvia's voice was triumphant. "We will make them fall in love with each other."

"What? How?" Benno sat up, startled. "They could not be more unlike each other!"

"Exactly! That is what will make the spectacle so diverting!" she said, her eyes gleaming with mischief. "This Kate, she's the type who always has her nose in a book, yes?" Silvia lowered her voice. "Can you imagine Giacomo trying to woo her?"

"Maybe he won't," Benno said. "Maybe he'll just let her yearn for him from afar."

Silvia gave a little snort at that. "You know Giacomo. He loves a challenge. And he can't resist the idea of being adored."

"That's true," Benno said thoughtfully. He and Giacomo had been friends since they were five years old. Good friends, of course, stalwart friends, loyal friends . . .

On the other hand, it did get tiresome, having a friend who made love look so easy. He gave a malevolent chuckle. "And after all, it is just a joke."

"Exactly," Silvia agreed with satisfaction. "All in good fun."

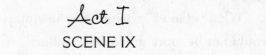

Act I
SCENE IX

The only value this seminar would ever have, Giacomo thought to himself, would be if one day he was threatened with life imprisonment by a clever lawyer who was intent on twisting his words, misconstruing his meanings and showing that every opinion he had was false, not only in its conclusion, but in its very premise. Perhaps, in that unlikely event, he would be able to use this experience to out-argue the lawyer and emerge from his dank prison cell into the sunshine of a new day.

He took a moody sip of espresso and silently counted up how many days he was expected to spend in this purgatory. The answer was appalling. Determined to wallow in gloom, he then figured out

the number of hours and had just moved on to cal-
culating the actual minutes when he was abruptly
interrupted.

"Giacomo, good, I'm glad I found you. I have to
talk to you!"

He looked up to see Kate standing next to his
table, her posture as straight as a sentinel, her eyes
snapping with righteous indignation.

"Of course," he said warily. In his experience,
conversations that began, "I have to talk to you"
rarely ended well. "Please, sit down."

"Grazie." She pulled the chair back and sat down,
jostling the table.

His elbow had been propped on that table.
Sighing, he looked down at the coffee stain on the
cuff of his pristine white shirt, then waved for the
waiter to bring two more espressos.

Kate didn't seem to notice. She crossed her arms
and leaned in to him. "I just overheard Silvia and
Benno talking!"

He dipped his napkin in his water glass and
dabbed at his sleeve. "You were eavesdropping?"
Perhaps there was some hope for her after all, he
thought. After all, eavesdropping was a sin, if a
minor one. From what he had observed so far, this
Kate was too saintly for comfort. He glanced across

the table and saw her straighten up in her chair, blushing.

"Not on purpose, of course!" she said.

Ah, well. "Of course not."

"I just *happened* to go back to the seminar room to get my notebook."

He gave her a look of polite interest.

"And I just happened to be in the cloakroom when they started talking."

He shaded that look with a hint of disbelief.

"And then I couldn't leave without them thinking that I was hiding there."

He increased the disbelief to outright incredulity.

"And so I waited and it's good that I did, because that's when I heard them decide to play a prank on us. A really stupid, humiliating prank."

"Oh, yes?" he said, as he continued to rub at the stain on his shirt. The waiter brought their espressos to the table; Giacomo nodded his thanks. "Well, Benno is always playing jokes, he was born a clown."

"It wasn't his idea at all," Kate said, miffed by his reaction. "It was Silvia's."

He stopped paying attention to his sleeve. "Silvia?" Giacomo knew the way Silvia's mind worked; it was subtle and cunning and malicious.

"Yes," she said. "They're trying to pull a Beatrice and Benedick on us."

"I'm sorry?"

"*Much Ado About Nothing*," she said, as if it was obvious. "Beatrice and Benedick are two characters who are always insulting each other, so their friends decide to make each think that the other has fallen in love with them and then—"

"Yes, I know the play," he said, with an edge in his voice.

"Well, they want to fool us into thinking that we've fallen in love with each other. They seemed to think it would be like watching a farce."

"A farce?" A slight frown appeared on Giacomo's face. "Why?"

"Oh, because we were arguing in class, I suppose." She took a sip of her espresso. "I, apparently, am too serious!" she said, clearly outraged.

"Well, eavesdroppers seldom hear good things about themselves," he said in a pious tone.

Kate glared at him. "And *you* are too—" She stopped abruptly and smiled down at her espresso. "Well. I suppose I really shouldn't pass on what they said about you." She took a little sip. "That would be *most* unkind of me."

She smiled sweetly at him. Strands of hair had

come loose from her braid; in the light from the window, he could see them floating around her head like a golden halo. But the eyes that looked at him over the edge of her coffee cup were too challenging to belong to an angel, he was sure of that. And the way she just waited, with that knowing look on her face, as if she knew he wouldn't be able to resist asking her. . . .

"What did they say about me?"

He would have thought it impossible, but she looked even more smug. "*You* are too frivolous," Kate reported with satisfaction.

"Hmm." A slight frown appeared between his eyebrows.

"When it comes to girls, that is," she went on, watching his scowl deepen. "In fact," she added, enjoying this report, "Silvia called you a *farfallone*."

He looked annoyed.

"What does that mean, anyway?" She had been wondering ever since she had heard Silvia spit out the word as if it were the vilest insult she could utter.

"A man who chases women," he said.

"Oh. Well, I can see why you wouldn't appreciate that, but—"

"I do not dislike the term because of its *definition*," he interrupted. "I dislike it because it is *inaccurate*."

He took a tiny sip of espresso before adding complacently, "I do not chase women. They chase me."

She just said, "Oh, *right*," but he could see her nose turn pink and knew that he had annoyed her. "Anyway, they kept going on about how we were total opposites and that was what would make the whole spectacle so funny."

"Really?" He looked at her speculatively. "Well, it's often said that opposites attract."

"You're thinking of magnets," she corrected him. "Not people."

He opened his mouth to argue, but she was still talking. "It's completely ridiculous!" she was saying. "As if *I* would ever be attracted to *you*!"

"Or I to you," he said, stung. Then he took another sip of his bitter espresso, and gave the situation more thought. The idea that Silvia and Benno could even contemplate tricking him in this way made him flush with anger. The idea that they had chosen Kate — serious, pragmatic, down-to-earth Kate — as his potential love interest irritated him beyond belief. And the mere fact that they believed that he would fall for their simple trap made him determined not just to avoid it, but to retaliate with his own plan. A plan that was so cunning and clever that they would be the ones to end up thoroughly hoodwinked.

So he said, "Here's what I think we should do: turn the tables on Silvia and Benno. That would teach them a lesson!"

She gave him a glance—half wary, half interested—over the rim of her coffee cup. "How would we do that?"

"We would pretend that their prank is working," he said, as if this were obvious. "We would pretend that we were falling in love."

"But all the time they thought they were fooling us, *we* would be fooling *them*," she finished slowly, a small smile flickering across her face. Her eyes met his, and for the first time, Giacomo saw that there was a hint of mischief hidden somewhere inside Kate.

He smiled back and took a thoughtful sip of coffee. He could have fun pretending to fall in love with Kate, he thought. It was so amusing to tease serious girls. He liked the way they condemned his every move. It made him feel worldly and depraved.

Still, this plan sounded like a lot of work, and he had been looking forward to doing as little as possible this summer. Perhaps it would be wiser to let it go. . . .

But Kate had been watching him closely and seemed to sense his second thoughts. "Of course, we may not be able to pull it off," she said. "But it would be a shame for Sylvia and Benno to think they were right. . . ." Her voice trailed off suggestively.

He gave her a cool look, but he couldn't help asking. "About what?"

She gave him a smug smile. "They said," she reported carefully, "that you would never see the trap they set until it was too late. They said that you were, well, a little too caught up in yourself, perhaps, to notice that a trick was being played."

The image of Silvia and Benno sniggering behind his back stiffened his resolve. He set his coffee cup down, rather harder than he meant to, and it rattled in the saucer. Kate's smile widened.

"Then let's let them think that, and use their self-confidence against them," he said, forcing himself to smile back at her. "If this is a battle of wits, I have no doubt that we will end up the winners."

Entr'acte

"They're going to pretend to be in love?" Sarah was smiling into the distance.

Actually, she was gloating. A very unattractive quality, in Annie's opinion.

"He sounds completely obnoxious," Annie said. "Not at all Kate's type."

"Kate doesn't have a type yet. She's only dated Jerome," Sarah protested.

"Exactly. Introverted genius boys with no social skills," Annie agreed. "That's Kate's type."

"Then it's time she found a different type," Sarah said stoutly. "And I think Giacomo sounds like the perfect guy to change her ways."

"Or drive her to homicide."

"We'll see." Sarah had gone back to smiling her Mona Lisa smile. "But in the meantime, they're going to pretend to be in love. This is promising. Very, very promising."

Act II
SCENE I

"I understand from Professoressa Marchese that you all know the play quite well, so I'm sure you will have great fun as we embark on this adventure," Mr. Renkin said, smiling at them encouragingly. "Great fun, indeed!"

Mr. Renkin—he had told them to call him Dan—had a mop of brown hair, lively dark eyes, and a merry expression. He was a British director, temporarily based in Verona to scout locations for his next film. He had been immediately dragooned by Francesca Marchese to provide coaching, dancing lessons, and fight direction for her students—at a nominal fee, of course, since he would be furthering the cause of education. He had stayed politely quiet as Professoressa Marchese had unveiled the enormous piece of paper that was her casting chart and briskly announced what parts they would play.

"First, Benno and Tom," she had said briskly. Tom looked tense, Benno wary. "You will play Mercutio and Tybalt." She gave them a smiling glance and added, "I'm sure you will enjoy the duel greatly."

They both sighed with relief and grinned at each other.

"Giacomo, you will play Romeo's part in their fight scene—that shouldn't be too taxing, since you just have to watch them and look horrified," she said. "As for Juliet—"

She flipped through the casting chart, which was covered with livid squiggles and dramatic crossouts. Kate saw Lucy surreptitiously cross her fingers, biting her lip with anxiety.

"Lucy, you will play Juliet in the scene where you first meet Romeo at the party," Professoressa Marchese announced. Lucy let out the breath she had been holding and smiled with pleasure. "And you, Kate, will play Juliet in the balcony scene." She glanced over her glasses at her son. "After going over the schedule many times, I have decided that it would make the most sense if Giacomo plays Romeo in both those scenes."

"Better him than me," Tom whispered to Benno, even as Giacomo raised a hand to protest.

"I'm not sure that's quite fair," he said quickly. "I mean, after all . . . Romeo! It's the part that everyone wants, isn't it?" He gave Tom and Benno a glinting look. "And I would hate to deny others whose acting skills are surely far superior to mine —"

"*Basta!*" His mother clapped her hands once, sharply, glaring at him. "I'm also considering the fact that you already know the part."

"Indeed I do," he said glumly. "I could recite every blasted line of that play while juggling blindfolded."

"Precisely my point," she replied. "And since our rehearsal time is limited, I believe that this is the most sensible solution."

Giacomo folded his arms across his chest, looking martyred, and Benno gave him a patently insincere look of sympathy.

"Now Sylvia," Professoressa Marchese went on. "You, I think, will be perfect as the Nurse." She glanced up sharply, as if expecting protest. "It's an earthy, comic role that you will play to perfection, I am sure."

But Sylvia shrugged one shoulder carelessly and said, "Fine. I would never want to play Juliet, she is far too dull." Then she added stubbornly,

"But I still don't see why I can't *fight*."

Professoressa Marchese frowned. "I agreed that you could learn stage sword fighting, but I have many male students that I need to cast. The duel scene can only be presented so many times, Sylvia! Now, I don't want to hear any more arguments. I was up until midnight creating this chart, so for now—*è fatto*! It's done!"

Professoressa Marchese had then turned to the others, ignoring Silvia's sulking, clapped her hands twice, and said, "Remember, everyone, *surrender to the experience*! Now I must go deal with a catering crisis and a plumbing disaster, but I leave you in the best of hands. Carry on, Signor Renkin!"

When she had left, Dan turned to his cast. "Right," he said. "Let's begin by running lines. Giacomo, Kate, why don't we start with your scene? In your own time . . ."

"But soft! What light through yonder window breaks? It is the east, and Juliet is the sun." Giacomo reeled off his lines with polish and flair, aware that he had an audience. They were, he was quite sure, admiring his delivery.

At the far end of the room, Lucy and Tom were supposed to be running lines, with Tom standing in as Romeo, and Benno and Silvia were supposed to be doing stretching exercises. But they had all stopped what they were doing to listen.

For the next few lines, Giacomo's voice became louder, his stance more self-assured, as the rhythms of the poetry took over.

But when he got to "Her eye discourses. I will answer it. — I am too bold. 'Tis not to me she speaks," Dan interrupted.

"Nicely done, Giacomo," he said. "Marvelous voice, very resonant. Clear articulation, very good."

Giacomo looked gratified. Dan moved closer and murmured, "But if I could just make one or two notes. . . ."

Giacomo frowned. "Yes?"

"Your delivery is perhaps a little . . . glib. I feel that you're not quite connecting yet with the character's emotions. Romeo has fallen instantly in love with Juliet and they've met and shared a kiss, but he doesn't really know how she feels about him. He's so intent on finding out that he's come to this dangerous place, he's standing right under her balcony! So Romeo is bold, daring! But at the same time" — Dan's voice softened, paused, stuttered. "He's hesitant. Look at the text: 'I will answer it.' He's determined to get her attention. Then the next line: 'I am too bold.'

Backing off. You see? He's like any young man who is approaching the girl of his dreams and wondering whether he'll be greeted with a smile or told to shove off."

"Mmm." Giacomo nodded in what he hoped was a thoughtful manner. "I see."

"So what you could do here, I think, is recall a time when you felt that way," Dan suggested. "When you tried to talk to a girl you fancied, and you weren't sure of what to say, or the words came out all wrong. Can you remember a moment like that to help you connect here?"

Giacomo tilted his head and stared intently at the ceiling, as if the answer might be written in the cobweb that was strung across the corner. "Well," he said after a long moment, "no, actually."

From the other side of the room, he heard Silvia give a little snort. He glanced over and saw Benno glaring at him, and realized that his answer, although true, was not calculated to make him friends. He was slightly cheered to see that Tom looked impressed and that Lucy was smiling at him in a friendly way. . . . But when he stopped to think about it, that didn't mean much because it didn't take anything at all to impress Tom, and Lucy always looked friendly.

Kate, he noticed, was yawning behind her script.

He turned back to see that Dan was looking at him with a rather befuddled expression. "I see. Well, let's leave it for now, but give it a thought, will you, Giacomo? Some time when you felt unsure of yourself, it doesn't have to be anything to do with love, you know, just a moment of insecurity and self-doubt. You're doing brilliantly, of course, but I think that will help your performance really come alive."

Dan turned to Kate. "Right! Kate, let's start again and see how you do."

"Romeo, Romeo, wherefore art thou Romeo?" Kate intoned. "Deny thy father and refuse thy name." She went on, secretly proud that she had read the play so many times that she hardly needed to refer to her script.

She barely paused long enough for Giacomo to say his line — "Shall I hear more, or shall I speak at this?" — before continuing.

"'Tis but thy name that is my enemy," she said. Word perfect, of course. She wouldn't even need her script by this time tomorrow. "Thou art thyself, though not a Montague. What's Montague? It is nor hand, nor foot, nor arm, nor face, nor any other part belonging to a man—"

"Yes, Kate, very good, thank you so much for that." Dan was sitting in front of one of the large windows, straddling a chair backward, watching her intently. "Your memorization skills are very impressive."

She smiled complacently. "Well, I know it's important to get all the words right."

"Absolutely, and you're going to do splendidly, you've done a lot of preparatory work already, I can tell," he said.

She hesitated. Something about the way he said that was not reassuring. "But?"

"Very nicely done, really, but you do sound a bit as if you're doing a trial summation. Rather brisk and to the point, if you know what I mean."

"But if you look at Juliet's dialogue, it *is* almost like she's making an argument to a jury," Kate said eagerly. As soon as she heard she had won a place in the seminar, she had gone through the play several times, underlining passages and making notes in the margins. Now she picked up her copy and opened it to the speech she had just said. "Look, here, Juliet says, it's your *name* that is my enemy, not *you*. And you would still be you, no matter what your last name was, so who cares about the name Montague anyway?" She lowered the book. "I thought it was a very logical point."

Dan nodded. "That's true, throughout this scene Juliet is practical, down-to-earth, grounded—"

Giacomo sighed heavily.

"Yes, Giacomo, you have a comment about that?" Dan asked politely.

"Well, yes," Giacomo said. "She's got Romeo standing under her balcony spouting gorgeous poetry and promising her undying love, and all she can say is 'How did you get in here?' and 'Who told you which balcony was mine?'"

"Right. While *Romeo*'s speeches just get more and more extravagant," Kate said, rather testily.

"He is expressing his soul," Giacomo said coldly. He was about to go on, but he caught a glimpse of Silvia exchanging glances with Benno, and Tom nudging Lucy, and remembered, just in time, that he was supposed to be falling in love with Kate.

So instead of countering her argument with a withering remark, he took a deep breath, smiled, and moved a little closer to her.

"Here, for example," he said, pitching his voice so that it was low and intimate, yet carried across the room for the benefit of his listeners. "O, speak again, bright angel!" He looked deeply into Kate's eyes. Fortunately, he was blocking her from the others' view, so they couldn't see the way she was lifting one eyebrow sardonically at him. She did not look at all like someone who was falling in love.

Undeterred, he pressed on. "For thou art as glorious to this night, being o'er my head, as is a winged messenger of heaven unto the white, upturned, wondring eyes of mortals that fall back to gaze on him when he bestrides the lazy-puffing clouds and sails up upon the bosom of the air."

From across the room, he heard Lucy sigh. He cut his eyes over without moving his head to see the others' reactions. Silvia was regarding him with what looked like disgust, but he knew Silvia well and he knew that she was, however unwillingly, impressed. Tom's mouth was hanging slightly open—he was either struck by the words or Giacomo's delivery or both—and Benno was shaking his head slightly in disbelief.

All in all, a most satisfactory response. Giacomo turned back to Kate.

"See, that's exactly what I mean," she said in an accusing tone. "It's too much! Everything Romeo says is so over the top, any sensible girl would run away as fast as she could, because she'd never be able to live up to his expectations!"

"Perhaps," Giacomo said, "Romeo does not *want* a sensible girl."

"He should," she said tartly. "He needs *someone* to help him keep his feet on the ground."

"Why? Because he has a heart? Because he has a soul? Because—"

"—he's an idiot. Look!" She flipped her book open to the first pages. "When the play begins, he's moping because Rosaline doesn't love him. Four scenes later, he sees Juliet and falls in love at first sight. And two scenes after *that*, he's swearing undying love to her. And then—"

"Yes, we all know the plot." Giacomo was trying to keep his temper.

They stood still, glaring at each other until Dan stepped forward, smiling. "Very interesting discussion, thank you both. I'm sure we'll make many discoveries together in the days to come. But perhaps it's time for a small break to really absorb the connections you've made today. So! Let's regroup after lunch, shall we?"

"Are you absolutely, positively sure this is a good thing we're fixing to do?" Lucy worried, even as she followed Silvia along the manicured paths in the garden behind the Villa Marchese. "I mean, you are absolutely, positively a hundred percent sure that Giacomo told Benno he likes Kate?"

"Shh!" Silvia stopped so abruptly that Lucy bumped into her and almost sent her sprawling into the lavender border that edged the walkway. "Yes, I told you! Giacomo and Benno went to the cinema last night and that was when Giacomo revealed his true feelings."

"Now what exactly did he say, again?"

"*Stai zitto!* Keep your voice down!" Silvia hissed. "I already told you!"

Fifteen minutes ago, Silvia had spotted Kate from an upstairs window, sitting down to eat her lunch in a secluded bower at the end of the garden. It was the perfect moment to implement the first phase of her plan, so she had grabbed Lucy and they had hurried down the three flights of stairs to the terrace. Now they were trying to creep behind the bench where Kate was sitting, surrounded by bushes and lemon trees, where they would then talk about Giacomo's supposed love for her, pretending that they didn't see her.

But this brilliant plan would only work if they actually made it to the end of the garden sometime this century. Right now, Lucy was standing in the middle of the path as if she had put down roots, waiting for Silvia to repeat, for the thousandth time, the fiction that she and Benno had created last night.

She tugged impatiently on Lucy's arm, but Lucy could be stubborn when she wanted to be. A small frown creased her forehead as she went on insistently, "It just seems so *odd*. I mean, the way the two of them argue in class! And they're always quoting Shakespeare to score points—"

"Exactly." Silvia pounced on this. "A mutual love of literature binds them together."

"Well, I was *going* to say that I never knew Shakespeare could be so sarcastic." Lucy's voice held a hint of reproof, and Silvia gave a slight shrug as apology for interrupting. "Although I suppose," Lucy went on, thinking out loud, "I *suppose* Giacomo could just be afraid that Kate doesn't return his feelings."

"Exactly," Silvia said with relief. It had taken some time, but Lucy had finally gotten there. "He's masking his true feelings, that's exactly what he told Benno. Now, come, she will finish eating and be gone if we don't hurry!"

Lucy seemed convinced by Silvia's urgent delivery. "You're right, of course! Oh, I really hope this works!" she said as she hurried down the path.

Silvia followed, silently congratulating herself on her truly superb acting skills.

❖   ❖   ❖

A few moments later, she was even more glad that she was a wonderful actress because Lucy, despite years of training in her high school's drama club, was unbelievably bad.

They had approached the leafy bower, talking casually—or they would have been, if Lucy had not made every slight statement sound like a pronouncement from Mount Olympus.

"Oh! Silvia!" she cried. "Are you SURE that Giacomo LOVES Kate that much?"

Silvia looked at her in disbelief and answered, in resolutely normal tones, "That's what Benno told me. They went to the cinema last night and Giacomo confessed all."

"It does seem STRANGE, though!" Lucy said. "After all, she's always ROLLING HER EYES at everything he says and telling him that he's committed another LOGICAL FALLACY and then explaining EXACTLY where he went wrong in his reasoning."

No human being who had ever drawn breath on this earth talked like that, Silvia thought, but she seized the opening that Lucy had offered with wicked glee. "You're quite right," she said smoothly. "In fact, he told Benno that that's why he knew that what he felt was true love, because it made no sense at all! He said that Kate is a shrill, argumentative, humorless girl with rather plain looks and no fashion sense at all."

There was a thump from the other side of the bushes as if someone had slammed a book shut. Silvia smiled her pleased, catlike smile and went on. "He says that he only acts rudely to her in order to hide his true feelings, because he knows that she would just mock him."

"Oh, that's so sad!" For a moment, Lucy was so caught up in the story they were telling that she responded in a natural, heartfelt way. Then her eyes darted toward the bushes as she remembered Kate's presence and she began projecting for the balcony once again. "But maybe we could TALK to her and LET HER KNOW how much he LOVES her and get her to BE NICE TO HIM!"

Silvia shook her head sadly, quite enjoying herself as the scene played on. "I'm afraid that won't work. After a week together, we know her too well. She's too proud of how smart she is, and completely unable to act charming."

Lucy frowned and whispered, "Don't you think that's a little mean?"

"Fine!" Silvia whispered back. "The next line is yours."

"Um…" Lucy looked momentarily frightened, as if they were truly acting in a play and she had missed her cue. Then she got back in the groove and said, "It's really TRAGIC! Giacomo is so good-looking, and charming, and intelligent, and funny."

"Yes, yes, he's stuffed, as they say, with honorable parts," Silvia quoted bitterly.

"What?" Lucy whispered, lost.

"Never mind," Silvia murmured. "Let's bring this scene to an end."

Obediently, Lucy called out, "OH! It is almost TWO O'CLOCK! We'd better get back to class!"

"Yes," Silvia said, pleased now that they had accomplished their mission. "We wouldn't want to miss rehearsal."

As they ran back up the path, Lucy tried, without much success, to stifle her giggles, and even Silvia found that she was almost smiling.

Act II
SCENE II

Giacomo sat on a bench in the church courtyard and gazed at the small poster that had been pasted on a nearby wall to announce the death of a Verona resident. Despite the somber surroundings, he was trying not to laugh. He had amused himself for the last hour as he had watched Benno and Tom try to figure out how to maneuver him into a position where he would be sure to overhear their staged conversation.

First, they had entered the café where he was enjoying an afternoon espresso and tried to skulk in without his seeing them. That plan had been doomed to failure, of course, since the café was only big enough for eight tables, each of which was only inches from the other.

"Ciao, Tom," he had said. *"Ciao,* Benno."

Their faces fell at being discovered, and Giacomo had to bite his lip to keep from laughing.

He went on smoothly, "On your way to the football field?"

"What?" Tom had asked blankly.

Benno gave him an exasperated sidelong glance and tossed the soccer ball he was carrying from one hand to the other.

Tom's face cleared as he suddenly remembered their cover story. "Oh yes! Right! We're going to go play soccer with some, um, guys. But we came in here because"—he glanced wildly at the menu written on a chalkboard—"we were thirsty!"

Benno nodded at the waiter. *"Due aranciate, per favore."*

Giacomo had smiled to himself and waited until they were served their orange drinks. Then he had taken a last sip of his espresso and said, "I have to go now. A few errands to run for my mother. *Ciao!"*

He had chuckled all the way to the *pasticceria* at the memory of how crestfallen Benno and Tom had looked as they had been forced to sit at the table and finish their drinks. He leaned against the counter as the *pasticceria* owner slowly wrapped up the loaf of bread he had bought. Fortunately for Benno and

Tom, the man moved at a glacial pace. Usually this drove Giacomo wild, but now he hummed under his breath as he gazed out the window, watching the street for the next scene to begin. Sure enough, Benno and Tom came running up, red-faced and panting in the heat, just as Giacomo stepped outside.

"Hello!" he said, pretending great surprise. "How odd to run into you again."

"Verona is not so big," Benno pointed out.

"True. But weren't you going to play football? And isn't the football field where you usually practice in that direction?"

Tom shot Benno a wild glance. Giacomo had to stop himself from shaking his head reprovingly at this. Really, Benno couldn't have chosen a worse person to involve in this conspiracy! Every thought that went through Tom's mind was written on his face for all to see.

"Yes, but I have to stop by my aunt Bettina's to, er, get some tomatoes she picked from her garden," Benno said quickly, clearly improvising. "*Then* we're going to play football."

"Ah." Giacomo nodded. "Well, I have to meet my grandmother at church now. *Ciao.*"

He sauntered back in the direction that they had just come from, pretending not to notice as they trailed behind him. He could have kept playing this game all day, but the afternoon was hot and the thought of going home and sipping a cool drink in the shade sounded very appealing. He finally decided to take pity on them and put himself in a position where it would be easy for them to sneak up on him.

He hadn't been lying, exactly, about going to the church. He did plan to head there, not because his grandmother had asked him to, but simply because it would take Benno and Tom so far out of their way.

The inner courtyard had high walls to provide shade, weathered stone benches to provide rest, and the sound of droning bees and church bells to provide a contented and meditative atmosphere. It seemed like a quiet and pleasant spot to while away the time it would take for Benno to coach Tom on his lines and then slip up behind him.

He settled onto a bench and let his mind drift until he finally heard approaching footsteps.

"That's what I'm telling you, Tom," Benno said, rather too emphatically. "Kate told Lucy that she has a—how do you say this in English? A crush?—on Giacomo!"

"I can't believe it!" Tom was doing a credible job of sounding amazed. In fact, Giacomo was impressed.

He wouldn't have thought, given Tom's performance so far, that he had any acting ability whatsoever. "Giacomo doesn't seem like Kate's type."

Giacomo smirked a little at this. No girl had ever said he wasn't her type.

"In fact, she kind of acts like she hates him," Tom went on. There was a brief silence, then a whisper, then Tom's voice again, unnaturally loud. "Oh! But maybe she's just *pretending* she hates him!"

"Yes, I think she is a very good actress," Benno said. "Because Lucy tells me that she sits in her room at night and writes his name over and over in her notebook, then she sighs and even cries a little over the fact that she can never have him."

"But why doesn't she just tell him how she feels?" Tom asked.

"As you said, she has treated him so badly since they first met," Benno replied. "That was before she realized she loved him, of course. She says she would be embarrassed to confess her true feelings now. Afraid, even!"

"Afraid?"

"You have heard how Giacomo treats her," Benno pointed out. "He mocks her constantly. She does argue with him, but you must admit that he also disagrees with every point she makes."

"Hmm," Tom agreed. "Well, maybe it's better that he doesn't ever know that she likes him."

"I agree," Benno said. "You know Giacomo is my friend."

"You guys seem really tight," Tom agreed, and Giacomo smiled.

"But still, even I have to admit," Benno went on, "he does have some faults."

Giacomo raised his eyebrows at this.

"Everyone does," Tom said fairly. "No one's perfect."

Giacomo nodded approvingly at this sentiment.

"Very true," Benno said. "Although . . ."

Giacomo sat up a little straighter and turned his head to make sure he heard what came next.

"Although Giacomo, perhaps, has more faults than most people," his friend went on. "In fact, if I'm being honest, I would have to say that he has a lot more."

"Really?" A note of genuine interest entered Tom's voice. "Like what?"

"Well, I don't like to say it, but he is a little vain about his looks. Have you noticed how he dresses?"

"Well . . . no, not really," Tom said. "I mean, his clothes always look just like, you know . . . *clothes*."

Benno snorted. "Extremely expensive clothes,

believe me. And his sense of humor . . . well, sometimes he enjoys mocking people."

"That's not very nice," Tom said thoughtfully.

"He's always at least fifteen minutes late. He's very forgetful." Benno sounded as if he were ticking the points off on his fingers. "And he sometimes borrows people's CDs and then forgets to return them. Actually, he does that pretty often. Once a month, at least."

And *you* are such a paragon of virtue, Giacomo thought, fuming. He had only forgotten to return Benno's precious CDs twice. Three times at most.

"And then, when it comes to girls, he is *incostante*," Benno said. "I think the word in English is fickle? It is shameful, everyone says so."

Benno's tone sounded quite severe, Giacomo thought, even condemning. And what did he mean, everyone said so? What had he ever done that was so bad? Of course, he flirted with girls, but, to be fair, he also flirted with the perpetually tired waitress at his favorite café, who often slipped him extra biscotti. And the sour-faced secretary in the school office, who usually unbent enough to give him a late pass and a small smile. And even his second cousin's four-year-old niece, who now shyly offered him a small bouquet of wilted flowers at every Sunday dinner as a token of her love. And where was the harm in any of that?

"If she won't tell him how she feels, maybe we should," Tom suggested.

Giacomo could hear the shrug in Benno's voice. "What good would that do? He would just lead her on, break her heart, make her miserable, ruin her life." He sighed heavily. "It's a shame that someone like Kate who is, as you said, *molto gentile*, should fall for someone who will never return her affection."

Tom sighed heavily as well. "You're right. He's crazy not to like Kate, though. She's so nice and pretty and smart—"

"Yes, very smart," Benno agreed. "Except, of course, for loving Giacomo."

Act II
SCENE III

"I can't believe it!" Giacomo was storming around the seminar room, running his hands through his hair in an agitated manner and glaring at anything that stood in his path. "I simply can't believe it! *I cannot believe* what Benno said about me!"

"Yes, that's what you've been saying for the last ten minutes," Kate said. She was seated at the table, flipping through the pile of letters to Juliet. She gave him a wicked glance and quoted his own words back to him. "You know, eavesdroppers never hear any good of themselves."

"Yes, I believe I've heard that somewhere before," he snapped. "But still, I can't believe —"

"Calm *down*. The others will be here any minute."

He stopped and whirled to face her. "Calm down!" he shouted. "Why should I calm down? I have been most foully perjured!"

She stopped rifling through the letters and tilted her head to one side. "'Foully perjured'? Who said that?"

"I said it! Just now!" He looked at her as if she were mad. "Weren't you even *listening*?"

"I could hardly help listening, the way you've been shouting!" Kate said, her voice tart. "I thought you were quoting Shakespeare, and I didn't recognize the line, that's all."

"Oh, of course." He threw himself into the chair opposite her, crossed his arms, and slid down until his neck was resting on the back of the chair. "I should have guessed. My best friend has slandered me behind my back and all you can think about is whether I'm quoting Shakespeare!"

"It's not slander," she pointed out, "if it's true."

He glared at her. "Betrayed at every turn," he muttered.

Before she could respond to that, she heard the sound of the others approaching. "Never mind," she said quickly. "They're coming. Just remember to play your part."

❖ ❖ ❖

They began their second day by answering Juliet's mail. "Read each letter carefully," Professoressa Marchese advised. "And as you write your reply, remember to answer in the spirit of Juliet!" She opened the box of letters and tipped it onto the table. Letters with stamps and postmarks from dozens of countries spilled out.

"Wow." Tom looked daunted. "That's a lot of letters."

"It's hard to believe so many people need help with their love lives," Benno said with a sly glance at Giacomo.

"Yes," Giacomo said, giving him a burning stare in return. "How fortunate that you are here to offer counsel. Given how perceptive you are about other people."

Lucy plucked a letter from the pile. "This is going to be such fun."

Professoressa Marchese left them again, saying she had to meet with the German translator of her books and have lunch with the president of the university. Once the door closed behind her, everyone except Lucy looked at one another, then at the stack of letters. Lucy was busily reading the letter she had picked up.

"Oh, listen to this one," she said. Then she read it out loud.

Dear Juliet,
   I really like a girl in my school. How can I tell if she likes me? I've already asked my friends, but they don't have a clue.
   Sincerely,
   Joel P.

"Dibs on this one," she said. "It'll be a breeze to answer."

Silvia frowned at her. This was something else that annoyed her about Americans. They acted as if everything in life was so clear-cut and straightforward, whereas Silvia knew to the depths of her being that life was murky, unpredictable, and extremely complicated.

"Fine," she snapped. "Then you answer it."

Kate leaned forward to pull another letter from the pile.

Dear Juliet,
   I like a boy in my math class, but I can't tell if he likes me. He doesn't ever talk to me unless I say something to him first. And every time I do, he asks me what my name is, even

though I've told him five times now. But my
friends think I should ask him to the school
dance. What do you think? I will follow any
advice you give me!
    Sincerely,
    Samantha B.

She looked at Tom. "You want to take this one?"

"I guess so," he said reluctantly. "But I don't know what to write. I mean, I don't know anything about this guy she likes."

"Well, obviously," Lucy began, "he *does* like her, so you just have to reassure her a little bit."

"*Uffa!*" Silvia said in disgust. "You must be joking!"

Lucy looked puzzled. "What?" She looked around the table and saw a ring of skeptical faces. "What?"

"I hate to say it, but I think we should write back and suggest that she start thinking about someone else," Giacomo said, sounding truly regretful.

Benno nodded, but added brightly, "Maybe we should give her advice on how to meet other guys, though! That would probably cheer her up!"

"Nothing will cheer her up." Silvia pronounced in a hollow tone, sounding like an oracle of doom. "She loves him, he does not love her. Nothing could be worse."

Kate clucked her tongue with annoyance. "Really? How about failing a class, breaking an arm, losing a wallet—"

"Those are only problems." Silvia waved a hand dismissively. "Problems can be fixed. But unrequited love is a tragedy."

"I don't know why you insist that it's unrequited!" Lucy said indignantly. "I think we should encourage her to at least try to find out his true feelings! Tom, you agree with me, don't you?"

She gave him an imploring look, as if she were being led to the stake and he offered her only hope of rescue. "Um, well . . ." As Tom tried to gather his thoughts, Benno found himself gazing at Lucy as if hypnotized. A beam of sunlight shone through the window, casting a golden halo around her blond hair. Her blue eyes—no, he thought, the mere word blue was not enough. Her eyes were the deep, dark blue of the ocean or the midnight sky, filled with unfathomable depth and mystery—

"Benno!" Tom almost shouted.

Benno came to with a start and saw that Tom was giving him a desperate look. "What do you think?"

Benno hated to disappoint Lucy, who had now shifted her imploring look to him. "Well, I guess he could just be *pretending* to not notice her," he suggested shiftily, ignoring Giacomo's doubtful expression.

"Exactly!" Lucy beamed. "That's exactly right! I think this could be a situation like the one you see in the movies, where someone acts like he doesn't like someone because he wants to hide the true nature of his feelings! But secretly, *way* deep down inside, he really *does* like that person! So actually the more someone doesn't pay attention to someone the more he probably likes her!" She paused for breath, then added, "Now if you look at it that way, the fact that he keeps forgetting her name is actually a very good sign! No one who didn't like somebody a little bit could ignore someone that completely!"

There was a brief silence as everyone took that in.

Then Giacomo said, "You've obviously given this more thought than the rest of us. Maybe you should answer this letter as well?"

Lucy smiled and, quite contented, wrote two letters filled with impassioned advice to send out in the next day's mail.

By the end of the class, each member of the Shakespeare Seminar had managed to meet their quota of answering two letters a day. After an hour, they had agreed to stop discussing every letter, since it was clear that otherwise they would still be in the seminar room at midnight.

Occasionally, they would pass a letter around the table for comments. Kate noticed that not only was each person's handwriting as individual as their personalities (Lucy's looping and carefree, Silvia's a black scrawl, Benno's almost indecipherable, Giacomo's spiky and angular), but the tone of their advice ranged from blithely optimistic to doom-laden gloom. They didn't seem to be learning anything about Shakespeare and, moreover, they were probably actively damaging relationships around the world. Kate shook her head at the wisdom of this exercise, but she dutifully kept working until the church bells chimed three o'clock.

Giacomo threw down his pen with relief and flexed his fingers. *"Basta,"* he said. "Enough."

The others followed suit, yawning and stretching.

"What's everyone going to do this afternoon?" Lucy asked. "Does anyone want to go shopping?"

Kate made a point of looking at Giacomo, then hurriedly glancing away before answering. "Sounds like fun," she said in an elaborately casual voice. "But I think I need to take a nap."

"I have some other things I promised to do," Giacomo said.

"Oh, too bad." Lucy's voice was innocent, but

Kate saw the knowing look she gave Silvia and smiled to herself.

Tom said he wanted to check out the city's soccer pitches, which clearly didn't interest Silvia or Lucy, so they all went their separate ways.

Only Benno lingered in the seminar room, saying that he had to write one last paragraph to finish his letter and that he felt duty-bound to mail it as soon as possible.

"It is a very sad case," he had explained dramatically. "Adrian from Birmingham, England, suffers from unrequited passion for his older sister's best friend, who does not know he exists! In fact, she loves another! I really think I should send an answer today."

Giacomo had given him a suspicious glance at this unexpected devotion to duty, but Lucy had beamed at him. "I'm sure your advice will help that boy *so much*," she had said. Benno had tried to look modest.

As soon as he was alone, he had begun rooting through the trash can until he found what he wanted: Lucy's rough drafts. She had a habit, he had noticed, of writing pages and pages of advice, filled with numerous cross-outs and scribbled margin notes. She would chew thoughtfully on the end of her pen as she wrote (he found this habit delightful).

Sometimes she would forget which end of the pen was which, resulting in an ink stain at the corner of her mouth (he thought the smear of dark blue was charming). She would furrow her brow, and sigh, and gaze absently out the window as she considered what advice Juliet would give (he found this seriousness of purpose quite admirable).

He kept searching until he had snatched all of Lucy's discarded letters from the trash, then turned to go. But as he was about to leave the room, he glanced back at the table where his letter—with, in truth, only one sentence written—lay half hidden under his notebook.

I only said I *should* reply today, he thought. I didn't say I *would*.

Then he thought of how Lucy had smiled at him so warmly. She seemed to think he was a kind person. Moreover, she seemed to *like* the idea that he was a kind person. He sighed, sat down at the table, and began to write.

His advice to Adrian had been succinct and realistic. Whether it would be helpful or not was another matter, and not one that he had time to think much about.

"Dear Adrian," he had written, "it is indeed painful to love someone who does not love you in return. I suggest you find out what she wants in a guy, then demonstrate that you are exactly what she's looking for. For example, most girls like—"

Here he had stopped, his pen hovering over the paper as he tried to figure out how to finish that sentence. Benno had the advantage, if one could call it that, of having grown up with three opinionated older sisters. Over the years, he had often heard them dissecting various boys' looks, personalities, and intelligence in a matter-of-fact way that had made him shudder. Angie had always claimed she wanted someone who made her laugh, while Gisella said she would only go out with athletes, and Rosaria's constant quest was for a boy with a devilish smile. "Especially," she would say meaningfully, "if he looks like he can back it up with action."

But then Angie married a very serious lawyer, Gisella started dating a video-game designer who spent ten hours a day at his computer, and Rosaria—well, Rosaria hadn't yet found a smile that lived up to her expectations.

Benno had to face facts. He had no idea what girls wanted. And, now that he thought about it, he suspected they didn't know, either.

He crumpled up the letter and started over with a fresh piece of paper. Perhaps a more imaginative approach was called for. "Dear Adrian, I've heard that women often fall in love with men who have rescued them from danger. Perhaps you could arrange for this girl to encounter some small peril which would then give you the opportunity to save her."

Not a bad suggestion, actually. His black eyes narrowed with thought. Perhaps Adrian could lure this girl into a field where a mad bull resided? And then save her when the mad bull (inevitably) charged her?

But then there was the question of speed. Benno had no idea how fast Adrian could run.

No. This plan was too fraught with difficulties. He stared balefully at the blank paper for several minutes, then began writing once more.

"Dear Adrian," he wrote, "All I can tell you is to be yourself. If it's meant to happen, it will."

Then he tossed the envelope in the mail bin and headed off with Lucy's letters in a pocket close to his heart.

Act II
SCENE IV

"Silvia and Lucy have taken up a position across the piazza." Giacomo stretched out his legs in a leisurely manner that almost tripped a waiter who was rushing by. "Don't look."

"I didn't intend to," Kate said crisply. "And anyway, I saw them, too."

They were sitting at an outdoor cafe in the late afternoon sun. Conversations in a half-dozen languages swirled around them, punctuated by occasional bursts of laughter. It was Giacomo's favorite time of day, when people decided that they had done enough work or enough sightseeing and were ready to relax into the evening.

Kate, however, looked anything but relaxed. She

was perched on the edge of her chair, her back perfectly straight, studying the menu as intensely as if it were written in Croatian. Watching her from the corner of his eye, Giacomo thought that their little plan, which had seemed so delightfully entertaining yesterday, might turn out to be more work than he had thought.

"You seem nervous," he said.

She glanced up just long enough to say, "Not at all. Why would I be nervous?" before turning back to the menu.

Giacomo closed his eyes briefly. *Saint Rosaline, help me out here.*

When he opened his eyes again, he saw the waiter standing behind Kate and surveying them with a knowing look. *First date*, his expression said. *Not going well at all, what a pity.*

Waiters never gave him that kind of look. On the contrary, he was used to getting looks of admiration and good fellowship, something along the lines of "Well done, our side!"

He gave their drink order in a distant tone — *"Acqua minerale, per favore"* — and turned his attention back to Kate, who was holding the menu so that she could glance over at Silvia and Lucy. "May I make a suggestion?"

She eyed him cautiously but nodded. "All right."

"You want to deceive our friends into thinking that we are beginning a romance, yes?" he said. "Then you need to look relaxed, as if you're having fun. Not like . . ."

"Like what?"

"Like someone who is being held hostage."

"I don't know what you're talking about," she said. "I'm perfectly relaxed."

"Well." He chose not to comment on that. "Perhaps if you sat back in your chair."

Kate glanced down and seemed to realize for the first time that she was perched uncomfortably on the edge of her seat. She slid back.

"Excellent. Now uncross your arms," he added. "Good. Now, smile at me as if you think I'm incredibly charming."

She glared at him.

"Okay." He sighed. "We'll work our way up to that."

"What's she doing now?" Lucy hissed to Silvia. She was wearing oversized sunglasses and a straw hat to disguise her identity. "Can you tell what's going on? I can't see a single blessed thing!"

"No wonder," Silvia said tartly. "It would be easier

to watch them if you weren't holding your menu up in front of your face."

"I don't want them to recognize me," Lucy muttered from the side of her mouth. "And I don't want to attract any attention."

"I think it's too late for that." Silvia was all too aware of the amused glances directed toward Lucy.

"They look like they're really getting along," Lucy said. "I would just *love* to be able to hear what they're saying, wouldn't you?"

"Kate," said Giacomo.

"Yes, Giacomo," said Kate.

He sighed. They had been sitting and regarding each other in silence for three full minutes. And not just any silence. It was tense silence, the kind that usually erupted into tearful breakups, emotional confrontations, or sudden confessions.

"Perhaps we should try some light conversation," he said. He offered her a charming smile without much hope that it would work.

He was right. It didn't.

"Conversation about what?"

"Oh, I don't know," he said. Giacomo thought with some exasperation that what was supposed to be a lark was turning into rather hard work. In fact, flirting with Kate was beginning to feel more like trudging up a hill.

"Tell me about your family, your friends, where you live."

She frowned. "You can't possibly be interested in that."

A very steep hill. In a torrential rainstorm.

"I would be if I were interested in you," he pointed out. "If that were the case, I would be fascinated with everything you said."

"But you're *not* interested, there's nothing to say about my life, and Lucy and Silvia can't hear what we're talking about anyway, so I don't really see the point," she said.

Wearing heavy, mud-encrusted hiking books and carrying a backpack filled with bricks.

"Well, we have to talk about something or people will think we're looking for work as living statues," he snapped.

"Okay, fine." She sounded just as testy. "My parents are divorced, my mother is a law professor, you know my father. I live in Lawrence, Kansas. My two best friends are named Annie and Sarah."

"Well. Thank you. Brisk and to the point."

"I told you there wasn't much to say," Kate pointed out. "Your turn."

"All right, let's see. First, family. Well, you've met my mother." He gave her a martyred look. "I grew up awash in Shakespeare. Even her motherly advice was stolen from old Will. You know—"

"'Have more than thou showest, Speak less than thou knowest, Lend less than thou owest.'" Kate nodded. She paused, realizing that, for the first time, she felt a spark of fellowship with Giacomo. "I *hate* being quoted at."

"Me, too. And somehow the iambic pentameter makes it even worse. Now my father, he's also a professor. History, though, which means that *his* parental lectures usually involve Great Men and Where They Went Wrong."

"Divorced?" Kate was becoming a little interested in spite of herself.

"Mmm." Giacomo nodded. "When I was two. But I visit him in Oxford every summer and—"

"—alternate holidays," Kate said. "He's British?"

"Yes, I think that's why my mother fell in love with him, actually. He spoke the language of the Bard." He said the last two words in a lofty tone to show that he was being sarcastic, and she grinned.

"Oh, that explains your British accent. When you speak English, I mean."

Giacomo made a mental note. She had noticed his

accent, that was very good. She seemed to be relaxing, even better. Now it was time to move to the next level.

He tilted his head toward Lucy and Silvia. "I think it's time to demonstrate our growing affection, don't you?"

Silvia continued her unwavering observation of the café table across the square. Benno, of course, had wanted to come along on this surveillance, but Signora Conti had rung his mobile to ask him to pick up a few things for her at the *farmacia*. Signora Conti was ninety-one, lived with twelve cats, and rarely left her apartment. She called Benno as often as five times a week to run little errands for her, and he never refused.

With a quick apology, he had dashed off right after the seminar ended. Silvia was stuck with Lucy, whose starry-eyed belief that they were furthering the cause of true love was making Silvia cranky, even though Silvia had planted that belief herself. Silvia glanced at the menu, saw the exorbitant prices that tourists were willing to pay for a slice of pizza, and felt even crankier. Then she glanced across the square and saw Giacomo put his hand on Kate's arm, and felt—well, cranky was no longer *quite* the right word.

She searched her mind for the exact word to describe the way she felt right now. Ah, yes. *Assassino*. She felt ready to kill.

Giacomo put his hand on Kate's arm. She jumped in surprise, which made him jump, and their little table rocked from the movement, spilling water on the tablecloth. He felt ridiculous, especially when he saw that the waiter had noticed and was hiding a smirk.

"Haven't you ever flirted before?" he asked as he gave the waiter a sharp look.

"Of course," she snapped. "But never for an audience."

"Right." He took a deep breath and readjusted his smile. "This is an unusual situation. So, let's, I don't know, let's think of ourselves as actors who are playing a scene."

He let his fingers brush her wrist and glanced at her from the corner of his eye. "Actors who are pretending to seduce one another, when in fact we are really wooing the ones who are watching us."

He lifted his hand to her cheek and let his fingers drift down to her chin and waited for her to blush. . . .

"That's *very* good," she said approvingly. "I can tell you've practiced."

He only kept from pulling his hand back through sheer force of will. "This only works," he said tightly, "if you play your part as well."

"Oh, I see." She gave him a satirical look. "I'm supposed to *swoon*."

He took a deep breath. "Well, yes," he said. "It would be helpful if our charade is meant to convince." His eyes slid sideways to where Silvia and Lucy were sitting, then back to her. He gave a tiny, meaningful nod.

Kate smiled serenely. "By all means." She leaned forward, propping her chin on one hand, and gazed into his eyes.

From a distance, Giacomo reflected—say, the distance from their table to Silvia and Lucy's table—her gaze might look adoring.

From close to, however—say, the distance across this table—it most definitely did not.

"Oh, this is going so well, don't you think?" Now that Lucy had finally lowered her menu, Silvia realized that it had served a useful purpose. Surely even two people who were as totally engrossed in each other as Kate and Giacomo might notice Lucy's beaming smile. "Silvia, this was *such* a good idea of yours!"

Silvia muttered something under her breath in Italian. Fortunately, Lucy did not ask her to translate.

"Kate is really going to thank us when she hears how we set this up," Lucy went on blithely. "I mean, to come to Italy and have someone like Giacomo fall in love with you . . ." A faint cloud moved across her face, but Silvia didn't notice it, because she was still staring across the piazza, reminding herself that Giacomo was going to feel like a real idiot when he learned how he had been set up.

"I mean, it's the kind of thing that people dream will happen to them, but it hardly ever does. Not to most people, anyway." There was a slightly vexed note in Lucy's voice, but Silvia didn't hear it, because she was too busy imagining how she would reveal that she had made a fool of Giacomo, who richly deserved it, and of Kate, who probably deserved it.

"So?" Kate asked crisply. "Do I look as if I've fallen under your spell?"

At least she was gazing at him with an expression that was . . . well, not enraptured, exactly. Giacomo certainly knew *that* look, and this wasn't it. But she did appear to be perhaps somewhat fond of him, which was an improvement over the trapped-hostage look.

He tilted his head to one side. "Almost. Now put your arms on the table and lean toward me slightly."

She rolled her eyes, but she did as he suggested. When she leaned forward, her face moved into a ray of sunlight that had managed to sneak through a gap in the umbrella over their table. For the first time, Giacomo noticed the light dusting of freckles across her nose, and the velvety darkness of her brown eyes, and the slight arch in her eyebrows. . . .

If only those eyebrows weren't raised in that sarcastic way, and those eyes weren't giving him a cool look, as if he had been measured against some private standard and found wanting.

"Stop tapping your foot," he snapped.

"I'm not—" she began, then caught herself. She took a deep breath, and smiled. "All right. Now what?"

"Now I lean toward you ever so slightly." He shifted forward and looked into her eyes. She looked away. "Yes, that's good, that little glance to the side, that makes you look modest and shy—"

"Oh, *please*." Her eyes snapped back to meet his.

"Right, and now you look back at me to show you're interested."

"*Pretending* to be interested." She corrected him automatically.

"Of course," he agreed.

His fingers were still resting on her wrist. He could feel her pulse beating.

Kate pulled her hand away. "I think," she said, still looking at him, "that Silvia and Lucy are leaving."

He leaned forward slightly and held her gaze. He said softly, "And then I'll whisper something to you. An endearment of some sort."

"I don't think that's necessary—"

"The sort," he continued, "to make a girl blush."

"Really?" she said coolly. "And that would be . . . ?"

In answer, he leaned forward and whispered in her ear.

And Kate blushed.

Act II
SCENE V

Benno eyed the soccer ball lying on the grass, then ran toward it. A straight shot, he thought, right into the goal. He kicked it hard and—damn. The ball veered wildly to the left. He ran after it, cursing to himself, and kicked it again. It shot off to the right. Frowning darkly, he chased it down.

Fortunately, the soccer pitch was always deserted at this time of day. That, in fact, was why Benno was here. He preferred to practice on his own, so that the inevitable distance between the way he imagined himself playing (with fluidity and speed, scoring goal after goal in front of a cheering audience) and the way he actually performed (not so well; witness his complete inability to kick a ball in a straight line) was not on display for jeering onlookers.

Most of the time, he actually felt quite happy, sweating in the heat of the midday sun while other people were sensibly inside, taking a siesta in their cool, dark bedrooms after lunch. He encouraged himself by narrating a mental commentary in the style of his favorite TV announcers ("And Benno Bugiardini scores again! *Magnifico!*") and by imagining a group of girls standing on the sidelines, watching him with admiration. But today, he was disgruntled, and even visualizing his most elaborate fantasies of victory and applause couldn't erase the feeling he'd had after reading the paper he had just pulled from the trash.

He had waited until he had finished his errands and reached the soccer pitch before pulling Lucy's letter from his pocket. When Benno read her response, he felt his heart sink with disappointment.

"Dear Joel," Lucy had written, "I totally understand why you don't want to just tell the girl flat out how you feel until you know if she likes you. The good news for you is that I'm a girl, so I can tell you exactly what to look for! First, does she pay attention to what you say? Does she care about your opinions?"

Unbidden, unwanted, the memory of Lucy leaning across the table and asking earnestly, "But Tom, what do *you* think?" came to Benno's mind.

Benno read on. "Does she pay you little compliments?"

He gritted his teeth as he remembered Lucy saying to Tom, just that morning, "That shirt looks great on you. It really makes your eyes look green!"

Disgruntled, he continued reading until the end of the letter. "Does she laugh when you make jokes? (Of course, that *may* mean that you're funny, but to be honest most boys *aren't*, so if she laughs it's probably because she likes you.)"

Benno sighed, a deep, despairing sigh. He had always thought that he was quite witty, but he had to admit that he had only managed to make Lucy laugh a handful of times. Well, to be totally honest, perhaps twice.

Or maybe just once.

Tom, on the other hand . . .

Benno recalled how Lucy had giggled when Tom had said—well, Benno couldn't actually remember what he had said, that's how incredibly *not* funny his comment was, but he remembered clearly how she gazed admiringly at the person Benno now realized was a snake in the grass, a wolf in sheep's clothing, a—

"Hey, Benno!"

He looked up to see Tom, the person he now hated more than anyone in the world, waving cheerfully at him from the sidelines. Benno picked up the ball and trotted over, trying to look casual and elegant, like the best players on the Italian national team. This effect was ruined when he stepped in a small rut in the field, tripped, and dropped the ball.

"*Ciao*, Tom," he called out. "*Come stai?*"

As usual, Tom looked flummoxed by this most basic Italian greeting. Benno imagined that he could actually hear the wheels in Tom's brain turning as he tried to remember the correct response.

"*Bene*," Tom finally said with an air of triumph.

A spark of mischief flared up in Benno's heart. "*Come parli bene, Tommaso. Ti congratulo,*" he said rapidly. "*Fra poco parlerai come un vero italiano!*" You speak well, Tom. Congratulations. Soon you'll be speaking like an Italian!

"Yeah, whatever," Tom said, abandoning the Italian language without ceremony. "So, listen, do you play on the local soccer, sorry, *football* team or something?"

Benno ducked his head modestly. "I play a little."

"Awesome. I was really hoping I'd find a game while I'm here. Who's your favorite team?"

Benno threw out his hands and gave an expressive shrug. "Milano, of course, who else? They are *fantastico*."

"Yeah, that's true," Tom said, nodding judiciously. "But you gotta admit, Inter is just as good—"

"Pah!" Benno's entire body seemed to express his disgust. "The way they play, it is ugly. Now compare them with Milano. . . ."

He kicked the ball over to Tom, who fielded it expertly and darted across the field, effortlessly dribbling with his feet until he was ten yards from the goal. Without missing a beat, he smoothly kicked the ball toward the goal. Even from a distance, Benno could hear the thwack that meant that the kick was solid and true. The ball sailed into the goal. Perfect.

Tom did not raise his arms in jubilation, as Benno would have done, or yell "Goal!" the way his friend Tony would have done, or turned to grin smugly at any onlookers as Giorgio would have done. Instead, he trotted over to pick up the ball, then loped back to where Benno stood absolutely still, as if he'd just been frozen into place.

Finally he thawed enough to say, "That was great."

"Well, you set me up with a great pass," Tom said offhandedly. "Thanks."

He wasn't even breathing hard, Benno noticed. And he kept bouncing the ball from one foot to the other in an easy rhythm, never missing a beat even as he continued talking. "This feels good. Actually, it feels great. I hate being stuck inside all day, don't you?"

"Yes," Benno agreed hollowly. "You look like you could play for Milano. Or Firenze, even."

"Really?" Tom's eyes lit up, then he shook his head modestly. "No, thanks for saying that, but I couldn't even come close to playing pro. I know that. College level, *maybe*, if I'm lucky."

"No, you're better than that." The note of authority in Benno's voice surprised both of them. He caught Tom's eye and shrugged. "I know a lot about football," he explained. He hesitated but couldn't help boasting a bit. "My great-uncle played for Italy in the 1960 World Cup."

"Are you kidding?" Tom had that eager look on his face again, the one that reminded Benno of large, shaggy, happy-go-lucky dogs with too much energy. "That's, that's . . ." He stopped, searching for a word to express the magnitude of this accomplishment, but ended up shrugging, as if acknowledging how useless words were to describe such an experience.

"I know," Benno said.

They stood for a few moments in reverent silence.

Then Benno, who was feeling friendlier toward Tom, said, "Most Americans don't know anything about football."

"I do. I know everything about it," Tom answered fervently. "That's why when I saw the announcement about the essay contest to become a Shakespeare Scholar I, um, . . ." His voice trailed off as if he was afraid he'd said too much.

Benno looked surprised. "You entered it because you love football?"

"Um, yeah." Tom's eyes had turned shifty. He looked down at the ball, which he was rolling back and forth on the ground with one foot. "Italy's my favorite team."

"Yes, they are the best in the world," Benno said slowly. He suspected there was something else going on here, but he didn't know what. He decided to test the waters a bit. "But you must also know a lot about Shakespeare to have written a winning essay."

"Well, yeah," Tom said weakly. "I guess so."

He looked over Benno's shoulder, as if hoping to see rescue in the distance. From the disappointed look on his face, it was apparent nothing was in sight. "So, what do you think about Italy's chances against Brazil next month?"

But Benno was not to be diverted. "So. You have studied Shakespeare for a long time?"

Silence. Then Tom sighed and said, "Okay, I'll

tell you something if you *swear* you won't ever tell anybody else."

Benno nodded, solemn as a priest.

"I didn't actually . . . well, I didn't maybe actually write every single word of the essay that won."

Tom stopped and didn't say anything for a long moment.

But Benno had experience confessing. He knew the drill. He simply waited.

The silence stretched out. Tom shuffled his feet, looked in one direction, then another, then down at the ground. Finally he said, "I didn't plagiarize it or anything."

Benno knew that trick, too: to keep from telling the truth about what you did do, simply explain all the far worse offenses that you *didn't* commit.

He merely raised one questioning eyebrow and Tom, who was clearly a novice when it came to interrogation, broke within five seconds.

"All the ideas were mine, or most of them, anyway, but my friend Serena? She's really, really smart, so I asked her to kind of just, I don't know, help me buff out the rough spots." Tom couldn't meet Benno's eyes. His ears were bright red. "And I really, *really* wanted to get the chance to play football in Italy."

"So this Serena," Benno said. "She wrote the essay for you?"

"No!" Tom was shocked. "That would be cheating. I told her what I thought about *Romeo and Juliet* and she helped me put it into words. But," he went on, more bitterly, "I had no clue when I entered the contest that we'd have to act in front of people! And wear costumes! And *dance*!"

"Perhaps that is your punishment for lying," Benno said, giving him a severe look that was an exact mimicry of the look Father Christopher gave him when he caught Benno drawing rude cartoons during catechism class.

"Maybe you're right." Tom gave the ball a moody kick. It shot off at an odd angle and landed in the middle of a group of mothers and young children. Tom winced, then yelled out, "Sorry! I mean, *scusate, scusate*," as he ran over to retrieve it.

Benno watched him go through narrowed eyes. What, he wondered, would Father Christopher have to say about this situation? Tom had done something very, very wrong. Clearly, he did not deserve the love of someone as beautiful, as kind, as openhearted as Lucy.

On the other hand, Lucy had just as clearly fallen for Tom. Benno didn't understand it, but then the things that he didn't understand about women were more numerous than the stars in the sky.

And yet, Benno thought that his feelings for Lucy could be classified as love, which should count for *something*.

But if true love meant anything, it meant that you wanted your beloved to have what she most desired. And in this case, if what Lucy wanted was Tom . . . well, Benno would have to help her get that.

Yes. He was decided. He would do the noble thing.

He paused to enjoy feeling gallant and chivalrous, and was disappointed to realize that he actually felt irritated and bitter.

Perhaps he had gone off track somewhere in his reasoning. He started over.

If true love meant anything, it meant that you wanted your beloved to be *happy*. That, at least, he had established to his own satisfaction.

But happiness, he suddenly realized, may or *may not* mean getting what she most desired.

Take this current situation, for example. Lucy thought she wanted Tom, but would she be happy with him? Benno considered this judiciously as Tom started bouncing the ball off his head to entertain his audience. Yes, Tom was an excellent athlete, but surely clumsiness also had its charms?

The ball landed on the ground and Tom trotted after it, not at all abashed at being laughed at by a crowd of five-year-olds. Yes, Tom was good-natured, but surely darker emotions added complexity and interest to a personality?

Tom offered to let one of the little boys kick the ball, which made the boy beam and his mother nod in thanks. And yes, Tom was kindhearted, but . . .

Benno could not, actually, think of any reason that Lucy would be happier with someone who played practical jokes, often felt spiteful, and was rarely described as kind.

His shoulders slumped as this line of reasoning, which had seemed so promising, crumbled into dust. So when Tom came to a halt in front of him, sweating and looking a bit happier, Benno said, "I have something to tell you."

"Tom! Benno! There you are!"

They turned to see Lucy running toward them.

"I'm so glad I found you guys," Lucy panted. "I just left Silvia at the café, can you believe it, Kate and Giacomo are *still* talking, it's been more than an hour already! I mean, honestly!"

"Our plan is working, then," Benno pointed out.

"Oh, yes, you should see the way he looks at her!"

Lucy's brow furrowed a bit. Kate didn't know how lucky she was, having someone like Giacomo looking at her like that.

"So Silvia's still there," Tom asked casually, as he kicked the ball from one foot to the other with practiced ease. "At the café, I mean?"

Lucy shrugged. "I suppose so."

Benno gave Tom a sharp look. Hadn't he just been told that Lucy was falling for him? Why wasn't he smiling at her, flirting with her, making her laugh? Why wasn't he *seizing the moment*?

Benno repressed a sigh and decided to help Tom out.

"What are you doing now, Lucy?" he asked. "Tom was just saying that he wanted to get a gelato."

But Tom was looking toward the bridge that Lucy had just walked over, clearly lost in his own thoughts.

Benno raised his voice slightly. "Weren't you, Tom?"

"Hmm?" Tom blinked and refocused his attention. "What?"

"Weren't you just saying that you wanted to go —"

"Oh, yeah, right, I've got to go and, um, do some stuff," Tom said quickly. "I'll see you guys later, okay?"

He kicked the ball neatly back to Benno, waved

to Lucy, and jogged off toward the bridge.

"Well." Lucy frowned as she watched him head away from her with an eager step. "Huh."

"He is very distracted, Tom," Benno said. "The workload is more than he expected. I think he wants to go study."

She turned and saw Benno standing in front of her, holding a soccer ball and giving her an intense and unreadable look. She had forgotten that he was there, actually, which made her feel guilty, so to make up for it she said, "Oh, right! Tom is such a hard worker!" and gave him a brilliant smile.

The ball slipped from Benno's fingers and bounced away. He ran after it and accidentally kicked it even farther, ran after it again and finally managed to grab it, and ran back to her, blushing.

If Lucy knew one thing, it was how to be polite, so she tried to smooth over the awkward moment by saying the first thing that came into her head. "So you guys were playing soccer?" Too late, she heard these incredibly idiotic words coming out of her mouth and tried not to wince. Of *course* they were just playing soccer, what a stupid thing to say! She added brightly, "Looks like fun!"

She didn't mean it, of course. Nothing that involved running around, chasing small round objects and getting sweaty counted as fun in Lucy's world.

But her completely insincere comment made Benno's face light up as if a wondrous vision had just appeared to him. "Yes, it is! Would you like me to teach you?"

Lucy sighed. This was the problem with being polite. It made you say things you didn't mean, which other people believed, of course, because they didn't know you were just being polite, and then they said something back that you had to agree with because otherwise you would have to admit that you hadn't meant a word of what you had originally said, and the next thing you knew you were baking five hundred cookies for the choir fundraiser and resenting every moment.

And now Benno was holding out the ball with a hopeful look in his eyes. So she said "Sure" and tried to listen carefully as he told her how to kick it toward the goal.

But as Benno went into a lengthy explanation of how this seemingly simple action was to be accomplished, Lucy's mind drifted off. Somehow, she had thought that her trip to Italy was going to be quite different. Of course, she'd only been here a few days, but still. She had imagined flirtations in cafés, walks in the moonlight, chance meetings in the square. She had expected romance.

It wasn't, she felt, an unreasonable expectation. After all, back home she was popular, she went on dates all the time, every guy in her school would absolutely love to go out with her. . . .

So why had she just spent an afternoon watching Giacomo flirt with Kate? And why did Tom just dash off as if he couldn't wait to get away from her? Lucy's mother had taught her from an early age that a pleasant expression would keep her from getting wrinkles, but right now Lucy didn't care. She frowned.

Finally Benno stopped talking. "Why don't you give it a try?" he said.

"What?" Lucy stared at him, then remembered, just in time, that he had been teaching her something about soccer.

Benno put the ball on the ground and smiled encouragingly. "It's a little tricky, so don't worry if you don't get it right the first time."

Lucy eyed the ball grimly.

"Just get a running start—"

She took three fast angry steps.

"And shoot it toward the goal—"

She kicked it as hard as she could.

Benno watched it sail through the air and land squarely in the net.

"Hey!" Lucy sounded absolutely astonished. "Did you see that?"

He nodded slowly, his face blank. "Yes," he said. "Well. Perhaps it's not as tricky as I thought."

An expression of shy delight dawned on her face as she murmured, "I'm really terrible at sports." Then she shrugged and gave Benno a smile that made him momentarily forget his own name. "That must have been beginner's luck."

He cleared his throat. "Beginner's luck? There is no such thing," he assured her. "Would you like me to teach you how to pass?"

Act II
SCENE VI

Silvia stared balefully at the biscotti and espresso that the waiter placed on the table in front of her. He backed away slowly and exchanged a meaningful glance with the barista behind the counter.

Steer clear of that one, their expressions said. She's nothing but trouble.

Silvia saw the looks they shot at each other, and she knew what they meant, and she finally smiled. True, it was a bleak smile, but that was the best she could manage these days. Ever since last summer, in fact.

Her best friend, Elena, couldn't understand it. "You look amazing, Silvia!" she would say. "Such a change in just one year! I wish that I—"

"No, you don't." Silvia would scowl at her. "Believe me." Silvia and Elena had been best friends for years. Their connection had been based on the unhappy realization, the year they turned ten, that some girls were prettier than others and that they both belonged with the others. By twelve, they noticed that they were, perhaps, a little heavier than most of their friends. When they were thirteen, they got pimples and braces. By fourteen, Silvia and Elena knew what it felt like when boys' eyes slipped by them to focus on Bianca Donatelli, already as gorgeous as a supermodel, or Isabella Rossi, who had perfected the art of the hair toss and the coy smile.

"It's like we're invisible!" Elena would complain.

"Perhaps we should become cat burglars, then," Silvia used to joke, back in the days when she could still find the humor in dark situations.

"I'm serious!"

"So am I. At least we would reap a financial benefit from our looks," Silvia would say, laughing.

And then, the summer Silvia turned fifteen, she blossomed. She grew three inches, she discovered she had a figure, her braces came off, her skin cleared up. Her older cousin took her to a really good hairstylist, her parents finally agreed to replace her glasses with contacts, and boys started turning their heads to look when she walked down the street.

"You're so lucky," Elena would sigh, half admiring, half envious. "You're not invisible anymore."

"Yes, I am," Silvia would argue. "They still don't see *me*. Now they just see this—" and she would wave her hand at her hair, her face, her body.

Elena would just look puzzled. "But that's good! That's great! That's what we always wanted, to look beautiful!"

Silvia finally gave up trying to explain why she felt just as resentful when boys noticed her because she was pretty as she had when they ignored her because she was plain. Instead, she started wearing all black clothes, torn fishnet stockings, and heavy boots; teasing her hair until she looked as if she'd just survived a tornado; ringing her eyes with black eyeliner; and putting away the pretty jewelry she had collected over the years in favor of silver skull rings and necklaces featuring daggers and razor blades.

Elena didn't hang out with her much anymore, but that was all right. Silvia had decided that she liked being alone.

She saw the waiter eyeing her from his safe spot behind the counter. She sneered at him and pulled a journal out of her handbag. Before she could jot down even one black thought about her life, however, the door to the café opened and Tom bounded in.

"Hi! Silvia!" he cried happily. "What are you doing here?"

She cast her eyes to the ceiling. Why was he always so *bouncy*? "Having an espresso," she said, pointing sarcastically at her cup. "This is a café, after all."

"What a great idea! Can I join you?" Without waiting for her response, he pulled up a chair and kept chatting. "I haven't had much of a chance to talk to you yet. Except when we're in class, of course. Which doesn't really count, because—"

He stopped, arrested by the basilisk stare she was leveling at him. After a long moment, he waved down the waiter. *"Un cappuccino, per favore,"* he said in a flat, nasal American accent.

Silvia made a small sound of amused disgust.

"What? Did I say it wrong?" he said. His green eyes looked worried.

She wanted to ignore him, but he looked so crestfallen that she found herself saying, entirely against her will, "It's not your pronunciation. Your pronunciation is—" She stopped. His Italian truly was execrable. "Well, anyway. It's just that, in Italy, people only drink cappucino in the morning. For breakfast. At this time of day, it is always espresso. Always."

"Oh, okay." He nodded slowly as he filed that away for future reference. She turned back to her journal, content with the thought that she had, ever so slightly, put him in his place.

Then he smiled at her, a big, cheerful, American smile. "Thanks a lot, Silvia! I would never have known that if it hadn't been for you! And that's exactly why I came here, to learn more about a different culture! So!" He earnestly bobbed his head up and down a few more times. "Thanks!"

"Try saying *grazie*," she suggested wearily. "You are in Italy, after all."

His smile flickered for a moment and she regretted her tone, which was sharper than she had intended, but she couldn't help it, he was just so irritating. For Silvia, for whom the sunniest morning was only a cause for dark suspicion—after all, if the day started off so well, it could only get worse—Tom was a complete conundrum. She couldn't understand why he was so happy all the time when he had so many reasons to be gloomy. After all, he was so naive. So uncultured. And the way he dressed!

Still, as she sipped the last of her espresso and listened to him butchering the word *grazie* over and over, shooting her quick looks to see how he was doing, she couldn't keep a small smile from tugging at her lips. She felt quite mature and sophisticated next to Tom. It wasn't an unpleasant feeling at all.

After Silvia left, Tom stared down at the dregs of coffee in his cup, mentally replaying everything she had said.

She had criticized his choice of drink. She had corrected his pronunciation. She had sighed and rolled her eyes and looked put upon any time he ventured an opinion.

Tom possessed a relentlessly optimistic personality, but even he couldn't make himself believe that their meeting had gone terribly well.

Faced with the problem of unrequited attraction, Tom decided to order some food. He knew this response proved that he did not possess a complex emotional life. A girl back home had told him this. She had seemed to think it was a problem. But at times like these he didn't care, because it meant that he could make himself feel much better simply by eating a grilled cheese sandwich or rather—he squinted at the menu chalked on a blackboard—a panino with tomato and mozzarella. There were advantages, after all, to being an uncomplicated person.

He was just about to wave for the waiter's

attention when a rich, amused voice said from behind his left shoulder, "So, Tommaso, I see you and Silvia are getting along well."

He turned to see Professoressa Marchese smiling down at him. "Um, not really," he said. "I mean . . . do you think so?"

"I know Silvia quite well," she said. "The fact that she did not throw her espresso in your face is an excellent sign."

"Really?" He felt momentarily buoyed by this, and then he remembered. The professor had studied Shakespeare all her life, practically. That had probably totally messed with her head when it came to the real world. Like, she probably thought this was some kind of play, where people who act like they hate you actually love you.

He sighed. It would be nice if life were like Shakespeare, but he was wise enough to know it wasn't.

"I think she was just being polite," he went on, feeling that the professor needed to be set straight. "Everything I say makes her mad."

"Mmm." Professoressa Marchese nodded gravely. "I can see why that would be disheartening."

Somehow, the way she was looking so thoughtful, as if she was taking him so seriously, made him open up a bit more. "And it's not as if I even say much," he confided. "I'm not very good with words."

Professoressa Marchese looked as delighted as if she had just walked into a surprise party. "Ah, but words are not the only way to speak from the heart," she said. "In fact, one might even say they are the least important."

Tom nodded as if he understood, but in fact he had a feeling that often overcame him in the middle of conversations, especially with teachers or parents or any of those kids in the AP classes. They talked and talked and talked, an ocean of talk, and he nodded and pretended to get what they were saying. And all the time, he knew he was just floating along on the surface while all kinds of hidden meanings flowed by on some deep underwater current that he could never hope to reach.

"You're absolutely right," he said agreeably, knowing from experience that this response usually worked.

Sure enough, she beamed with pleasure. "I have an idea for you," she said, patting him on the shoulder. "Read *Henry V*."

His heart sank. *Romeo and Juliet* alone had been hard slogging. And now she wanted him to read *another* play?

She chuckled. "Don't look so dismayed, Tommaso! You will not be tested and you will enjoy it, I promise you. It is about a king who was a great warrior—yes, I thought that might get your attention. And what's more"—she gave him a mischievous wink—"I think you will find that certain parts will prove to be most helpful to you. Most helpful indeed."

Act II
SCENE VII

"Okay, let's try the beginning of the dance one more time. You remember what we did yesterday, right? We begin with three steps, the first two steps down, the third one up on your toes." Dan stood at one end of the ballroom wearing a faded T-shirt and shorts. His students stood in two groups at the other end. The college students clustered on one side of the room, and the high school students on the other, each divided into a row of boys and a row of girls. Full-length mirrors had been mounted on one wall so that they could study their reflections as they learned the patterns and steps.

This was not a good thing, in Kate's opinion. They had been practicing for almost two hours, and she still couldn't bring herself to look in the mirror. Other people, she noticed, did not have this problem.

Lucy, for example, smiled and winked and positively flirted with her own reflection. And it was no wonder, Kate thought grudgingly. Lucy was wearing a crisp white T-shirt and short blue sarong skirt and looked charming. She was also an excellent dancer.

As was Giacomo, who possessed both physical grace and the superior air of a natural courtier; Silvia, who moved through the steps with haughty ease; and, somewhat surprisingly, Tom, whose balance and agility on the soccer field translated effortlessly to the dance floor.

Kate, on the other hand, held herself too stiffly and couldn't stop staring at the floor. She consoled herself with the fact that she was not as bad as Benno, though that was small comfort, considering that Benno was a disaster. He couldn't remember more than two steps at a time. He tripped over his own feet when he had to do a turn. And, when put under pressure, he forgot how to tell his right foot from his left.

"Excellent," Dan said in a bright voice. "So! Let's begin! One, two, three, four . . . and down, down, *up*! Down, down, *up*!" As he counted out the beats, his voice got steadily louder with frustration.

They all managed to make it down the length of

the room in this manner. Then it was time for the dancers to stop, turn to their partner in the opposite line, and bow. Kate came to an abrupt halt, turned a meticulous ninety degrees, and bowed exactly as Dan had shown them.

"Look at me," Giacomo whispered.

"What?" Startled, she glanced up.

He smiled and held out his hand. "That's better. You seemed afraid to look me in the eye."

"That's ridiculous." She frowned as she took his hand, and they walked around each other until they both were facing the opposite way.

Then it was time for them to do a double skip to the side and clap their hands, a move that was supposed to be executed in a high-spirited manner and *in unison*, as Dan kept reminding them, but which once again ended up with Benno tripping, the serious Jonathan and Erik clapping as if they were ordering an execution, and everyone else finishing at different times. Kate took a quick peek in the mirror and was dismayed to find that her face was bright red, there were damp patches of sweat on her T-shirt, and a piece of hair had come out of her braid and was sticking out over her left ear at an odd angle.

"Not bad, not bad at all," Dan called out. "If I may make a few *small* suggestions . . ."

As he walked over to talk confidentially to Benno, Giacomo leaned closer to Kate and whispered in her ear, "We are supposed to be falling in love, remember?"

"I remember," she said, exasperated. "But I can't do that *and* think about learning this stupid dance."

"There's nothing to it, I promise you. Just relax. Smile when I take your hand and laugh at things I say as we dance," he said. "Oh, and try looking at me when my attention is elsewhere, as if you can't keep your eyes off me. That will be very persuasive."

Kate surveyed him coolly. "You're enjoying this, aren't you?"

"Enormously." He grinned at her, his dark eyes sparkling. A few brown curls were clinging damply to his forehead, but otherwise he looked completely unruffled. He stepped even closer and put a hand on her arm. "Our spies are keeping very close watch," he murmured.

Kate glanced over his shoulder and saw Lucy and Silvia standing together, watching them. Lucy looked pleased, but Silvia, Kate was happy to note, was glowering darkly. Today she wore a black leotard, silver tennis shoes, and a gray skirt that had apparently been shredded with a butcher knife. Three lug nuts dangled on a leather thong around her neck, heavy black kohl surrounded her eyes, and all her fingernails were painted black. She looked like a malevolent fairy.

Giacomo followed Kate's gaze, then whispered in her ear, "Why don't we give them something worth seeing?"

Kate turned her head to hide her smile. "Excellent idea."

He stepped back and said, a little more loudly, "Would you like to practice the turn now? The one that goes like this"—Giacomo stood opposite her, then stepped forward, turning to the side so that his right shoulder was facing her. Kate did the same thing so that they were standing close, their shoulders almost touching, looking into each other's eyes.

"And we flirt," he said in a low voice and winked.

She smiled and they both stepped back and then repeated the move, stepping forward and swinging the opposite way so their left shoulders were touching. Close again, she said in his ear, "And we flirt." He turned his head and she noticed for the first time that his nose crinkled up a little bit when he smiled. Then he twirled her around and she sank down into a curtsy and he bowed with a flourish of his arm and then he pulled her up and said, "Once more?"

As they repeated the move, Kate meant to glance over and see how their audience was enjoying the play she and Giacomo were putting on. But somehow, as they spun around, first close together, then apart, again and again, she completely forgot to look.

"You're late." Giacomo's grandmother spared him one quick glance, then turned back to the flour she had heaped up on the counter. She made a small depression in the flour and, scowling, cracked an egg into it. "Again."

"Perdonami, nonna," he said in his most contrite voice, which often got him out of trouble. "I was tired after the dance lesson. I took a nap."

"Hmmph." She didn't look up from the flour, which she was now mixing into a sticky dough. "You are always sorry, Giacomo, and yet you always have much more to be sorry for."

"Sì, you're right. I really must change my ways." He gave her the charming smile that almost always got him out of trouble.

She slapped the dough sharply. "I only hope I live that long. Because that would mean I live *forever.*"

Giacomo couldn't help it; he had to laugh at that. Then he gave her a quick kiss on the cheek, which never failed to get him out of trouble.

She gave a reluctant chuckle that sounded like a rusty iron door creaking open, and he knew he had been forgiven. Then she pinched his cheek with floury fingers. He winced. It was a hard pinch; his nonna was not as easily hoodwinked as he would like.

"You are a rascal, Giacomo," she said, her voice rough with both irritation and fondness. "Now start chopping the vegetables."

He moved over to the end of the counter where a chipped yellow bowl was piled high with plump tomatoes. He grabbed a knife and a tomato and began slicing with the ease of long practice.

He smiled to see the neat stack of newspapers on the wooden table. His grandmother read four papers every day, hunched over a heavy brass magnifying glass, diligently scanning the columns of type for stories of disaster and destruction. As a child, she had lived through World War II; as a young woman, she had scrabbled for a living as a cook or maid; as a young wife, she had nursed her clumsy husband through numerous broken limbs, then went back to work when they lost all their money in a confidence scheme. She was determined not to be caught off guard by any future calamity.

As a result, she was remarkably—if morbidly— well informed. They often had interesting discussions about the world's woes as he helped her prepare a meal. But before he could ask about the latest catastrophes, his grandmother said, "So, I saw you with that girl. The American." She slammed a pot of water onto the stove and turned on the burner.

"Kate?" he asked, striving to sound casual as he sneaked a quick peek at his grandmother. Her opinions of his girlfriends tended to be brutal; her predictions for his relationships were inclined to be dire. He braced himself.

"Hmmph." She rolled out the dough with a heavy marble rolling pin. After a moment, she said, "Yes. I think she will be good for you."

"You do?" He couldn't keep the surprise out of his voice.

"*Sí.*" She smiled grimly. "She will break your heart and leave you shattered and alone." She paused to think that over, then nodded approvingly to herself. "It will make you a man."

"She's not going to break my heart," he said, viciously stabbing a tomato. The tomato retaliated by squirting juice in his eye.

Muttering a curse, he wiped his face with a towel and wondered why everyone suddenly felt that they had to offer an opinion on his love life, although he was fairly sure he had never asked for anyone's views on the matter.

He returned to his chopping and added, "We are just playing a game."

"Ha!" his grandmother snorted with derision.

"What?" he snapped.

But just then, the door swung open and his mother swept into the kitchen. "Mama, what are you doing?" she cried.

Francesca Marchese was impeccably dressed, as always, in a silk jacket, skirt, and stiletto heels; her makeup was polished, her hair twisted into an elegant chignon, her jewelry understated and elegant. She stared at her mother, dressed in a shapeless black dress and black orthopedic shoes, her hands and arms covered with flour, her hair pulled back into an untidy bun, and shook her head in despair. "I keep telling you, you don't have to clean! You don't have to cook! I have a staff to do all that now!" She paused for emphasis, then said with great satisfaction, "I am rrrrich!"

"Today you are rich." Her mother shrugged. "Tomorrow you could be ruined." She began cutting the pasta dough into strips. "I will keep cooking."

Her daughter gave an annoyed shrug. "Fine. Do what you like." She turned to squint at her reflection in a copper tray hanging on the wall. "I just wanted to stop by and let you know that the caterers are coming tomorrow to look at the kitchen. Please don't scare them too much." She tweaked a stray lock of hair back into place.

"As long as they don't get in my way, they have nothing to fear."

"Yes, well." She turned back to her mother. "That is what worries me. However, I don't have time to argue with you. I have a meeting at the university in an hour and then I'm having dinner with my American publisher, so I must fly!"

She rushed over to kiss her mother's cheek, first one, then the other. "*Ciao*, Mama." She turned to Giacomo and kissed him, "*Ciao, tesoro*. I'll see you tomorrow!"

Then she whirled around and was gone, leaving nothing in her wake but the smell of her musky perfume. Giacomo stared after her. The perfume had awakened faint memories from childhood. Lying in bed at night, waiting for his mother to come tuck him in. Finishing his homework, hoping she would ask to see it. Eating dinner one slow bite at a time, trying to make it last so that she would be home in time to join them. And always, always, what he got instead was this: a quick rush into the apartment, a brief conversation, a kiss on the forehead, and then she would be gone, with only the lingering scent of her perfume as evidence that she had been there at all.

He looked up to meet his grandmother's shrewd eyes. She shrugged in an understanding way. He shrugged back, then nodded toward her newspapers. "So, what fresh calamities have struck the world today?"

"Oh, there is all kind of horrible news, everywhere you look." She shook her head mournfully, clearly enjoying herself. "Murderers roaming the streets, buses crashing off mountaintops, people getting hit by lightning! And the international money markets! Pah!" She made an emphatic gesture of disgust, and flour flew through the air. "Sure to collapse any day now."

Giacomo clucked his tongue and picked up another tomato. "What a world."

"And I have not even told you the worst!" she added.

"There's more?"

"*Sì!* Today there was a report from scientists who have spent their entire lives studying chimpanzees and you know what they said? They said the monkeys are learning to make spears! They've never been able to make weapons before but now, *now,* all of a sudden, they can!" She gave him an ominous look and took the lid off the pot of boiling water.

"Mark my words, Giacomo. They're doing it for a reason. The next thing you know, they'll be coming after *us*."

"Mmm. That will be bad."

"*Si*, very bad." She threw the pasta into the pot. "But I will be ready for them."

Act II
SCENE VIII

Kate stared resolutely at the computer screen in front of her, refusing to look out the library windows and risk being tempted by the golden evening. She had hurried to the library immediately after dinner, hoping to get there before Winnie. She had managed it, just. But even as she had rushed into the empty room, she had caught a glimpse of the sun beginning to set. The sky was a clear, pure blue with streaks of rose and pale apricot at the horizon, and Kate couldn't help thinking that it was a shame to waste the last of the light. . . .

No. It had been days since she'd written to Sarah and Annie. By this point, they were sure to be feeling neglected and resentful, if not homicidal.

She had forced herself to sit down at the desk, logged on to her e-mail account, and clicked to open a new message screen.

The door opened.

"Kate! What are you doing here?"

She looked up to see Winnie standing in the doorway, looking accusatory.

As if I don't have as much right to be working on this computer as she does, Kate thought indignantly.

But she gave Winnie a big smile and said cheerfully, "I have a few e-mails to send! It'll just take a minute!"

Winnie scowled as if she didn't believe this story for a moment. Kate quickly tapped some nonsense words to stave off her wrath.

"All right," Winnie said. "I'll come back in half an hour and then you'll have to log off. The computer is for everybody's use, you know."

Kate resisted the temptation to say something very rude, and Winnie left, slamming the door behind her.

"Dear Sarah and Annie," Kate wrote. "Sorry it's taken me so long to write. I've been really busy. We had our first dance lesson today. I think I told you that we're supposed to perform an Elizabethan dance at the party that ends the conference? It actually turned out to be rather fun—"

The scent of lilies drifted through the windows on the evening breeze. Kate paused, gazing at nothing as she remembered the feel of Giacomo's hand on her waist, guiding her through the dance. She found that she was looking out the window again. She could see the lilies nodding, ghostlike, by the weathered stone wall.

" —and even though I'm not the best dancer in the world (stop snickering, Annie!), I managed to learn all the moves, including one called *la volta*. It involves the girl leaping into the air with the guy's help — "

She stopped again, remembering how Giacomo lifted her into the air. She had been nervous, sure that her leap would be clumsy and awkward, but instead she had felt almost graceful —

"I was surprised at how much energy the dance took," she continued. "When Elizabeth I was queen, she and her ladies-in-waiting would dance every morning as a form of exercise. I can see why. Your heart does beat quite fast, I've found — "

The door opened.

"Kate! What are you doing here?"

She looked up to see Tom standing in the doorway, looking self-conscious.

"I'm working," she said, a bit impatiently.

"Oh, sorry. I didn't mean to interrupt." He edged

his way in. "I just wanted to, um, get something."

"Fine," Kate said, relieved that he didn't want to chat. He began looking at the bookshelves. From the corner of her eye, she could see him glancing over his shoulder at her every once in a while, but she ignored him.

"Giacomo is my partner, which I was dreading, as you can imagine. It ended up being better than I had expected, though. He was actually almost likable." It was interesting how different his smile looked when he wasn't striking an attitude, Kate thought idly. When he was just enjoying himself, his expression was much more open and pleasant and . . . well, *friendly*.

"See you later." Tom was halfway out the door, clutching a small volume, by the time she looked up.

Strange, Kate thought. He seemed almost embarrassed to be seen with a book. With a mental shrug, she looked at the last words she had written, then added, "Of course, I think it probably helps that he can't *talk* much while he's dancing."

She was smirking to herself when she heard her father's voice, saying, "Yes, indeed, I think this room will do nicely."

The door opened.

"Kate! What are you doing here?"

She watched as the grin on his face disappeared, only to be replaced by a strangely furtive expression.

"I. Am. Working," Kate said evenly.

The door eased open a little farther and Professoressa Marchese stepped into the room behind Kate's father, looking cool and amused.

"How admirable," she said. "We certainly don't want to disturb you." She put one slender hand on his shoulder. "Dr. Sanderson, perhaps we can continue our discussion about next year's conference somewhere else?"

"Well, yes, I suppose so." He sounded grumpy.

"In fact, it's such a lovely evening . . . perhaps we should sit outside with a glass of wine?"

"Oh, yes!" He sounded happier. "Excellent idea!"

"Much better than sitting inside on a night like this," she was murmuring as she softly closed the door behind them.

And then they, too, were gone.

Kate propped her chin on her hand and looked wistfully out the windows. The last sunlight still slanted through the trees, the lazy sound of conversation and laughter could be heard in the distance, and all of Italy—Italy!—lay right outside her door, yet here she was, staring at pixels until she was about to go blind. She grumpily studied what she had written so far. One paragraph, two at most. No color, no detail, none of the "you-are-there" reporting she had sworn she would send back.

Gritting her teeth, she placed her fingers on the keyboard.

The door opened once more.

"Kate . . ."

"I'll tell you what I'm doing here, I'm *working,* that's what I'm doing!" Kate said as she turned to glare at the latest interloper.

It was Giacomo, wearing a white shirt and jeans. One last ray of sunlight turned his dark hair gold, then vanished.

"Good for you," Giacomo said mildly. "I was just going to say that I've been looking for you. Do you want to go into town to get a gelato?"

"That sounds great," she said, surprised to feel a little flutter in her stomach. "Let me just send this."

"Lucy and Tom have already gone to meet Silvia," he went on. "It's the perfect chance for us to stage another little scene. This time, it will be an accidental meeting. You will look flustered, I will look annoyed, they will think they have discovered us in the midst of a secret assignation."

"Oh." She felt unaccountably dashed. "Right."

She cleared her throat and added, "But we did have lunch in the garden yesterday. And we walked by the river the day before that. Won't they suspect that something's up if we go out again tonight?"

"Yes," he said. "They will suspect that we like each other, which is the idea. Besides," he added persuasively, "you can't work on a beautiful evening like this, *cara mia*."

His warm voice seemed to caress the last two words. She wavered. "I really do need to send this e-mail."

"Fine. I will wait until you finish, then we will go."

"Sounds like a plan." Kate made her voice brisk. As she returned to typing, the cursor seemed to blink a little faster on the screen, as if in rhythm with her pulse.

Giacomo threw himself into a chair, picked up a book and examined the title with a quizzical look. "*Alchemical Symbolism in the Age of the Renaissance*," he read out loud. "Lord." He dropped it back on the table. "Tonight is not a night for studying! It is a night for walking in the moonlight and laughing with friends and *living*."

She glanced over, but the room was filling with shadows and she couldn't see his expression. Only his shirt glowed white in the gathering dusk.

Was it her imagination or was the cursor now blinking impatiently?

She quickly typed a few words, hit send, and stepped out into the summer night with Giacomo.

Entr'acte

Sarah and Annie bent over the computer. They read Kate's latest e-mail. Then they looked at each other and, in unison, screamed.

"I can't believe it!" Sarah said.

"I'm going to *kill* her!" Annie muttered.

They turned again to the screen and read the words displayed there with disbelief.

"Oh, Giacomo just came in, hold on . . . we're going to get gelato, trying to make everyone believe we're in love, ha ha, I'll let you know how it goes, *ciao*, Kate."

"No punishment," Annie pronounced solemnly, "is bad enough for our Kate."

Act II
SCENE IX

"You villainous knave!"

"You putrefied, lily-livered lout!"

"You loathsome, vile, motley-minded milksop! Have at you!" Laughing, Tom leaped at Benno, whirling his sword around his head. Then he lunged.

Benno parried with a clang of steel (or, at least, a lightweight aluminum alloy). But then he tried a cutting thrust of his own. Tom dodged it easily, and Benno only succeeded in knocking over a chair.

The crash made Lucy jump. "Are you sure," she asked Dan, "this isn't dangerous?"

The director was standing at the side of the room, his arms folded, watching the action closely. "Not as long as they follow the choreography," he said absently.

He had spent the morning teaching all of them the basics of stage fighting, then had led them through the moves of a simple fight, with each move flowing logically from the previous one. Once they had learned that, he had paired them up and had them all repeat the pattern several times to get the feel of it.

"On the stage, the fight should look real," he had said, "but in reality, the fight should always be under complete control."

For most of the morning, they had all dutifully fought controlled fights. Then he had asked everyone to sit down and let Benno and Tom—his Mercutio and Tybalt—take the stage.

Now Dan winced as Benno swung wide with his sword. He raised his voice. "Perhaps that movement could be a *little* smaller!" Benno tried again, and a vase crashed to the ground.

"Let's take a quick break," Dan called out hastily.

As he pulled Benno and Tom aside for a private discussion, Lucy said, "I swear, this sword fighting is making me nervous as a June bug." She cast an accusing look around the seminar table, which had been pushed against the wall to allow room for fighting. "I don't see how y'all can just sit there writing letters when Benno and Tom are killing each other!"

Giacomo was perched on a corner of the table, one

leg propped up on a chair, the other swinging lazily. "They're using stage swords, not real ones," he pointed out. "They won't get hurt."

Kate added prudently, "God willing."

"Duels are *supposed* to be dangerous," Silvia said. "They're supposed to end in *death*."

Lucy looked even more distressed at this thought, so Kate said hastily, "It's already eleven o'clock and we haven't answered any letters yet. Here, I'll pick one this time." She reached into the pile of letters, pulled one out, and read it aloud:

> *Dear Juliet,*
>
> *I am so unhappy. The guy that I've known for five years is going away to college. I have always liked him, but I didn't know I loved him until a year ago. I love him so much and I can't bear to see him leave. The other night we were at the swimming pool and he was being so sweet to me, and I felt happy because I was with him, but I also felt like my heart was about to break. Every time I see him, I fall more madly in love with him. Then he goes home and I get so depressed because I think pretty soon he'll go away forever and I'll never see him again. This hurts so much*

*that I almost wish I had never fallen in love
at all. What do you think, Juliet? Would it
have been better for you in the long run if you
had never met Romeo? I know he was the love
of your life, but if you'd never met him, you
wouldn't know what you were missing and
you wouldn't have suffered all that tragedy.
You probably would have married Paris and
had a pretty okay life. I would like to know
what you think because I am really thinking
right now that falling in love is not worth it.*

    Rose K.

"This is a tough one," Kate said. "I mean, she makes a good point."

"What?" Lucy was shocked. "Romeo and Juliet were meant to be together!"

"They did end up dying," Kate felt compelled to say.

"And immortal," Giacomo pointed out.

"Yes, as *characters* in a *play*!" Kate said. "But we're talking about real life! Why set yourself up to get your heart broken if you can avoid it?"

"Everyone's heart gets broken," Silvia said darkly, even as she kept her attention on the sword fight, which had started up again. "It is unavoidable."

"But you don't have to invite heartbreak in," Kate argued. "And this girl, Rose, she seems to be setting herself up for unhappiness."

"But don't you see?" Lucy asked. "That's the whole reason people are still writing to Juliet! Because everyone who falls in love ends up living her story."

They all looked at her in surprise, and Lucy looked embarrassed.

"How so?" Giacomo asked, interested.

"Well, it's just an idea of mine," she said. "I mean, after we read the play in my English class, I started thinking about my uncle Dub and aunt Zinnia. They fell in love in seventh grade and got married right after high school and stayed married for seventy years! Then Aunt Zinnia died, and even though they'd been married for such a long time, it was just like Juliet dying for Uncle Dub. So I was kind of thinking about that, and I realized that Romeo and Juliet meet and fall in love and get married and die in three days, which is like a super-condensed version of what happens to most people over their whole life. One way or the other, you end up losing the person, but you still are happy that you loved them. I mean, Uncle Dub wouldn't have wished that he had never met Aunt Zinnia, just because he knew that one day she wouldn't be in his life anymore."

There was a brief silence, then Kate said, with some surprise, "That's good."

"Really?" Lucy asked. "I mean, it's just a crazy idea I had."

"It's very good." Kate nodded at her. "You should write that down."

Lucy blushed. "I did, actually. That was my contest essay. I was kind of surprised that I won, even though Uncle Dub said he really liked it —"

She was interrupted by a yell from Benno. "You deceitful dog-hearted dolt!"

He lunged at Tom, who backed away. Benno, sensing victory, decided to try a thrust to the heart, missed, overbalanced and crashed to the floor.

"Ha!" Tom moved quickly to press his advantage. Benno managed to scramble to his feet and get out of the way, but not before crashing into a standing lamp. Then Tom was right on top of him again, so Benno spun out of the way, ducked under a sword thrust, and ended up by the window when —

"Gentle Mercutio," Dan called out, moving forward to the center of the room, "put thy rapier up."

"What?" Benno was trying to unwind the window-shade cord from around his head. "I can keep going! Don't worry about me!"

"I'm not, believe me," Dan said. "The furnishings, however—" He gestured to the rumpled rug, the vase lying on the floor, the chair tipped over on its side, the shade hanging askew. "Let's start again tomorrow."

"Oh. Sure." Panting, Benno walked over to the table and grinned at Giacomo, Kate, Lucy, and Silvia. "Hey, were you watching us fight? I think I looked pretty good!"

Act III
SCENE I

"Oh!" breathed Lucy, her eyes wide with astonishment. She had taken two steps into the costume shop before stopping dead in the middle of the floor. "*Oh!*"

"Wow," Kate said, gazing around her.

Beside her, Silvia made a curious little sound in her throat. It sounded almost as if she were purring with delight.

"Doesn't this all look just simply . . . scrumptious?" Lucy asked.

Although Kate didn't consider herself susceptible to swooning over clothes—Sarah had often complained about her unwillingness to accompany her to the mall—she had to agree with Lucy. When they first stepped into the shop, the contrast between the bright sunshine outside and the dim, cool interior made them blink. Then their eyes adjusted, and they beheld an Aladdin's cave of colors—scarlet, gold, midnight blue, sea green, ivory, silver, purplish black, rose. Billowing silk and taffeta dresses hung on the walls as if they were works of art in a museum. Mannequins were posed around the room wearing satin waistcoats and velvet doublets; scarves, gloves, ties, belts spilled out of drawers; jewelry was scattered inside glass cases; and the walls were lined with shoes tied with ribbon laces and high, cuffed leather boots.

"Scrumptious? What does that mean?" Silvia asked absently. Her eyes were gleaming as they took in the room, and her voice was, if not friendly, at least not scathing.

"*This,*" Lucy said, picking up a long cloak made of dark brown velvet, "is scrumptious."

As definitions went, this was a long way from being complete or useful, Kate thought. But even as she thought that, she found herself drawn to a pair of high-heeled gold shoes. She picked one up and held it near the window. The buckles were encrusted with crystals that caught the light and cast rainbows on the whitewashed walls.

Lucy was right. This was just . . . scrumptious.

Silvia reached out to stroke the cloak, which Lucy had put down on a counter. Her touch was slow and careful, almost as if the cloak were a wild animal that she was trying to calm. *"Bellissimo,"* she murmured, sounding completely unlike the Silvia who had presented herself at the villa each morning. She moved to touch a satin dress hanging on the wall. It was the color of rubies, with an embroidered bodice edged in gold lace, a long, billowing skirt, and full sleeves. *"Molto bellissimo,"* she said again, sounding almost as if she were in a dream.

For a few moments, the three of them moved slowly around the room, pulling out dresses with languid gestures, speaking in hushed voices, completely and utterly entranced.

Then the door burst open and Professoressa Marchese strode inside, followed more slowly by Benno, Tom, and Giacomo.

"Ah, excellent, you are here already!" she cried. "Forgive me for being so extremely late, I had many urgent items to attend to at the villa, not to mention taking on a class for Signora Napoli, who woke up this morning with a bad head cold, and then the caterer called to say he foresees some sort of problem with the ice sculptures for the ball . . . But enough!

We are all here now, ready to be made dazzling for the big night, yes?"

Lucy and Silvia were already rifling through the dresses that hung on racks in glittering rows, and Kate was inspecting a display of costume jewelry on the counter. Benno and Tom seemed less sure. They exchanged uneasy glances and didn't move into the room. Giacomo strolled over to a mannequin, lifted the black hat from its head, and placed it on his own. He instantly looked piratical and dashing, despite the wrinkled linen shorts and faded shirt he was wearing.

"What do you think?" He smiled at Lucy, who was staring at him, then glanced in a nearby mirror. "Does it suit me?"

"It makes you look like a black-hearted scoundrel, so yes." Silvia sounded as if she was trying to be cross, but her heart wasn't in it. She had already moved on to a rack of dresses against the far wall and was going through them one by one. She held up a silk dress, blue shot through with threads of silver, and turned it this way and that, watching appreciatively as the silver picked up the light.

"Kate," Professoressa Marchese said, "has anything caught your eye?" She noticed Benno and Tom, still huddled by the door. "Come, come, boys, you must pick out something as well! You mustn't let the girls steal the show. You know, men were quite the dandies in Elizabethan times. Yes, I assure you, they were peacocks! Velvet coats, silk doublets, plumed hats—"

"But no tights," Tom reminded Professoressa Marchese. "Remember, I asked you, did we have to wear tights, and you said no, we did *not* have to wear tights, and I remember it perfectly because there is *no way* I am ever going to wear tights."

"Of course, of course! Not to worry, Tommaso. You will wear breeches and you will look quite gallant, I assure you."

Tom wasn't sure he wanted to look gallant. It sounded beyond him, somehow. "What," he asked suspiciously, "are breeches?"

She waved a hand dismissively. "Oh, just pants," she said. "More or less."

Tom frowned and opened his mouth as if he wanted to question her more closely on this point, but Professoressa Marchese's attention had been caught by something she saw through the window. A small smile curved her mouth, then she turned back to them and clapped her hands.

"Excellent! Well, I will leave you to it, while I go and deal with the florist," Professoressa Marchese said briskly. "When Signora Ceraso returns, simply tell her to put everything on my bill and send the costumes to the villa by tomorrow morning. *Ciao!*"

She whirled around and went out the door, leaving only a faint trace of her perfume in the air. Lucy and Silvia barely noticed her exit; they were too deeply entranced by the dresses they were pulling off the racks.

"Well." Giacomo looked at Benno and Tom. "You'd better find something to wear, or my mother will pick out costumes for you."

Benno and Tom shot each other expressive glances and edged a little farther into the store.

"I just don't want to look like an idiot," Tom muttered. "It's bad enough we have to dance."

"And we need something we can fight in," Benno pointed out. He flicked a dismissive finger at a man's costume displayed on a mannequin. Knee-high cuffed boots, a dazzling ivory waistcoat with gold embroidery, a silk shirt with ruffles, and a large hat topped with an ostrich feather. "Pah! Anyone who tried to draw their sword wearing that would be dead within seconds!"

Silvia gave a catlike smile. "I could fight wearing that," she said loftily. "And I would win."

"Yes, Silvia, but then you could fight if you were

wearing a ball gown and high heels," Giacomo said.

"Hmmph," Silvia muttered, but she had a blank look on her face that meant that she was extraordinarily pleased.

Giacomo picked up a shirt from a stack on the counter and held it in front of him. "This might work." It was snowy white; in the dim light of the shop, it seemed to glow. It was simply cut, open at the throat, with long, full sleeves and floppy cuffs.

"Mercutio could fight wearing that," Benno said grudgingly.

"He'll still die, though," Tom reminded him. He grinned, feeling more secure on this familiar ground. "Stab, stab, stab, die, die, die."

Benno punched him in the shoulder. Tom punched him back. As Benno pulled back his arm, Kate hastily grabbed another item off the shelf. "Here, Tom, if you're going to start a brawl, you can at least test these out while you're hitting each other."

He stopped in midscuffle to look at what she was holding out to him. "What's that?"

"I think," Kate said, "they're breeches."

An hour later, Tom, Benno, and Giacomo had picked out their costumes. Actually, Tom had selected his clothes in fifteen minutes flat, and he could have done it in ten if he hadn't had to sit around and wait for Benno to be done in the fitting room.

All things considered, Tom was pleased with the way he looked. As it turned out, breeches were pants. A little close-fitting, maybe, considering he always wore baggy shorts or jeans, but at least they weren't tights. And even Tom had to admit, once he added the boots, shirt, and sword, that he wasn't going to be totally embarrassed on the night of the party.

In fact, he thought he looked rather dashing.

Not that he would admit that to anyone, even under threat of torture.

Benno, on the other hand, had gone over to the dark side. He was standing in front of a full-length mirror, turning this way and that, checking out his reflection, and asking for the hundredth time if he should go with the burgundy coat instead of the chestnut.

"Benno," Tom finally said. "Stop it."

Benno looked at him, eyes wide. "Stop what?"

"You're—you're . . . preening!" he finally said in exasperation. He had no idea where that word had come from, but he felt a little glow inside that he had come up with it.

Then he heard something. It sounded like a small, raspy chuckle—the kind of laugh that an ancient, wizened crow would make, if someone said something that an ancient, wizened crow found amusing. Tom shot a glance at Silvia, but she was intent on examining the lining of a skirt and didn't look up.

Silvia? Laughing at something he said? No. Couldn't be.

"I am not preening, as you say," Benno answered sulkily. "In Italy, we take fashion and appearance very seriously. It is important to, well . . . *fare bella figura*."

Tom felt his jaw tighten. This summer was turning into a tutorial on all the things in life he didn't know, starting with Shakespeare and sonnets, continuing right down the line to Renaissance dance and waistcoats, and finishing up with the Italian language. All of Tom's friends back home knew him as the most laid-back guy in the world, but now he had to admit that he was beginning to feel just a little bit fed up.

"Oh, yeah?" he said. "What's that?"

"It's, um, the way you dress, only more than that, it means style and and and . . ." Floundering, Benno gestured toward his reflection. "Everything!"

Tom tilted his head inquisitively to one side and waited.

Benno opened his mouth to go on, thought for a moment, then shrugged. "I can't explain it."

"It means taking pride in how you look," Giacomo explained kindly. "A good haircut, nice shoes, the best-quality clothes, even if you're only wearing"—he indicated his own clothes—"shorts and a shirt."

"Oh." Tom nodded slowly. He wasn't the kind of guy who looked at clothes. So now he examined what Giacomo was wearing more closely. Just shorts and a white cotton shirt, but the shorts were linen and the shirt had a collar. And buttons.

He glanced down at his faded T-shirt and noticed, for the first time, several old stains and a small tear at the hem. He looked in the mirror. His shorts were old and baggy. And his running shoes were pretty battered. . . .

His thoughts were interrupted by Silvia handing him a dress. "Hold that up," she snapped. Startled, he did as she said. She shoved another dress at Lucy, the third one at Giacomo, and snapped her fingers. "Now stand over there, all of you! I must see each dress next to the other in order to make this decision."

Giacomo grinned at Lucy and shrugged one

shoulder; she grinned back in a knowing way. Watching, Kate felt an odd sensation in her stomach, but before she could consider what this meant, Silvia was telling Giacomo, Lucy, and Tom to move this way, hold that dress higher, stand closer to the window, twirl around a little to make the skirt flare out. . . .

"No," Tom said flatly. "No twirling."

"Oh, very well!" Silvia snapped. She stood in front of them, her arms folded, looking at the three dresses appraisingly. One was a deep, rich red silk; the second was gold satin with elaborate embroidery on the bodice; and the third was coal black velvet with a sprinkle of jet beads around the low neckline.

Dramatic colors, Kate thought. Just like Silvia.

"The red dress is the color of arterial blood," Kate pointed out astringently. "If that helps."

"Thank you," Silvia said. "It does not." She paced slowly back and forth, tilting her head to one side and the other, until her three assistants finally began to protest.

"I think you should just pick one," Tom said. "You'll look great no matter what."

She gave him a scathing look, and he blushed. "Of course I will," she agreed. "That is not the point."

"Surely the velvet is too hot for summer?"

Giacomo suggested. A faint sheen of sweat had appeared on his face, just from holding the black dress. "Perhaps you can eliminate this option, at least."

Lucy sighed and shifted from one foot to the other. "Silvia, honey, I know it's hard to decide, but my arms are getting really tired," she said.

"Mmm." Silvia didn't seem to hear her. "Just one . . . more . . . minute . . ."

As Silvia turned to examine the dress Tom was holding, Lucy caught Giacomo's eyes and made a comic, despairing face. He leaned over to whisper something in her ear, and she giggled.

Kate felt as if a small ice cube had slithered down into her stomach. She considered the dress she was holding. It was gray satin and relatively simple, with a modest lace edging on the bodice and a small amount of discreet silver embroidery. She seemed to hear Sarah's voice in her mind ("Honestly, Kate, are you *trying* to look like you're Amish?"). She looked back across the room. Silvia had finally listened to reason and eliminated the black velvet, but she was still frowning back and forth between the other two dresses. Giacomo was leaning over Lucy's shoulder and whispering; she glanced up at him and said something that made him laugh.

Kate impatiently thrust the dress back on the rack and began rummaging through the other costumes. No, the apple green gown would make her look as if she had jaundice. No, the lavender would make her look as if she had stomach flu. No, the white would make her look dead.

As she shoved the last offending gown to the side, Kate could feel tears begin to prick in her eyes. It shouldn't be this hard to find something that she looked halfway decent in, should it?

She bit her lip and considered grabbing the pale pink gown—the one she knew would make her look like a dish of raspberry ice cream—and hurling it to the floor and stomping on it.

Just then, a voice behind her said, "Do you need some help?"

Kate looked into the mirror and saw Giacomo, who lifted one eyebrow meaningfully. "We're back on stage, I think." She looked past his reflection in the mirror and saw everyone else, busily engaged in looking at their costumes or out the window or at one another—anywhere except at her and Giacomo.

Then Lucy sneaked a quick peek in their direction, caught Kate's eye, and startled as if a mouse had run over her foot. She turned hurriedly away to say something under her breath to Tom.

Kate's spirits lifted in spite of herself at the sight. She smiled up at Giacomo from under her eyelashes. "Thanks for the cue."

"You're welcome." He smiled back. "Oh, just a quick note—the way you looked up at me just then? Excellent flirting technique."

"But I wasn't trying . . ." She stopped.

"Even better," he said with approval. "Now, as for your costume . . ."

"I know," Kate said, trying not to sound dejected. "I *know*."

Her voice trailed off. He had walked away from her, but only to begin sorting through the rack of dresses at the far end of the store. "Now this," he said finally, bringing a gown over to her. "This might do."

He turned her to face the mirror, then swung the dress in front of her with a flourish, holding it with his right hand. His left hand rested lightly on her waist. She glanced in the mirror and saw that he was looking at her. In the store's soft lighting, she saw that his brown eyes had flecks of gold. It was strange, she thought, that she hadn't noticed that before.

She forced herself to look back at the dress. It was a subtle fawn silk with ivory lace at the neckline. Dark gold embroidery and pearls were sewn on the bodice.

Kate stared at herself. The dress seemed to make her blond hair look golden, her skin rosy, her eyes a deeper, richer brown. And she felt all sparkly and confident and alive. . . .

It was amazing, she thought, how much difference the right dress makes.

"What do you think?" she asked, a little breathless.

Giacomo glanced over his shoulder. Benno and Tom had their backs to Kate and Giacomo as they carefully examined a plumed hat. Lucy's eyes were fixed on the two necklaces she was comparing, and Silvia had turned her head away, elaborately uninterested in anything Giacomo might be doing.

He lifted Kate's hand to his lips, then turned it over to kiss her wrist. His eyes met hers in the mirror. He smiled.

"*Perfetta,*" he said.

Act III
SCENE II

Silvia walked up the three flights of stairs to her family's apartment, feeling strangely cheerful. This wasn't an emotion she had experienced much lately, so it took her several blocks to identify it and most of the long walk home from the costume shop to accept it.

As she pushed the door open, she was still dreamily remembering the way the long skirt had swayed around her ankles, the rich color glowed in the light, and the silk felt brushing against her body. When she smelled the familiar homey scent of cooking pasta and simmering tomato sauce, her heart lifted even more.

Then she heard the cheerful babble of babies. Her

smile disappeared. She slammed the door behind her and walked down the hall toward the living room, where the causes of her current discontent were crawling on the rug, looking adorable, as always. Silvia stopped just outside the doorway and silently watched her father. As usual, once he stepped inside his own home, he was a changed man.

The short, pompous mayor with the red sash that the world knew was gone. In his place was a man with a vacant, doting look on his face, a man who could spend hours staring at three babies, a man who was captivated by the smallest, most insignificant action, as long as it was performed by someone under the age of two. Tonight he was watching the triplets attempting to stand and failing miserably.

"I see we are in for another entertaining evening," she said. "No need for television, eh, Papà? Not while we have the Baby Channel. All babies, all the time."

"Silvia, *cara*, how are you?" he asked, not even bothering to look up. One of the triplets threatened to tip over. He caught the baby quickly and set her upright again, cooing, "There you are, you're all right, aren't you?"

Silvia shot him a poisonous glare. "Terrible, thanks for asking."

"Ah, good, good," he said. He hurried over to where Giovanni was reaching for a light plug. "No you don't, little man," he admonished, lifting the baby and placing him at a safe distance from the outlet.

Giovanni's mouth formed a perfect square, his wispy eyebrows drew together, and he took in a deep lungful of air. Silvia, who recognized the warning signs, put her fingers in her ears.

The anguished wail that echoed around the room brought her mother and grandmother on the run. "Ah, no, my poor Giovanni, what is the matter?" her mother cried, lifting the little boy in her arms.

Giovanni's wail had set off his siblings, Rosa and Lorenzo, who were now crying even more loudly than Giovanni. Nonna picked up Rosa, Silvia's father picked up Lorenzo, and the living room was filled with the hiccupping snuffles of babies who were reluctantly letting themselves be calmed.

Silvia came close to stamping her foot in disgust.

"My day was more than terrible," she continued. "My life has been ruined, my future shattered, my hopes and dreams dashed to pieces!"

Her grandmother murmured to Rosa, "There, there, little one, all is well!"

Her mother lifted Giovanni above her head and

made a face at him that was so ridiculous that he burst into giggles.

Her father did that silly thing with his lips, the thing that sounded like a motorboat sputtering and that always made Lorenzo laugh and laugh.

Silvia hesitated. Part of her wanted to go to her room, slam the door and leave the rest of her family in the happy little cocoon they had created. Another part of her knew that going to her room would feel like exile, even if it was her decision.

After a brief inner struggle, she stepped into the living room just as her two little brothers and her little sister were put down on the floor. As they caught sight of Silvia for the first time, they greeted her with happy cries and crawled rapidly in her direction, occasionally tumbling over in their haste.

"Oh, how sweet, they are so happy to see their big sister!" Silvia's mother said, beaming and casting a look of hope in Silvia's direction. "They can't wait to say hello!"

Silvia bit her lip before she made a snarling response that she was sure to regret. After the triplets had arrived so treacherously on the scene, she had discovered that babies have the power to turn every adult within fifty meters into complete idiots. Case in point: All grown-ups insisted on attributing motivations and inner lives to infants who clearly only cared about three things: eating, sleeping, and pooping. They did not, Silvia was quite sure, count the minutes until she arrived home so that they would be sure to awaken from their nap in time to greet her.

Rosa, the youngest, took two tottering steps, fell over, and chortled madly. Lorenzo, the middle triplet, managed to stand, then put his head on the floor and flipped over in a neat somersault that would have been quite impressive had it actually been planned.

"Oh, look at that!" Silvia's father said. "They're showing off for you!"

Silvia gave her father a stony look. She refused to be charmed. These triplets were, after all, usurpers. Tiny, innocent usurpers—they hadn't asked to be born—but usurpers nonetheless.

Then Giovanni, the oldest, asserted his leadership role by crawling across the perilous expanse of living-room rug, grabbing the arm of the couch, and pulling himself upright. He reached up to place one small hand confidingly on her leg and proceeded to make a long, involved and earnest speech. No one, of course, had any idea what he was saying. Some of his phrases sounded vaguely Japanese.

"Oh, listen, he wants to tell you all about his day!" her grandmother cried.

His day? What about *her* day?

"I'm going to my room," she muttered.

But Rosa chose that precise moment to reach for a glass candy dish, so her departure went completely unnoticed.

Silvia stomped down the hall to her bedroom, locked her door, and threw herself on her bed, not even bothering to take off her black boots. She gazed at her latest creation, hung on the wall like a work of art. Well, of course, it *was* a work of art. A dress, certainly, but also a work of art. She had taken a relatively simple pattern and added her own touches: slashed sleeves, an asymmetrical hem, dozens of tiny buttons, a winged collar . . . it looked like something that a time-traveling Edwardian might wear on a visit to the year 2039.

Silvia sighed. Usually anything to do with her fashion creations made her happy, from sketching her initial ideas to sitting at her sewing machine until late in the night. Even looking around her room, which was a riot of color, with fabrics tossed everywhere and various projects in different stages of completion, usually gave her a contented and quiet feeling that was totally at odds with her normal emotional state.

But lately even her room, her projects, her fabrics and buttons and ribbons, did not soothe her soul. She considered the dress on the wall more thoughtfully. It was the best thing she'd ever done. But there was something a little unnerving about the way it hung there, empty, like a dress worn by an invisible girl.

She tore her gaze away and stared up at the ceiling, where she could still see the faded constellations her father had painted for her eighth birthday. The luminescent paint had faded over the years, but there was the pale outline of Orion and the faint tracing of the Big Dipper. She remembered the thrill of joy that had run through her when she had first seen them. Her parents had led her into the room at bedtime, smiling the excited smiles of grown-ups with a secret. Then they had turned off the lights, and it was as if the roof had been lifted off the house and she was staring straight up into the universe.

The stars blurred in front of her eyes. She jumped up and tore off her tattered black cotton jacket, which had been too much for the hot day, really, but which she had been determined to wear because she fancied that it made her look sultry and dangerous.

She had just leaned down to unlace her boots when she heard a soft knock at her door.

"Silvia? Are you hungry?" her mother called.

"No!" Silvia shouted back, even though she could have eaten everything in the house and then gone out for a pizza.

"Are you all right, *cara*?" Her mother's voice was troubled.

Silvia smiled grimly at herself in the mirror that hung next to the closet. She was quite pleased with the way her wind-tossed hair, smeared black eyeliner, and cynical expression made her look. In fact, she fancied that she looked like the reincarnation of one of the Borgias, a family known for its expertise in the fields of poison and murder.

"You must eat something!" her mother tried again. "You'll waste away to nothing!"

Silvia sneered at that, even as her eyes flicked over to the small photograph wedged into the mirror frame. It was a picture of her at fifteen. Surely her mother remembered how she looked then? A long, heavy braid of dark hair, scraped back from her round face. Thick black-framed glasses. Lips firmly clamped over the mouthful of metal that her orthodonist had subjected her to for years. And, of course, fat.

"Silvia?" There was an edge of anxiety in her mother's voice now, touched with a shade of irritation. "Did you hear me? Are you all right?"

"Yes!" Silvia said, in the loud, impatient tone of someone who can't believe she has to waste so much precious time explaining the most basic concepts over and over again. "I'm fine! I just have a lot of work to do!"

"But you need to eat something. And dinner tonight is your favorite." Her mother was cajoling her now. "*Maccherine e ragu,* your nonna made it special."

For a moment, Silvia wavered. Her nonna made the best *maccherine e ragu* in the world. . . .

Then a sudden piercing cry split the air (Silvia recognized the voice of Giovanni, the most vocal of the triplets), followed immediately by two more. She heard her mother gasp with concern and start down the hall toward the latest catastrophe, only stopping long enough to call back hurriedly, "I'll put something in the refrigerator for you for later."

Silvia slammed the closet door shut. Distantly, she could hear the babies' screams gradually diminish to hiccupping sobs as a chorus of adult voices murmured and clucked and soothed them.

Of course, Silvia thought bitterly. She had locked herself in her bedroom in obvious despair. Did anyone care? No, not as long as the terrible triplets ruled the household.

At least her plan to trick Giacomo was going well. It had been quite amusing to see him flirting with Kate in the costume shop and Kate flirting back. Really, quite, quite amusing.

In the mirror, Silvia could see her lip tremble. She bit it hard enough to taste blood, then turned sharply away and threw herself on her bed. She stared at the ceiling once more, imagining herself fading away into nothing, then floating away into a sky of vanishing stars.

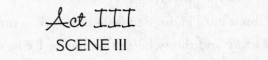

Act III
SCENE III

"Benno is over there. In the *farmacia*," Kate reported. "He's doing his best to lurk, but—"

"Yes, I see him." Giacomo grinned.

Kate and Giacomo were sitting on a bench in the piazza, sipping lemonade and people-watching. They were watching one person in particular: Benno, who had trailed them from the villa and through the town for the last half hour.

"He would make a terrible spy," Giacomo added, shaking his head. "Does he see us?"

"Oh, yes." Kate chuckled. It was a lovely sound, full of mischief, like sunlit water running over rocks in a stream.

"Excellent," Giacomo said. "Then let's begin."

* * *

Across the square, Benno peered at Giacomo and Kate through the *farmacia* window. Their trick seemed to be working, although Benno was less gratified by this than he would have thought. For one thing, he was hot and sweaty after following those two all over Verona. They hadn't spotted him, of course; he was far too clever for that. Although there had been a few moments when Giacomo had taken such a roundabout route to the piazza that Benno had wondered whether his friend was leading him on a merry chase on purpose. . . . But just as he was thinking that, they had all finally reached the piazza. Kate and Giacomo had settled down on a bench. And Benno had decided that his imagination was playing tricks on him.

The second reason he was in an ill humor had to do with what he was watching through the window. He could see Giacomo's dark head bend toward Kate's blond one. He could see Giacomo's hand lightly brush her arm. He could see—

But actually, he thought, he had seen quite enough. When he had agreed to this prank, he had told Silvia that he would enjoy watching Giacomo and Kate being tricked into love, but he had expected Giacomo to fail; Kate, he thought, was simply too serious to be won. In fact, he had devoutly *hoped* that Giacomo would fail.

And yet there they were in the piazza, acting so sweet to each other that it made him sick.

"What's so interesting out there, Benno?" Signora Lombardi, the owner of the *farmacia,* leaned over his shoulder to peer out the window. "Ah, a pretty girl, I should have known. But isn't that your friend Giacomo with her?"

"Si," Benno said glumly.

Signora Lombardi gave him a knowing look and a consoling pat on the shoulder. "Never mind, Benno. Remember, *botte piccola fa vino buono!"* A small cask makes good wine.

Benno began to scowl, then forced a smile instead. It wasn't Signora Lombardi's fault that she was perhaps the five hundredth person to quote this proverb to him in the past few years. It was supposed to be a nice way to compliment someone who was short, but somehow Benno never quite saw it that way.

"And anyway," she added, "I'm sure you'll get your growth spurt any day now. My Christopher was the shortest boy in his class until he was sixteen, and then, overnight, he shot up five inches!"

He decided not to point out that he had turned sixteen several months ago.

"So, listen," she went on, "Signor Moretti's heart medicine is ready. Can you take it over to him?"

"*Ma certo*," Benno said. A quick glance out the window told him that Kate and Giacomo were still sitting in the piazza. He could slip around to Signor Moretti's *gelateria* while still keeping them in sight and probably get a free scoop of *cioccalato* as thanks as well.

"Look over there, at the woman in the green flowered dress," Giacomo said, pointing to his left.

Kate leaned in front of him slightly and looked. "Where? I can't see — " She felt his arm go around her shoulders.

"No, don't pull away from me," he said. "Relax."

"All right, fine." She relaxed, somewhat gingerly, against his arm. "That was very clever, the way you did that. Do you often use the woman-in-the-green-flowered-dress approach?"

"Only when there really is one. See?" He gestured toward a nearby bench, where a middle-aged woman was sitting down. Even from some distance, Kate could sense her sigh of relief as she eased herself back into the seat. Her feet probably hurt, poor thing. Kate looked her over more carefully. The woman's hair was pulled back severely from her forehead and fastened with bobby pins. Her large round glasses winked in the sun like oversized bug eyes. And that dress . . .

"She's had that dress for thirty years," she said out loud. "She has to have it altered every year, of course, because she can't seem to stop gaining weight. But she can't give it up."

"Not surprising," Giacomo said easily. "After all, it was the dress she was wearing when her husband proposed. She didn't know he was going to propose, of course, or she would have worn something much nicer."

"But they were going on a picnic and she thought it wouldn't show the grass stains as much." Kate stopped and turned sharply to Giacomo. "I thought I was the only one who did that!"

"What? Making up stories about complete strangers? I used to do it all the time," he said. "When I was younger. Hanging about at some boring conference with my mother—"

"Trying to sit perfectly still and not make any noise and not get into trouble," Kate said, adding indignantly, "even though it's impossible to get into trouble in a room of two hundred English lit professors!"

"Well, not *impossible*," he said. "But you do have to

try quite hard." He gave her a mischievous sideways glance. "But back to our subject."

They both turned to examine the woman through narrowed eyes.

"Her name is Cornelia, I think," Kate said. "Her parents are dead now, of course. They were quite old when they had her."

"Yes, yes, they were so happy when she was born," Giacomo agreed. "They had almost given up hope."

"And so they started spoiling her from the day she was born."

"Her father called her his little princess and gave her whatever she wanted."

"So she grew up expecting everyone to treat her that way," Kate said. "And then one day, she met, um—"

"Cesare," he offered.

"Yes, perfect!" Kate could see this Cesare in her mind's eye. He had a bold nose, like the Emperor Caesar, and a willful, stubborn personality to match. "He was also an only child, also spoiled, also used to getting his own way."

"It was love at first sight," Giacomo added.

"Naturally," Kate agreed.

"They met at the disco."

"At the festival of Santa Lucia," Kate corrected him. "They shared a passion for parades and marching bands."

He considered this, then nodded. "Yes. Each secretly imagined that the celebration was being held in their honor."

Kate laughed at that and added, "But after two months of happiness, they faced their first real test. Cornelia wanted to go to France on vacation."

"But Cesare hated France, ever since the time a Parisian maître d' had sneered at him," Giacomo said gleefully.

"Yes, he had never had anyone sneer at him, not ever!" she said dramatically. "He still thought about what he should have said, even though his scathing comeback was years too late!"

"So he suggested a holiday in Greece," Giacomo went on.

"But Cornelia had her heart set on Paris." Kate sighed. "Neither one would give an inch."

"So the love affair ended." Giacomo's tone was mournful. "No ring on her finger, no beautiful wedding to make her friends jealous, no *bambini* for the parents to spoil."

"She began going to the piazza to throw a coin in the fountain, wishing that she would find a love like that again," Kate finished. She sighed, feeling unexpectedly sad at the ending they had written.

"Hmm." Giacomo seemed to sense her mood. He tilted his head to one side, squinting at the woman as if he were a painter trying to decide if his canvas was finished. After a moment, he said briskly, "And her wish was answered. One day a young man appeared, as if by magic."

"Yes, that's good," Kate said, her face brightening. "He had golden hair and blue eyes and a winning smile."

"But he wasn't perfect," Giacomo cautioned. "He snored, for example."

Kate gave a little shrug. "Cornelia could forgive that. After all, *she* had a tendency to hum under her breath."

"But he insisted on having his supper every evening at five." Giacomo shook his head sadly. "She hated to say it, but her new love was a barbarian. The only civilized hour to dine, of course, is nine o'clock. And he watered his wine, and he picked his teeth, and he used up all the hot water every time he took a bath."

"But she loved him anyway," Kate interrupted hastily, determined to bring this story to a happy conclusion.

"She did?" Giacomo quirked an eyebrow at her. "Because . . ." He paused invitingly, waiting for her to complete his sentence.

And Kate stared back at him, completely at a loss. Finally, she threw her hands up in the air. "Because she loved him," she said simply. "She couldn't explain it, she knew it made no sense, her friends and family thought she had lost her mind, but there it was."

He smiled and shrugged. "There it was. She loved him."

They stopped and looked at each other. Without realizing it, they had stood up and started walking, engrossed in their story. They had ended up in the small parklike area in the center of the piazza, where tall trees cast a cool, green shade.

"Benno is still watching, yes?" Giacomo whispered.

Kate looked into his eyes and nodded slightly.

"Then I think we should kiss now."

"Do you?"

"Well." Giacomo pretended to give this serious thought. "Benno will be expecting it."

Kate nodded judiciously. "Yes," she said. "If we don't he may begin to wonder."

On the other side of the piazza, Benno gaped at the sight of Giacomo kissing Kate.

Then he saw Kate kissing Giacomo back.

"No," he said under his breath. "I don't believe it."

He threw his half-eaten dish of gelato in a nearby trash can. Somehow he no longer had the taste for it.

Entr'acte

"Those boots will look perfect with my black coat," Sarah said dreamily.

She rolled over on her stomach and hung her head over the edge of her bed, the better to see Annie, who was stretched out on the floor and sulkily rereading the latest e-mail. "You know, the long black coat with the faux fur collar?" She smiled sweetly at Annie, then flopped on her back again.

Act III
SCENE IV

"I'm just saying Paris seemed like a nice guy," Tom said the next day as he casually kicked his soccer ball from one foot to the other.

"Yes, he was," Benno said, as mournful as if they were discussing the fate of a close friend. "And you know what happens to nice guys. They finish last. Or, in this case, dead."

Tom persisted. "So why didn't Juliet want him?"

"Because he was not Romeo," Silvia said with finality.

The morning's rehearsal had ended. They had eaten a picnic lunch in the garden and were enjoying a well-deserved rest while Dan rehearsed with the other Shakespeare Scholars. Lucy was sitting in the shade, while Silvia and Benno were lying in the sun. Tom, who didn't want to sit on the ground and risk getting dirt on his new shorts, started bouncing the ball off his head. Kate had carefully selected a spot that was close, but not too close, to where Giacomo was leaning against a tree trunk. She gazed down with satisfaction at the new cotton dress she was wearing, which Lucy had helped her pick out the day before. It was simple, yet flattering, the exact pale apricot shade of the flowers that bloomed under her window. . . .

Kate glanced up to see Giacomo smiling at her, and looked away, blushing.

"I agree with Kate," Tom said. "Romeo was an idiot."

"What?" Kate asked, trying to remember what they were talking about. "When did I say that?"

"The first day we met," Tom reminded her. "You were saying that Romeo and Juliet took everything too fast, they didn't stop and think things through."

Silvia sniffed with disdain.

"You said," Tom finished, "that they were impulsive in the worst way, because all they thought about was themselves."

Giacomo grinned at Kate. "That is so like you," he said. "Because Romeo and Juliet are not practical, they must be idiots."

"Well, you know what I meant," Kate said, forcing

herself to meet his eyes. "When you really read the play closely—okay, the poetry is amazing, I admit that, but when you look at the *plot*, the whole thing is ridiculous! In fact—"

"Please!" Benno groaned and put his arm over his eyes. "We're not in class now!"

"Yes, can't we stop talking about *Romeo and Juliet* for a few minutes?" Lucy begged.

"I thought it was your favorite play in the world," Kate teased her.

"It still is. Except when I'm falling asleep, like right now."

"No, no, you can't fall asleep." Giacomo reached over with a stalk of grass to tickle her nose. Lucy giggled. "The day is too beautiful to sleep through."

"It's also too hot to sleep through," Silvia said crankily. Then she glanced from Giacomo to Kate and added more sweetly, "Tell me, Kate, have you explored the villa's gardens?"

"A little bit," Kate said. "Lucy and I walked to the grape arbor when we first got here."

And she and Giacomo had whiled away a few afternoons on a bench hidden behind a riot of rose-bushes, but she wasn't going to mention that. Especially since it was one of the times they had slipped away from their watchers.

"Oh, but there are acres and acres to explore! Giacomo, I don't think you've been fulfilling your duty as a host!" Silvia said, mock-chiding. "Your guests haven't seen the Greek temple, or the secret grotto. I would wager they haven't even tried their luck in the maze."

"Oh, right, I read about that when we first got here," Kate said.

"And you didn't try to find it?" Silvia gave her a sly look. "It's called the Lover's Maze, you know."

"It is?" Lucy was suddenly more alert. "Why?"

"Oh, yes." Giacomo leaned back against the tree, settling in to tell a story. "That was the reason my mother bought the villa. Not just the maze, the whole garden, really. The house itself—" He shrugged. "Seventeenth century, not very important or distinguished. But acres of land that have been cultivated for three hundred years—that is what she set her heart on."

"Yes, but the *maze*," Lucy insisted.

"It's very old, the oldest part of the garden—"

"Don't tell me," Kate said. "There's a legend."

"But of course!" he said, and Lucy sighed happily. "It's a complicated maze with two entrances. The legend says that if two people enter the maze, each at a different place, and manage to find each other at the center, they are destined to be together."

"That's beautiful!" Lucy said.

"But extremely difficult," he warned. "There are all kinds of cul-de-sacs and paths that double back on themselves. There are even enclosed areas with a tree and a bench that make you think you've reached the center, but you haven't. My mother commissioned marble statues of Shakespeare's characters and put them in the false centers. You see Rosalind standing there or Puck or good old Henry V and then you know the maze has defeated you again."

"And how do you know you've reached the center?" Kate asked.

"You see Shakespeare's statue, of course," Giacomo said. "Because in the end, all paths lead to the playwright."

Kate entered the maze with confidence. This was simple, really. She had read about it. To get to the center of a maze, or to get out of one, you place one hand on the leafy wall and then walk, always keeping your hand in place. You might walk into a dead end, but you would walk right back out, as long as you didn't take your hand off the hedge.

So she rested the fingers of her right hand on the wall and started down the path, humming to herself.

One turn to the right. One to the left. Another to

the left, and then again to the right . . .

In the distance, she could hear the others laughing and calling out to each other in mock dismay as they got more and more lost. She had hung back, wanting to go last so that she could walk the labyrinthine paths alone with her thoughts.

To the right, to the left, to the left . . .

The voices sounded much farther off now. Well, the maze was quite large, and they could certainly move through it more quickly than she could, given her methodical approach. That was all right, she'd get to the center before any of them, and she wouldn't have wasted time getting lost, either.

Another two turns. It was so quiet now that she was aware of the sound of her footsteps, scrunching along the gravel path, and the faint rustle of a lizard slipping through the leaves. The world had shrunk to a hallway of green under a bright blue bowl of sky filled with sunlight. Kate almost felt that she was dreaming as she walked through the shimmering hot afternoon, always with her hand brushing the hedge beside her, keeping her on course.

Another turn to the left and then to the right, and now she was in an enclosed space, and Portia was smiling down at her from a pedestal, shining cool and white under the spreading branches of an olive tree.

"Kate." Giacomo sounded as if he was right behind her.

She whirled around but saw nothing but green leaves hemming her in.

"Where are you?" she said.

Nothing but silence. Then the breeze shifted and, in the distances, she could hear Tom say, "I know I saw this tree before! This is the third time, at least!" Benno was laughing, and Lucy was saying, "Lord, I'm just so turned around, I don't know where in the world I am!" Then their voices faded away again.

"Giacomo!" Kate's voice sounded sharper than she meant it to.

"Yes, I'm right here." Now his voice sounded as if it were coming from the other side of the statue. Kate started in that direction, then realized she'd have to go out the way she had come in and turn to the left to get to him, if, indeed, he was standing where she thought he was.

"Where's right here?" Kate turned in a circle.

"Right here is right here," he said. "Behind this hedge."

"Oh, that's helpful. *Which* hedge?"

There was a pause. "Well," he said, and she could tell he was laughing, "it's tall and green."

"Thanks, that narrows it down," she said, smiling.

"Hold on, I just need to go back the way I came, I think."

But when she held up her right hand, she realized that she couldn't remember exactly which hedge she had been using to guide her. Idiot! she thought. You were so sure you had the trick to this puzzle that you weren't even paying attention to your surroundings.

She shut her eyes and tried to remember. She knew that when she came into the enclosure that Portia was looking down at her, with a lively, humorous expression. Excellent. So all Kate had to do—she opened her eyes. Hmm. Portia was posed so that her head was slightly turned. Had she been looking straight at Kate? Or over her shoulder?

"Kate?" Giacomo's voice sounded even farther away.

Kate hesitated, then decided to take the plunge. If she didn't do something, she'd be stuck here forever. She put her hand on the hedge closest to her and started walking.

One turn, then another, then back the other way . . .

That branch lying across the path seemed awfully familiar. Didn't she pass that before? Kate stared at it almost fearfully. Of course, there were probably other branches on other paths; there was no way to tell whether this was the same branch. And maybe she had seen it coming into the maze, which would mean that now she was headed out. Maybe.

Kate took one step forward, hesitated, then turned to go back. Unless going back was the wrong thing to do.

No. Her first instinct had been to move forward. That's what she would do.

She strode forward, around a corner, into a dead end and out again, around another turn —

And she was back in front of Portia's statue.

Kate felt a wave of panic sweep over her. Which is ridiculous, she told herself sternly. People know where you are, you won't be lost forever, someone will manage to come into the maze and find you. . . .

"Kate?" Thank goodness. Giacomo's voice sounded very close.

"I'm here!" She hated the way her voice trembled, but she was so grateful to hear him that she didn't care.

"Stay where you are," he suggested. "I'll try to come to you."

There was a sound of footsteps walking down a path. Kate sat down on the bench to wait, feeling more confused and lost than she had in her whole life.

❖ ❖ ❖

Kate and Giacomo gave up on finding the center of the maze after being confronted by Portia's clever face for the third time. They hadn't heard the voices of the others for some time, so they decided to wait to be discovered.

"After all, that's the first rule about what to do if you get separated from the people you're with," Kate said. She stood next to the statue with her hands on her hips, her face flushed from both exertion and frustration. "Stop moving and stay in one place. That's the only way others can find you."

Giacomo nodded solemnly, but there was a glint of laughter in his eyes. "Assuming, of course, you want to be found. Well, we might as well be comfortable while we wait." He took her hand and pulled her gently to the ground.

The tall hedges made the enclosure into a green, leafy room, with a grass carpet starred with flowers. Kate was lying on the grass next to Giacomo, acutely aware of her hand still clasped in his. She stared up at the bright blue ceiling of sky, her heart beating fast, and watched a bird wing its way swiftly through the air.

She cleared her throat. "So. Do you think the others are still trying to find their way out? Or did they leave us here?"

She could hear the smile in his voice as he answered. "You sound nervous, Kate."

"Not at all." The afternoon light was still dazzling. Kate closed her eyes against the brightness. "I was just wondering, that's all."

"Relax," Giacomo murmured. His voice was low and warm. "There is no record of anyone vanishing forever in the Lover's Maze."

"There's always a first time," Kate said, but she was smiling. She could feel the sun's heat pressing down on her, her muscles loosening until her body seemed ready to melt. Her heart slowed down, and she could hear the humming silence all around them.

For a time, neither of them said anything. Then Kate sighed.

"Actually, it's not so bad," she said dreamily. "Being lost, I mean."

"We're not lost," he answered with some surprise.

Kate turned her head to look into Giacomo's dark eyes. "Actually," she said, "we are."

"Speak for yourself." He smiled back at her. "I'm right where I want to be."

Some time later, Giacomo sat up and said, "Shh." He nodded toward one of the hedges. "I think they've found us."

Kate stopped in the middle of pulling a piece of grass from her hair and sat very still. At first, she could hear nothing. Then a soft rustle, as if someone were creeping down a leaf-strewn path. And a crack, as if someone clumsily stepped on a small branch, followed by a hissed warning.

Giacomo motioned for her to move closer. "Ready? Ask me what my favorite speech is from Shakespeare," he prompted her in a whisper.

Kate cleared her throat. "You know, Giacomo, I was wondering," she said rather loudly. "Out of all the brilliant, poetic speeches in Shakespeare's plays, which one would you say is your absolute favorite?"

"Oh, that's easy." Giacomo spoke clearly, so as to be heard, but he was looking into Kate's eyes as he said:

What is love? 'Tis not hereafter,
Present mirth hath present laughter:
What's to come is still unsure.
In delay there lies no plenty,
Then come kiss me, sweet and twenty:
Youth's a stuff will not endure.

A little breathless, Kate said, "I don't remember what comes after that."

"No? So now we improvise."

Then he reached for her again.

Tom edged his way into the library, looking over his shoulder to make sure he wasn't observed. He slipped *Henry V* back into its place on the shelf and thought about a plan he had hatched last night. It was a plan that scared him quite a bit, although Henry V would have scoffed at his fear. After all, Tom wasn't planning to raise an army, he wasn't going to war against the French.

On the other hand, he was going to try to win Silvia for himself. He considered, for a moment, what England's most valiant king might have done when faced with Silvia di Napoli. He had a feeling that even good King Harry might have said, "Better you than me, mate," and run for the hills.

"Stiffen the sinews," he said under his breath. "Conjure up the blood."

"Not a bad motto," a voice said from behind him.

Tom jumped, then cursed himself as he turned to see Dan standing by the computer.

"Sorry, didn't mean to sneak up on you," the director said. "Just wanted to send a couple of quick e-mails."

"No problem," Tom muttered. "I was just,

um—" He waved vaguely at the bookshelf.

"Trying out something besides *Romeo and Juliet*? Good for you." Dan walked over to scan the shelf. "So, did you like *Henry V*?"

"Yes." Tom tried to put everything he felt about the play into one heartfelt monosyllable, because he knew he could never, if he lived to be a hundred and twelve, find the words to explain in a way that someone like Dan would understand. At first, he had struggled with the language. He had to look up every footnote just to understand what was going on. It was hard, slow slogging, and he wondered what he had been thinking, to take on this task when he had never been that good at understanding difficult books, especially something as difficult as a Shakespeare play. There had been all that back and forth between lords and bishops about politics and then an incredibly long speech about honeybees. And that stupid chorus kept coming onstage and talking everyone's ear off.

But then a character appeared uttering wonderful curses ("O viper vile!" Tom would say while practicing his fencing. "Thou prick-eared cur of Iceland!"). Several lords were arrested for treason. And King Harry and his men invaded France. After that, the play really picked up speed, and then there was that scene with Queen Katherine of France near the end, when Harry so eloquently apologized for not being eloquent—

"It was really good," he added.

But Dan was watching him with an astute eye. "'I speak to thee plain soldier,'" he said with an understanding nod.

"Yeah, exactly." Tom hesitated, then launched into another passage in turn. "'For these fellows of infinite tongue, that can rhyme themselves into ladies' favors, they do always reason themselves out again. . . . But a good heart is the sun and the moon.'"

Dan clapped Tom on the shoulder. "Well said! I think you've stumbled onto a little secret that it took me years to discover. Shakespeare always tells you what you need to know when you need to know it. It's really rather spooky. I remember one time—" He stopped short and stared out the window. "My goodness."

Tom turned and saw Silvia, changed into slim black pants and a black T-shirt, her hair pulled back in a businesslike ponytail. She was racing up and down the terrace with a sword, slashing furiously left and right, whirling to fight off imaginary attackers, then leaping onto the stone balustrade and launching a fast and ferocious counter-attack. She looked like a madwoman.

"My goodness," Dan said again, his voice awed.

"Wow. She looks really good," Tom said.

"Yes, she does." Dan hummed thoughtfully, then added under his breath. "Yes, as I was saying. Shakespeare always offers a solution to every problem."

"What?" Tom wasn't really listening.

"Never mind," Dan said. "Just talking to myself. I'll see you later, Tom. Keep up the good work."

The door slammed shut behind him.

Panting, Silvia slumped into a chair to rest.

After a few seconds, Tom forced himself to look away. He felt as if he were invading her privacy, somehow, by watching her when she didn't know she was being observed. He turned his attention to the bookshelf and ran one finger along the spines of the other plays.

Shakespeare always tells you what you need to know. . . .

It sounded a little New Age-y to Tom, but Dan was a smart guy. His eye fell on a title embossed in gold: *Two Gentlemen of Verona*. Tom grinned and pulled it off the shelf. After all, his mother was always telling him to act like a gentleman, and he'd been standing right here with Dan, who clearly *was* a gentleman, when Dan had told him the secret of

Shakespeare, and then, at that very moment, they had been vouchsafed a vision of beauty.

With a devil-may-care spirit, Tom flipped the book open and read the first lines his eyes fell on.

What light is light, if Silvia be not seen?
What joy is joy, if Silvia be not by? . . .
Except I be by Silvia in the night,
There is no music in the nightingale.

Tom felt the hair rise on the back of his neck. He slowly lowered the book, then turned to stare out the window at Silvia, who was now practicing lunges with her sword. She looked terrifying, deadly, and completely gorgeous.

She stopped suddenly to look at her watch. Then, between one breath and the next, she had run down the terrace steps and was gone.

Tom stood still, watching the now empty space where she had been and saying the words over to himself. "Except I be by Silvia in the night, there is no music in the nightingale."

Lucy danced. She danced with her hand resting lightly on top of Benno's, which he held out shoulder-high, and glided across the ballroom's polished wooden floor, her long silk skirt swaying to the rhythm of the music. She twirled, she turned, she curtsied. She took three quick steps to the left and clapped, then three steps to the right. Then, along with the other dancers, she swept across the floor in a wide circle, until she was back at the beginning, ready to move through the pattern again.

Lucy danced, catching quick glimpses of herself in the mirror: her head tilted at such a charming angle, her arms held out so gracefully, her movements so fluid and quick.

Lucy danced, and she watched herself dancing, and she wondered, somewhat petulantly, why no one else seemed to be watching her at all.

"*Perdonami*, my fault, I'm sorry—"

Benno had missed a step. Again. She gave him a warm and forgiving smile (again). He looked away.

She bit her lip. It was so strange. Benno was her dancing partner, yet he could hardly meet her eyes. He was always staring at the floor or over her shoulder, as if he wanted to be anywhere else but here with her.

It made it very difficult to dance together. And she was beginning to feel snubbed.

He's probably just embarrassed, she consoled herself. *We've been practicing forever and he still* can't take three steps without tripping.

"Down, down, and *up*, down, down and *up*." Dan had noticed Benno's mistake, of course. He began counting the steps again, the way he had when he was first teaching them the dance. It seemed to steady Benno, and the dance continued.

As Lucy curtsied to Benno's bow, she glanced to her left and saw Giacomo and Kate smiling into each other's eyes as they did the same move. Then it was time to do the little sidestep that brought each couple close together. Lucy turned, still watching, and saw Giacomo whisper something that made Kate smile.

Another sidestep, and it was time to dance the length of the room once more in a stately double line.

"One, two, and *up*, one, two and *up*." Lucy danced, not bothering to listen to Dan's counting; she had learned these steps in the first five minutes of the first day. She moved automatically, her thoughts still with Giacomo and Kate.

It was so amusing to watch them, trying to pretend that they weren't falling for each other, when everyone could see that Giacomo couldn't keep his eyes off Kate and that Kate stole a look at Giacomo whenever she thought no one was watching. It was delightful to think that Silvia's scheme had worked, and that they had been able to bring true happiness to two people who would have never found it other-wise. And it was charming to observe Giacomo and Kate together, so happy and in love.

Lucy sighed as Benno twirled her around. This move had been difficult at first, since she was an inch or two taller, but now, as she glanced in the mirror, she saw that they were doing it perfectly. This should have made her happy, but Lucy was twirling with a heavy heart. The golden summer days were slipping away, and all her dreams about an Italian romance seemed to be slipping away with them.

In order to banish this thought, Lucy smiled even more brightly as she turned to face Benno. He gave her a stunned look in return, then tripped. The trip was even more impressive considering that he was standing still at the time.

"Never mind, Benno, keep going," Dan called. "Remember, learning to cover a mistake is as impor-tant as getting everything right."

Benno nodded, frowning in concentration as he led Lucy in the circle back to the beginning. They made it back safely and started through one more round. Tom and Silvia were in front of Lucy; she had to repress an unworthy stab of jealousy when she saw how well they danced together. It had come as something of a surprise to find that they were the best dancers in the room. Both were graceful and had a natural sense of rhythm, and Tom's pale gold hair and Silvia's raven black hair make them a striking pair.

Tom was gawking a bit at Silvia, Lucy noticed thoughtfully, but Silvia was intent on watching Giacomo and Kate. She would turn her head as she moved through the dance to keep them in her line of sight. Then she would frown or snap at Tom or just look downright peevish, which Lucy didn't understand at all, since it was clear as day that their matchmaking scheme was working beautifully.

The line of dancers stopped. Time to curtsy and bow.

Tom bowed to Silvia as if he were a lovesick knight paying tribute to a courtly lady.

Lucy found herself sighing again. Not that she was interested in Tom, of course. He was like every boy she had ever dated back home. She hadn't come to Italy to date another Tom.

But still, it would be nice if he noticed her once in a while, if he let her know, even by just a glance, that he thought she was pretty. Of course, Lucy didn't harbor any real doubts about her charms; she had been told about them often enough. She was fairly sure that she was adorable.

But then, that had been back home. A sudden dark thought struck her. Maybe she was only pretty by Mississippi standards! Maybe her charm only worked in a town where everyone had known her since she was a baby! Maybe in Italy *she wasn't adorable at all!*

This thought was so dismaying that Lucy felt quite dizzy. Only muscle memory, years of ballet training, and pure Southern grit helped her make it through to the end of the dance.

"Ha! Take that! And that! And *that,* you dog!"

Tom stood with his back against the wall, watching from a safe distance as Silvia, dressed in black tights and tunic, apparently took on ten swordsmen and won. "She looks good," he commented.

"She looks lethal," replied Benno, who was standing next to him.

Tom glanced over at him. "Are you sure you don't mind the recasting?"

Benno gave a little snort of amusement. "No, Signor Renkin is right. I am terrible at fencing, even pretend fencing. And now"—his face took on a beatific look—"I get to play Romeo opposite Lucy!"

"True." Tom was happy for his friend, he really was.

"And you get to rehearse with Silvia!" Benno went on, bright as a button. "What fun for you!"

"Yeah." Tom watched from across the room as Silvia lunged across the floor, darted forward with a series of rapid feints, whirled around, and finished with a savage thrust, straight through the heart.

Benno thought he knew who she was imagining as she dealt the death blow. Their adventure in the maze had not pleased her at all.

"Why are you so angry?" he had asked her as he walked with her across the bridge that evening. "Everything is happening as you planned it."

"Yes, I know!"

"Giacomo has been totally duped! He will feel like a complete fool when he learns the truth!"

"Yes, I realize that!"

"All that remains is to tell Kate and Giacomo how thoroughly they have been tricked and enjoy a good laugh—"

But at that point they had reached her apartment building. She snarled good night and slammed the door in his face.

Now, as he watched her whip her sword back and forth in a menacing fashion, he felt great sympathy for his friend Tom.

Even Dan had backed away a bit, but he called out cheerfully, "Very good, Silvia, nicely done," and gestured for Tom and Benno to join him. "Now I'll take you two through the choreography, slowly at first. Once you've got the moves down, we'll work on speed."

"All right," Silvia said. "I'm ready."

"Yes, excellent, the readiness is all, as they say." Dan hesitated, then said, "So, Silvia, I don't know if you've managed to read through the entire scene yet"—he grinned to show he was joking—"but you do know that you lose this fight, right?"

"Yesss," Silvia hissed. "I know."

"Excellent. So, no getting caught up in the moment and trying to fight back, right?" Dan raised his eyebrows meaningfully. "No spontaneous rewrites on the night that would result in a Mercutio victory."

"No," Silvia agreed through clenched teeth. "I will lose."

"Not that Mercutio could win," Benno put in. He was standing in front of the mirror, trying out various poses with his sword. If he couldn't actually fight, he thought, he could still look dashing. "Not against Tybalt."

"Exactly!" Tom thought it was about time to

assert some authority here. He tried a quick thrust, parry, and counter and was pleased to see Dan give him an approving wink. "You don't have a chance against me! Ha!"

"Only because you are sneaky!" she said hotly. Dan had spent some time explaining to them that most of the play's characters objected to Tybalt's style of fighting, which was more like fencing than an honest Elizabethan knife fight. "Otherwise I would win. I am sure of it."

"But you don't," Benno said again, feeling more cheerful as Silvia got more aggravated. "Stab, stab, stab, die, die, die —"

"Yes, I die, I understand," Silvia snapped. She added haughtily, "But I die beautifully. *And* I have the best lines in the play."

Dan grinned. "Spoken like a true actor. So. Let's begin."

Act IV
SCENE I

Time slipped by, as it always does. The members of the Juliet Club answered letters, and danced, and rehearsed, and fenced.

Kate and Giacomo found many chances to sneak away from the others. After a while, they stopped noticing whether anyone was still spying on them.

Benno continued to teach Lucy how to play football. Lucy learned to dribble, do head shots, and kick goals in record speed, and discovered that she didn't mind exercising after all.

Tom humbly asked Silvia to help him practice his Italian. Silvia scornfully agreed, then spent hours disdainfully correcting his pronunciation, grammar, and imperfect grasp of the masculine versus feminine.

Francesca Marchese had an espresso every afternoon, reflecting with great self-satisfaction that the Shakespeare Seminar was progressing marvelously well.

Kate's father found himself humming to himself and staring out the window when he should have been talking in a learned manner about verse and meter in Shakespeare's poetry.

Giacomo's grandmother went to church every evening and chuckled throughout the service, much to the displeasure of the people sitting in the pew in front of her.

And gradually, the golden days dwindled until, finally, there was only one week left before the final party that would mark the end of the first annual Shakespeare Seminar.

On her last week in Italy, Kate found herself feeling oddly at loose ends one evening after dinner. The air had cooled off and a slight breeze had stirred up, bringing the scent of roses and damp earth. Kate felt too happy, and the world was too luminous, to stay inside; she couldn't share the cause of her happiness with others and she was too restless to be by herself. Finally, after ricocheting purposelessly around her room for twenty minutes, she pulled on shorts and a T-shirt and set off on a run.

She started at an easy pace, jogging on the path that ran along the river. The willows on the bank swayed in the breeze, their leaves trembling over the swift water. She quickened her pace as she ran across the bridge and turned right onto the path that followed the other shore. Birds darted across the sky, the setting sun glinted on the river, her strides lengthened until she was flying, and her mind was empty of everything. All she felt was the joy of movement.

Kate followed the river for a while, then looped back toward the bridge. After thirty minutes, she had reached the old part of town. She decided to walk through the narrow streets as she cooled down, since there was always something interesting to see there. She walked past houses painted gold, orange, and bluish green, their windows opened to the night air, glowing golden in the dusk as lamps were turned on. The scent of tomato sauce, baking bread, and fresh coffee wafted out as people fixed their dinners; occasionally she could hear the murmur of conversation and low laughter.

The streets were quiet now. She turned a corner and found herself alone. Then, above her head, she heard the sweet, reedy sound of someone practicing the clarinet.

She stopped to listen, enjoying the tired exhilaration that followed a run. And suddenly, between one note and the next, everything around Kate—the soft shadows, the glowing windows, the faded stucco buildings, the smell of coffee and bread, and that thin thread of music—became so intensely real and vivid that it felt as if she had stepped into another, richer world where every sense was more acute and every feeling more concentrated.

Then a car horn honked. The spell was broken. Kate blinked and realized that she was standing in the middle of the street. She moved over to let the car pass, then began to walk slowly back to the villa. The moment faded, but the feeling lingered. By the time she got to the river, she realized that she had been smiling for a long time without even realizing it.

Lucy stretched out on her bed and held a letter above her, reading it for the fifteenth time.

"Dear Juliet," it said.

> *My name is Martha and I'm a junior in*
> *high school. My problem is that I've never*
> *been in love. I've never even had a boyfriend!*
> *My friend Merry is dating the quarterback,*
> *my friend Debbie is dating the captain of the*

*basketball team, and my friend Clare is
dating a senior! But no guy in this stupid
high school will look twice at me. So how am I
supposed to find a boyfriend? What should I
do?*

Yours sincerely,
Martha P.

Lucy sighed. She felt sorry for this Martha, she
truly did. Not that Lucy had ever had a problem with
dating. Boys loved her, they always had.

She lowered the letter and stared unseeingly at the
canopy over her bed. Everyone had loved her. Until
she came to Italy.

Maybe this was a sign. Maybe her best days were
behind her. Maybe she was doomed to a long, lonely,
loveless life. Maybe she never would have known
what a terrible future awaited her if she hadn't won
this contest and traveled to Verona and flung herself
into Italy, which she now realized was an utterly
hateful country.

This was such a horrible thought that she sat up in
bed. "Now you are being just totally ridiculous!" she
scolded herself, shaking the letter out so that she
could read it again. The thing to do, she told herself,
was to write an extremely sensible answer, then wash

her face and brush her teeth in a sensible way, and go to bed at a sensible hour. Surely, after all that sensible behavior, she would wake up tomorrow morning, fresh and bright and eager. Just like the Lucy she used to be, before coming to hateful, hateful Italy.

As she picked up her pen, there was a quick knock on the door, then Kate stuck her head in. "Hey, Lucy. I just got back from my run." Her face was glowing.

Lucy turned to get a better look. "What happened to you?" she asked, a trace of suspicion in her voice.

"Nothing." Kate looked surprised, then laughed. "It was a good run. Anyway, I wanted to take a shower. Do you need the bathroom for anything?"

She looked so radiant that Lucy fell back on her pillow in despair. "No, that's all right. You go ahead."

Kate looked her over, raising her eyebrows as she took in Lucy's appearance. Lucy knew exactly what she looked like: sweaty, hair disheveled, no makeup . . . and what was more, she didn't care. She met Kate's astonished gaze with a defiant one of her own.

"I thought you didn't like getting sweaty?" Kate asked.

"I don't," Lucy said. "But Benno's teaching me corner kicks."

"Lucy Atwell, soccer star," Kate said, teasing.

Lucy's mouth twitched into a small smile. "Well, it

is fun," she admitted. "But you know what's really crazy? I'm kind of good at it! Me! You know, I'm the only person in the history of Littlefield High School who actually failed gym *twice*."

"I guess you just needed the right coach," Kate said blandly.

But Lucy was frowning again. Was that what her time in Italy was going to come down to? Learning to play *soccer*?

Kate walked over to sit down on the edge of the bed. "Lucy? Are you all right?"

"Perfectly." Lucy's chin was trembling.

"Really? Because you don't seem —"

"Look at this!" Lucy thrust the letter at Kate.

Kate read the letter quickly. "Are you upset about this?"

"Yes!" Lucy cried.

Kate waited. Finally she asked, "Why?"

Lucy jumped up and began pacing around the room.

"Because this poor girl!" She reached the bathroom door and wheeled around.

"Is going to live her whole life!" Over to the window, and another turn.

"Without ever experiencing true love!" She finished on a wail, then flung herself down on her bed and stared mulishly at Kate. "I know you probably think I'm overreacting."

Kate bit back a smile. "Maybe just a little."

"You see why I'm so upset, don't you?" Lucy rushed on. "And I can't think of a single thing to say that will help her!"

"Well," Kate said. .

Lucy sniffed. "Yes?"

"She seems to be focusing a lot on the guys her friends are dating," Kate said, somewhat tentatively. "You know, the quarterback, the captain of the basketball team, seniors . . . the top guys in the school, in other words."

"Right." Lucy stared at Kate, who seemed to be making some kind of point although, for the life of her, Lucy couldn't figure out what it was.

"Well, all I'm saying is"—Kate gave an apologetic shrug—"maybe you should tell Martha to open her eyes. There are probably plenty of guys who would like her a lot if she would bother to notice they exist."

"Oh." Lucy held the letter up in front of her eyes, as if trying to read between the lines. "You think so?"

"I do," Kate said, quite firmly.

So when Kate went off to take her shower, Lucy sat down at her small desk, pulled out a sheet of

Juliet Club stationery, and after staring off into space for some time, began to write.

> *Dear Martha,*
>
> *I'm sure there are many boys in your school who like you, but I think the problem is that you don't see them. Because sometimes very worthy people are totally ignored by everybody for no good reason. My advice would be for you to open your eyes and look around. Maybe you'll find that your true love is right in front of you and you don't even know it!*
>
> *Sincerely,*
> *Juliet*

Lucy reread her letter several times. She still wasn't quite sure that this was good advice, but she had to admit, she had nothing else to offer. And so, satisfied that she had done her very best, she folded her letter, put it in an envelope, and set it aside to mail the next day.

Act IV
SCENE II

Tom entered Juliet's House as furtively as a spy, although most spies would have known not to glance over their shoulders every two seconds to see if they were being followed, or to jump when the woman selling tickets asked for money, or to dart past her as if they were making a run for the border. Heart pounding, he crept up two flights of stairs, afraid at every moment that he would be caught and his mission revealed to all the world.

Sure enough, he had just walked over to the bright red mailbox where people could drop letters to Juliet, had just glanced around to make sure that no one he knew was nearby, had just reached into his pocket to pull out the envelope that had been tucked away there all morning, when—

"*Buon giorno,* Signora Marchi!" Benno's voice echoed through the room as he climbed the staircase to the second floor.

Tom dashed upstairs and hovered in a corner of the large, bare room that offered, as he now realized to his dismay, absolutely no cover at all.

Fortunately he heard Benno chatting with Signora Marchi as he opened the mailbox and gathered the letters. Then he could hear both their voices drift away as they walked downstairs.

Tom counted to one hundred, just to be safe, then walked back down the steps to the room where the mailbox was. He stood there for a long moment, staring at it glumly. True, he hadn't been caught. However, his carefully laid plot had been ruined. Everything depended on his letter being picked up today, and he had come too late. The mail had been collected. His grand plan had been dashed to pieces.

He pulled the letter out of his pocket, where he had stuffed it when he had heard Benno coming, and took another look. He had worked hard on this letter. It was a good letter. He was almost tempted to put it in the mailbox anyway, even though it was, by now, pointless. Then he sighed, crumpled it up in his fist, and turned to leave Juliet's House.

If the letter couldn't serve its purpose, he thought, he might as well keep it, a painful reminder of what might have been, a bittersweet souvenir from his trip to Italy.

Head bowed, he walked down the stairs and out the door, oblivious to the laughter and swirling activity in the courtyard. He turned to trudge down the street, intending to head back to the villa, when someone leaped out at him, grabbed him, and dragged him into a side street.

"What the —" He stopped, his heart pounding, and glared at Benno, who was looking pleased with himself. "What are you *doing*?"

Benno shrugged. "I always wanted to try that," he explained. "Just like in the movies, you know, when someone's doing something sneaky and they think they've gotten away with it so they're just walking along and then — *bam!* The hero grabs him!"

Tom shook his head, confused. "I have no idea what you're talking about."

"Is that so?" Benno said in the cynical tone of a man who has heard every excuse and knows not to believe any. "Then why were you lurking in Juliet's House? And why did you duck out of sight so that I wouldn't see you? And what do you have in that pocket?"

He pointed an accusing finger at Tom's pocket. Tom looked down and realized that he had automatically reached for the letter, unnerved by Benno's interrogation. He looked back into Benno's triumphant face.

"Nothing." Tom sighed, surrendering to the inevitable. He handed the letter over. "Just this."

"Oh, Tom." Benno lowered the letter and stared at his friend in dismay. "This is not good."

"I know." They were sitting on a bench overlooking the river. Tom was resting his elbows on his knees and had his head in his hands. "It's terrible." He raised his head to look beseechingly into Benno's face. "Silvia makes me nervous."

"Only nervous?" Benno said. "She makes me fear for my life."

This made Tom smile slightly, but then his smile disappeared. "I know. But still, I kind of, you know . . . like her."

Benno stared at him, horrified realization dawning. "Perhaps my English is not as good as I thought. You like her? As in —"

"As in, I *like* her!" Tom said, exasperated. "I'm sorry, I don't know how else to say it!"

He stood up and began pacing back and forth in

front of the bench. "I know it's crazy," he said, running his hands through his hair.

"Insane," Benno agreed. "Mad, nutty, bonkers, completely barmy."

"Your English seems to be getting better." Tom had stopped his pacing long enough to give Benno a cold look.

"I'm sorry, those are words I've had reason to look up," Benno replied, injured.

Tom sat back down. "No, I'm sorry, I shouldn't take it out on you. I just . . . I don't know why I feel this way when I really don't want to feel this way, you know?"

Actually, Benno couldn't quite follow this sentence—he had a feeling even his English teacher might have struggled with it—but he nodded sympathetically. "Yes," he said, "I understand." He thought for a moment, then came to a decision. "Actually, I do not understand this at all, but you are my friend. If Silvia is the girl you want, what can I do but help you get her?"

Act IV
SCENE III

Dear Juliet:

I like a girl who hates me. At least, I think she does. She ignores me a lot of the time, and when she's not ignoring me, she's making fun of me. On the other hand, she does that to everybody. The thing is, I know she would like me if she gave me a chance. So, I have a favor to ask. Can you write a letter to her, telling her how I feel? I think it would mean more, coming from you. At least she might read it.

Mark B.

There was a brief silence after Benno finished reading, broken, predictably enough, by Lucy.

"Well, *I* think this girl sounds absolutely terrible," she declared. "We should tell this Mark to find another girl. One who likes him."

"That was easy." Giacomo took the letter from Benno and flicked it across the table to Lucy. "Next."

Tom looked alarmed. "Hey, wait a minute!"

Everyone looked at him with a questioning look except Benno. When Tom seemed unable to say anything else, Benno jumped in to help. "Yes, wait a minute!" he echoed, then stopped, unsure what to say next.

Puzzled glances were exchanged around the table.

"Wait for what?" Silvia asked, impatient. "Why waste our time on another stupid *letter*"—she took the letter opener from Benno and thrust it into the paper to emphasize her point—"from another stupid *boy*"—another thrust—"who is too stupid to see the *truth* that is *staring* him in the *face*!" The paper ripped in half, and Benno winced.

"But what if—" Tom began.

Silvia was still holding the letter opener, which was now pointed at him. He went on doggedly. "What if he likes this girl? Really, really likes her?"

"Oh, well then." Giacomo threw his hands in the air. "As long as he really, really likes her, that is all that matters."

"Tom is right," Benno said stoutly. "Another girl will not do. We must help, um, *Mark* win this one."

"How?" Kate asked. Love had a logic all its own, she was willing to concede that, but this situation sounded dire. "It sounds like a battle that's already been lost."

"I don't know, let's see. . . ." Benno pretended to think, then brightened. "I have an idea! Why don't we write a letter to this girl, explaining why Mark likes her, and she will be so moved that—"

"And how are we supposed to do that?" Silvia snapped. She snatched up the letter again and scanned it furiously. "He doesn't even say *why* he likes her!" She tossed it back on the table. "Typical."

"So we write a letter that says that her eyes are lovely and her hair is beautiful—" Benno had raised his voice. A tactical mistake, he soon realized.

"Oh, and it doesn't matter what color her eyes are, I suppose!" Silvia raised her voice even louder. She was almost shouting. "Or her hair!"

"Why should it? She knows what color they are, why should it matter whether that's in the letter?"

"Because it shows he's paying attention to her!" Silvia pushed her chair back and stood up, the better to yell at him. She was even waving her arms a bit. She looked insane, Benno thought as he sank back in his seat. Really, what did Tom see in her anyway? "Because anyone can say"—Silvia switched to a mocking, falsetto voice—"'Oh, you are so beautiful. I love you soooo much.' Even though"—back to the yelling—*"I've never even bothered to notice who you really are!"*

Silvia flung herself back in her chair, crossed her arms, and glared around the table. There was a brief, thrumming silence that, clearly, no one wanted to break. Finally, Lucy said cautiously, "But maybe he *has* noticed. And he just didn't write it in the letter. Shouldn't we at least give him the benefit of the doubt?"

The members of the Juliet Club looked at Silvia, holding their breath.

After a long moment, she gave a slight shrug, and they breathed again. "If you wish," she said offhandedly. "It is nothing to do with me."

"I don't know," Tom cleared his throat. "I kind of think you should write the letter for him."

The look she turned on him was scorching. "I should write the letter? For this imbecile who is too stupid to figure out whether this girl likes him? And too scared to talk to her himself? I should help an *idiot* like that?"

Tom could have cursed himself. He had said that

without thinking, as usual, and now he was sitting here with his mouth open, as usual, and he was frantically searching his mind for an answer, and, as usual, his mind was blank. "Well . . . yes."

She scowled, but she took the paper from him. "Fine! I will tell this girl to give him a chance," she said as she began writing with a fast, furious scrawl. "But only one. If he can't win her with my help, he doesn't deserve to win her at all."

Act IV
SCENE IV

Although it was almost ten o'clock at night, it had been a hot day and the evening was still warm. Giacomo wandered aimlessly in the streets near the church, too restless to go back to the villa and too preoccupied with his thoughts to be sociable.

Rehearsal had gone all wrong again. He wasn't sure why, he had been so good at the beginning, but now he couldn't seem to say a line without stuttering, he couldn't seem to take a step without tripping, he couldn't seem to make a move without Dan stopping them and suggesting, ever so kindly and gently, that perhaps they should start over.

Kate, somewhat to his surprise, had been quite understanding about all this. In fact, now that he thought about it, she seemed like a very different person than the girl he had met almost a month ago. She didn't lift her eyebrow sardonically when he made a mistake, or offer a minilecture on Shakespearean action when he forgot where he was supposed to stand. She just waited patiently until he regrouped, and then started the scene again.

But that, of course, was part of the problem, because Kate was playing her part brilliantly. She said Juliet's lines with passion; her timing was perfect. And she seemed lit from within; she glowed. Giacomo could see it, and he knew the others could, too. Yesterday, when they had been rehearsing in the garden, with Kate standing on the balcony, some of the college students had been on the terrace, reading and talking. They had stopped what they were doing to listen, and Giacomo wasn't an idiot; he knew they weren't paying attention to him.

When she had said the last line, "A thousand times good night," they had applauded.

Giacomo rounded a corner and suddenly stopped under a streetlight, struck by an awful thought. Was he jealous of Kate? Was that the reason that he was stumbling through their scenes, unable to say a simple sentence?

He worried about this for a moment, then he

thought of Kate's radiant face as she looked down on him from the balcony, and his worry vanished. In fact, he felt quite happy. . . .

Quite happy, that is, until Saint Rosaline appeared in the window of the drugstore he was standing in front of, looking exasperated.

Of course you aren't jealous! she said. *You are in love!*

Giacomo felt that he had walked for miles through the small, narrow streets of Verona, but still he couldn't go home.

He wanted to dismiss Saint Rosaline's comments out of hand, but this was impossible because he knew that the comments came from the recesses of his own mind. Either that, or he was truly going mad, which at this point seemed like an attractive option.

But surely one's subconscious sometimes got things wrong? Because it was clearly, obviously, patently ridiculous that he would really fall in love with someone like Kate. No, they were just pretending to fall in love, and his difficulty with the balcony scene was just an acting problem. He simply needed to find the key to solving it, and all would be well.

He turned another corner and found himself walking past a pastry store. Eager to think about something else, he stopped to examine the baked goods on display. After several moments, he suddenly realized that he was no longer staring at the biscotti but at his reflection.

It had taken him a moment to recognize himself. Perhaps it was the moonlight that made him look so pale and grim—

Suddenly, another face popped up in the reflection and a voice yelled, "Giacomo! There you are!"

Giacomo whirled around to glare at Benno. "What are you doing here?"

"Looking for you, of course. And it took forever, too. First, I went to the villa and your mother didn't know where you were, but I stopped in the kitchen and your nonna said you had left her at the church and headed toward the river, so I stopped by the comic shop and Angelo said he saw you walk toward the piazza, so then I went there because I thought you might have stopped at the café and Stefano said I had just missed you and . . . hey!" Benno stopped his rambling long enough to take a closer look at Giacomo. "Are you all right?"

"I'm fine."

Benno gave him a penetrating look. "So why have you been doing the grand tour of Verona, anyway?"

Giacomo did his best to make his voice light. "'A troubled mind drove me to walk abroad.'"

"Troubled about what? Oh, you're quoting again, aren't you?" Benno said in disgust. "Listen, I need your help. Where can we go that's quiet?"

"I'm telling you, this situation is terrible! Tragic! A disaster in the making!" Benno cried. He flung himself back in his chair and shot Giacomo an accusatory glance. "I can't believe I let you talk me into this."

Giacomo groaned and put his head into his hands. They were alone in the library. It was almost midnight. Moonlight was pouring through the windows, turning the room silver and gray; church bells chimed in the night; and he wanted nothing more than to be asleep. Instead, he was sitting at a table strewn with crumpled pieces of paper, racking his brain to find the right words to write in a love letter. And why?

Because Benno had decided he absolutely must commit his precious feelings and innermost thoughts to paper and that it must happen this very night, and because Benno was perhaps the most ill-equipped person in the world to take on that task, and because Benno had asked for his help, and because he, Giacomo, was softheaded enough to have offered advice and counsel for more than an hour, simply because Benno was his very good friend.

"I can't believe you call yourself my friend!" Benno ended bitterly.

Giacomo closed his eyes to send up a brief prayer to Saint Rosaline. Give me strength, he pleaded, because my friend is an idiot.

"Don't make it so difficult," Giacomo snapped. "Just write what you feel."

"But that *is* difficult!" Benno protested. "It is the most difficult thing of all!"

"Because you don't know how you feel?"

"No! Because what I feel is so enormous, so overwhelming, it's like, like . . ."

"Yes?" Giacomo prompted Benno.

His friend threw his hands into the air in despair. "I don't know! Like being swept out into the ocean by a huge wave, it's like waking up one morning and discovering that the world has been made brand-new, it's like, it's like . . ."

"Perhaps you should write that you're suffering from 'a madness most discreet, a choking gall, and a preserving sweet,'" Giacomo began. He had barely finished before Benno threw a pen at him.

"Stop quoting!" he yelled. "You know I can't understand you when you quote!"

"I was just saying, far more poetically and

beautifully, of course, what you've been rattling on about for the last forty-five minutes."

"Exactly! And everything you say is even more confusing, which proves my point!" Benno cried triumphantly. "What I feel cannot *possibly* be expressed in words!"

Giacomo gritted his teeth, closed his eyes, and imagined himself in church, staring up at Saint Rosaline's faded fresco.

Have patience, she advised. *Your friend is an idiot, but remember, he is in love.*

"What you are feeling is nothing new," he said to Benno, doing his best to at least sound patient. "Throughout the centuries—"

"Don't, don't, don't, *please* don't start talking about history, I beg you!" Benno clutched his head with both hands. "That's even worse than quoting Shakespeare. And don't even think of telling me that my problem will seem like nothing when one considers the great span of time, or I swear I will hit you."

"I was going to say," Giacomo went on, even more patiently, "that millions of other people have felt the same way that you do."

"I don't care about millions of other people!" Benno's eyes were blazing. "They're all dead, anyway, so what good can they do me?"

Giacomo counted to ten, then to twenty, and reflected that, since patience was a virtue, this session with Benno might just qualify him for canonization. "Fortunately for you, some of those useless dead people were poets." He paused, then added meaningfully, "Poets of love and romance."

"Oh?" Benno lowered his hands and looked at his friend with dawning hope. "Good poets?"

"The best," Giacomo reassured him. "And I was further going to suggest that perhaps you could take a page or two from some of them who have, after all, managed to write down what, er, cannot possibly be expressed in words."

"Hmm." Benno was nodding now, and looking somewhat happier. "So you have a poem I could copy?"

"Not copy, no. You should always use your own words when telling a girl that you love her," Giacomo said sternly.

Benno looked crestfallen, and Giacomo relented. "But perhaps you could paraphrase a poem in your own words, add a few little touches that would make it your own, that sort of thing."

"Oh." Benno was looking daunted again. He pointed out the obvious flaw in this plan. "But I already told you, I don't know what my own words are!"

"Yes, I know." Giacomo selected a book from the

pile on the desk, opened it, and pushed it across the table. "But perhaps you can find a sonnet that will fit your situation."

After much deliberation, Benno finally chose a sonnet, admitting—somewhat begrudgingly—that it just might articulate the monumental passion and adoration he felt for Lucy. Then, after a lengthy discussion about the poem's meaning, he managed to paraphrase the sonnet's sublime beauty into a few halting sentences of his own. And after a short but spirited argument, he got Giacomo to agree that quoting one other piece of poetry was permissible, given that, without such a quote, his letter would completely lack beauty, grace, or felicity of expression.

"But now I have to find *another* poem," he cried, clutching his hair.

"Here." Giacomo searched through the pile of books, grabbed a familiar volume, opened it to a fitting verse, and shoved it across the table. "That will do very well."

"Grazie," Benno said with relief.

Then he looked at his letter, which had many laborious cross-outs and corrections, and said sadly, "If only my handwriting wasn't so horrible. Even after I copy this out, it still won't look the way a love letter should."

Giacomo sighed and held out his hand.

Fifteen minutes later, Benno finally left, beaming, with a beautiful letter, written in beautiful handwriting, that he could drop at the beautiful Lucy's door on his way out.

Giacomo tilted his chair back to lean against the wall and closed his eyes. It was a wonderful thing to have reached such a deep understanding of the inner mysteries of love that he was able to help others. Now if only he had the faintest clue about how to help himself.

Act IV
SCENE V

"Oooh, you look wonderful!" Lucy gave Kate an approving nod as she stepped into the bedroom. Lucy was already wearing her dress, a filmy creation in several shades of blue, and she twirled around to show it off.

"So do you," Kate said. She smoothed down her hair and glanced at herself again in the mirror, feeling her heart beat a little faster. It was the night of the dress rehearsal. They would all be wearing their costumes, performing their parts, practicing the timing of each scene and dance and sword fight. Professoressa Marchese had been prowling the corridors all day, issuing sharp commands and dramatically throwing her hands into the air when she saw anything that wasn't quite right.

"Thank you!" Lucy dropped into a little curtsy, then frowned and rushed over to the window as a roll of thunder sounded. "The storm sounds like it's getting closer." She peered out through the curtains. "I sure do hope it doesn't rain. Everything will be completely ruined if it rains!"

"We'll just perform the scenes inside," Kate said, preoccupied. She was checking the way her new earrings — dangling gold loops with little crystals — looked with her dress. As Lucy had promised during their afternoon of shopping, they matched perfectly. "Anyway, better to have rain tonight for the dress rehearsal. It might clear up in time for the party tomorrow."

"I suppose so." Lucy stared out at the trees, which were beginning to whip around in the deepening twilight. She shivered and let the curtains drop closed.

Kate was looking in the mirror above her dresser and brushing on another layer of mascara as carefully as a surgeon performing a delicate and dangerous operation. But even in the midst of her concentration, she could sense Lucy moving restlessly behind her, walking over to her bedside table to pick up a book Kate had been reading, putting it down with a sigh, wandering to the other side of the room to examine a watercolor on the far wall, then tacking back to sit on the end of the bed for two whole seconds before jumping up again and —

"What is wrong with you?" Kate asked. She put down the mascara and turned to look at Lucy. "Are you nervous about your scene?"

Lucy and Benno had been struggling in rehearsals, most notably because Benno couldn't seem to remember any of his lines. But Dan had taught Lucy, who knew every word by heart, the useful art of cuing someone else under her breath, and their performance had become, if not riveting, at least coherent.

"Oh, no, we'll be fine," Lucy said. "Even if Benno forgets all his lines, I figure I can just jump to the last line and we'll be done."

"That's one way to finish the scene quickly," Kate admitted.

"Exactly. And I bet hardly anybody will notice anyway." Lucy plumped herself back down on the bed, looking so pleased with her solution that Kate didn't have the heart to tell her that Romeo and Juliet's first meeting was one of the most famous scenes in literature and that *everyone* would notice. In her shoes, with Benno as her Romeo, Kate would have been tempted to do the same.

"So if you're not worried about the acting —" she prompted.

"Oh! Right!" Lucy jumped up again and rushed over to Kate. "So, Kate, can I tell you something? Something really secret?"

"Of course." Kate uncapped her new lipstick and turned back to the mirror.

"And you swear you won't tell?"

"'If I lose mine honour, I lose myself,'" Kate remarked absently.

"No, Kate, say it in your own words, this is important."

Her attention caught by Lucy's tone, Kate stopped in the middle of cautiously trying out her new lipstick and looked over. "Of course I won't tell. What is it?"

Lucy took a deep breath, let it out and then said simply, "Look."

She held out a paper.

"A letter?" Kate asked as she took it. "What, from the box of Juliet letters upstairs?"

"No! A letter for me! I found it under my door this morning, I've been dying to show it to you all day, but there was never a moment." Lucy's hands were clasped in front of her. She looked excited, happy, and—Kate looked at her more carefully—a little scared. "Go ahead, read it!"

So Kate did.

"Well? What do you think? Isn't it wonderful?" Lucy's voice trembled.

"Yes," Kate said dully, her eyes still fixed on the familiar handwriting. "Wonderful."

"From a secret admirer," Lucy said dreamily. She kept gazing at the letter as if she couldn't bear to put it away. "Why do you think he didn't sign his name?"

Because he's a sneaky, underhanded, duplicitous, deceitful . . . Kate ran out of words. It didn't matter anyway. It didn't help much to just think the words. What she wanted to do was scream them from that damn balcony, rampage through the villa yelling them as she pulled over furniture and tore down tapestries, scrawl them on the walls with her brand-new rosy pink lipstick.

Instead, she said evenly, "The last line said something about seeing you tomorrow night. I imagine he wanted to see your face when he revealed who he was."

"Oh, do you think that's it?" Lucy took a few dancing steps toward the door. "I don't think I can wait until tomorrow night! I think I'll spritz on a little perfume before I go downstairs. I'll meet you in a few minutes?"

"Sure," Kate said. "I'll see you down there."

Alone, she stared at herself in the full-length mirror. Why had she thought this tan color looked good with her hair? It actually made her blond hair look dull. Her eyes no longer sparkled. And the dress itself looked positively drab.

She blinked a few times as she looked at her reflection. Then she squared her shoulders, lifted her chin, and resolved to get through this dress rehearsal with her dignity intact. After all, she only had to get through two more days, then she would be getting on a plane for the United States.

No. She did a quick calculation in her head. Less than two days. Only forty hours left until the plane took off and she could leave Italy behind. Forever.

Kate almost made it.

She danced in the ballroom with her skirt swirling gracefully around her and never missed a step. She managed to smile at Tom and Benno when she moved through the dance and was partnered with them. When the dance brought her back to Giacomo, she stared at his collar and concentrated on projecting an air of cool, unapproachable dignity.

When Silvia and Tom dueled, she stood with everyone else and applauded at the end. And when, finally, it was time for her to do the balcony scene with Giacomo, she dutifully recited her lines to a spot six inches above the top of his head.

She was aware of puzzled glances from the others. Her father pulled her aside at one point to ask if she wasn't feeling well, so she pleaded a headache.

"Well, you've been working hard, it's no wonder," he said. "Be sure to get enough sleep tonight, all right?"

She had nodded and moved through the evening with her chin held high, clinging to the thought that soon it would all be over.

She had just slipped away to go to her room when Giacomo intercepted her in the upstairs hall. He wore a severely cut maroon jacket with silver buttons, black pants, and tall, polished black boots. His hair had gotten a little longer in the last month, and it was pulled back in a short queue and tied with a black ribbon. Kate thought he looked dashing and rakish and dangerous, an impression that was only reinforced when he gave her a quick smile, then caught her hand and bent down to kiss her.

He loves Lucy, she reminded herself. *Not you.* She pulled her hand away from him and regarded him coldly.

"Is everything all right? You didn't seem like yourself tonight." His dark eyes looked concerned.

Of course they do, she thought furiously. He's a wonderful actor when his words don't mean anything.

"Everything's fine."

He smiled slightly. "I think our director would tell you to keep working on your delivery. It didn't sound quite truthful."

Kate caught her breath at the sheer outrageousness of this statement. *He* had the nerve to say *she* wasn't being truthful?

Of course, she wasn't, but that was not the point.

"Really, I'm fine." Her excuse to her father came back to her. "I'm just tired and—and I have a headache. That's all."

And everything would have been fine if he hadn't reached out to touch her arm, if he hadn't smiled at her in that private way that said they shared a secret, if he hadn't murmured, "Why don't we take a little walk? The evening air is supposed to be very good for headaches."

"So is aspirin." She jerked her arm away. "And I'm sure there are other girls you'd much rather take for a moonlight stroll, so why don't you go ask *them*?" Well, so much for her vow to treat him with cool, dignified contempt.

He looked at her as if she were insane. "What are you talking about? What girls? Where?" He made a great show of looking around the hall, as if perhaps he had misplaced an entire flock of girls.

"That isn't funny," she said through gritted teeth, and started to stalk off to her room.

But he was standing between her and the last flight of stairs. Beyond him lay her room and sanctuary—but she couldn't see any way to get to it without brushing against him in the narrow hall.

"Have I hurt you in some way?"

For the first time in her life, Kate understood what a "beseeching" look was. Giacomo looked upset and worried and just faintly cross. It was the crossness that almost made her almost believe the rest; that, at least, seemed absolutely authentic.

She hesitated, and as if he could sense her wavering, Giacomo stepped forward and put his hand on her waist. He leaned forward to whisper something; she could feel his breath on her ear; she caught her breath and then—

"Oh, hey, there y'all are!" It was Lucy, tripping down the hall from the other direction, daintily holding up the skirt of her blue spangled dress. "Come downstairs, Professoressa Marchese has refreshments for everyone and we're having such fun!"

Giacomo turned to Kate. "Shall we?"

She gave him a bitter, knowing smile in return.

"You two go on," she said. "Have a great time."

Then she picked up her own skirts, ran down the stairs, and fled into the night.

The storm broke just as she ran through the villa's courtyard, tears streaming down her face.

She had to plant her feet and pull to get the heavy wooden door to open it. Then, just as it did, her father and Francesca Marchese came in, arm in arm. She had a blurry impression of seeing her father's face, looking startled and somehow secretive. She heard him call out, "Kate! Is something wrong?" She noticed that Professoressa Marchese still had the ghost of a smile on her face, as if she had been interrupted in the midst of laughter. Then Kate pushed past them, stumbled, and began running.

Behind her, she could hear her father's voice calling to her, getting fainter and fainter until finally she didn't hear anything except the rain pelting on the sidewalks, the occasional crash of thunder, and the sound of her fancy high-heeled shoes clattering along the street.

Her thoughts whirled around her mind in time with her footsteps. I'm so stupid, she was thinking. I looked like an idiot, just the way Silvia and Benno wanted me to! After I swore that I would never, ever make a fool of myself because of love!

Lightning streaked through the sky. Kate jumped, her heart pounding, and turned another corner at random. She didn't know where she was running, but it didn't matter. Nothing mattered. Her face was wet, and she couldn't tell the difference between the tears and the rain.

The thunder crashed, only seconds after the lightning. Good, the storm was getting closer. Kate wanted it to break right over her head, she wanted the earth and heavens to shake, she didn't care if it killed her —

Well, actually, she did care. Even in her distraught state, a tiny part of her mind whispered, "Why should lightning strike you? Let it kill *Giacomo!*"

She almost smiled at the thought, until she remembered who she wanted dead.

Giacomo the betrayer. Giacomo the liar. Giacomo, the false friend, who whispered sweet nothings that were exactly that, *nothing,* in fact they were less than nothing. . . .

Now she was crying so hard she couldn't keep running; she could barely breathe. Her long skirt clung to her legs, sodden with rain. Gasping, she dashed under the portico of a building. It was a store of some kind, shut up for the night.

Kate wiped off her face, took a sobbing breath, and tried to get her bearings. She had run along the river, she remembered that much, but she had no idea how far she had run. She could smell the fresh scent of the rain, which was falling in sheets; it was as if the skies had opened and water was flooding the entire world.

She blinked, and the building across the street came into focus. Santa Lorenzo, where Giacomo went to church with his grandmother. She wanted to moan with despair, but she hiccupped instead. It was such a ridiculous sound, she might have laughed — but no. Tragedy had visited her life, it had come to stay, and she would never laugh again.

"Ciao, bella! Come mai ti trovi qui stasera?" a man's voice said with a definite leer.

She jumped and turned to see two older men leaning against the wall, smoking cigarettes and eyeing her up and down. The one who had spoken tossed his cigarette to the ground, stepped on it, and started toward her, grinning suggestively. *"Devo dire che stasera sono proprio fortunato di ricevere la tua visita, bella ragazza che sei."*

Kate didn't know what he was saying, and she didn't want to know. She plunged out into the rain and ran on.

❉   ❉   ❉

Silvia was pedaling her bike as fast as she could, as if she could outrace the rain. Which was rather ridiculous, since the jeans and T-shirt she had changed into after rehearsal were now drenched. Still, she pumped harder on her pedals, shot around a corner a little faster than she meant to, and almost tipped over. She threw her weight to one side and managed to stay upright, but she had barely regained her balance when someone came dashing into the street, right in front of her.

Silvia swerved, slammed on her brakes, and managed to stop with her front wheel only inches from the idiot who had almost made her crash. Panting, she still had enough breath to let forth with an imaginative stream of curse words.

"I'm so sorry." Kate was leaning over, her hands on her knees, breathing hard. "I didn't see you."

"That much," Silvia said frostily, "is quite obvious."

Kate looked up. "Silvia," she said. "Oh, good. Now my night is complete."

"I did not want to run into you, either," Silvia said pointedly. "Or rather, I did not want to almost *kill* myself trying not to run into you!"

Kate clearly wasn't listening. She straightened up and glanced down the deserted street, looking as bewildered as if she had just appeared from another world. "I'm lost," she said, almost as if she were talking to herself. She had lifted one hand to push her wet hair out of her face, and now stood motionless, still holding her hand to her head.

This was not the superior Kate of the seminar room, or the radiant Kate who had been making Silvia's plot develop far more successfully than she had hoped. In fact, this Kate looked miserable and frightened and—

"Completely lost."

Silvia bit her lip in exasperation as a small, and most unwelcome, spark of compassion flickered in her heart. "No, you're not," she said crossly. "I've found you, haven't I?"

"I can't go back to the villa!" Kate was sitting in Silvia's room, wearing one of Signora di Napoli's robes and sipping a cup of tea. She felt much better after drying off, eating a bowl of soup in the family kitchen, and being fussed over by Silvia's mother and grandmother. "Not while *he* is there."

Silvia felt that little spark of fellow feeling flare brighter. No need to say who *he* was. So, Giacomo had broken Kate's heart. How like him.

Looking at Kate's face, however, Silvia felt a small twinge of . . . well, she couldn't quite identify the emotion, but it was most unwelcome.

She hurried on. "He is a terrible person," she agreed, and waited.

After a few moments, it was clear that Kate was going for dignified reserve instead of a girlish heart-to-heart. Fine. Silvia didn't have to hear all the details; she could imagine them readily enough. In fact, her imagination supplied the pictures in a series of widescreen, high-definition close-ups.

And, as she heard Kate give a little heartbroken sniff, she realized that she really didn't *want* to know what Giacomo had done. The uncomfortable twinge tweaked her again, harder this time.

"No need to worry," she said briskly. "My mother called the villa to let your father know you were safe. You can stay here tonight."

Kate gave her a wary glance over the rim of her teacup. "Really?"

Silvia shrugged. "Because of the storm. It will be easier than going back to the villa."

"That's very nice of you." Kate looked truly grateful. "I'm glad I don't have to go tonight and see . . . anyone."

Silvia's mind flashed back to that moment when her plan to trick Kate into falling in love with Giacomo had popped into her head. It had seemed wonderfully amusing at the time. And really, it was not *her* fault that Giacomo had behaved so horribly to Kate.

"So. We will go to the villa in the morning, problem solved."

"*One* problem solved." Kate prodded the sodden silk mass that had been her costume for the ball, which was now lying in a heap on the floor. "I think my shoes will be fine once they've dried, but my dress is ruined."

"Mmm, you're probably right." Silvia held up the dress and examined it with a practiced eye. "Maybe it could be steamed and pressed, but it will never really look the same."

"It doesn't matter," Kate said bleakly. "I'm not going, anyway."

She stared down at her empty teacup. Silvia's heart twisted inside her and, before she knew it, she was saying vehemently, "No, no, you mustn't give up now, you *must* go!"

Kate looked up, surprised, and no wonder, Silvia thought, biting her tongue. After all, Kate didn't know about the prank Silvia had set into motion, so she didn't know that Silvia was now feeling a very unfamiliar emotion. Remorse.

"I mean," Silvia added more calmly, "you can always get another dress."

Desperate to find something to talk about — something other than Giacomo — Kate glanced around the room.

Her attention was caught by a dress hanging on the wall. It was a truly wondrous dress: several shades of rosy pink, fuschia, and gold, with a profusion of ribbons and a double row of glass drops with silver backing.

"That dress is amazing," she said.

To her surprise, Silvia blushed and glanced down shyly and even smiled, just a tiny bit. "Thank you," she said. "I . . . well, I made it."

"*You*? Made *that*?" For a moment, Kate was too astonished to speak. Then she said, "But it's not black!"

Silvia waved one hand dismissively. "Black is just what I wear outside. I must, you know, warn the world that I am on my way. But on the inside — "

She jumped up and opened the closet door. There were so much clothing packed inside that it seemed as if the closet had exploded, with a rainbow of colors spilling out. "This is me, too."

Kate stared, openmouthed. "You made *all* those dresses?"

"*Si.*" Silvia shrugged, clearly trying for nonchalance, but just as clearly pleased by Kate's admiration.

"I want to be a fashion designer some day. I made that"—she nodded toward the dress on the wall—"after we visited the costume shop." She stood still for a moment, biting her lip and looking at the dress thoughtfully. Then she turned to look at Kate.

"And that is another problem solved!" she said triumphantly. "You will wear that dress. Try it on right now, but I'm sure it will fit you."

"I don't know if I can wear that," Kate began, stealing another glance at the dress. It was so bright, so eye-catching, so attention-grabbing!

Silvia was still giving her that long, assessing look, her head tilted to one side. "Tomorrow," she said, "I will take you to my hairdresser, Giulia. Your hair is too long, too heavy. I'm sure it would be curly if you cut it short."

"Um, well, I don't know," Kate began. Things seemed to be moving rather quickly here.

Silvia ignored this. "Giulia is a genius, you will see."

"But I'm not even sure about the dress. Really, it's so nice of you and the dress is completely gorgeous, but . . ." But it looked like a dress that would be, onstage, under a spotlight, the focal point for every eye in the room. "It doesn't look like me at all."

"That is exactly why you must wear it," Silvia replied. "You will look stunningly beautiful, and you will make every man at the ball fall in love with you! And that," she finished with great satisfaction, "will show Giacomo!"

Something about her utter certainty made Kate feel reckless and brave.

"Okay," she said quickly, before she could have second thoughts. "You're right. I'll do it."

Act V

Villa Marchese seemed to vibrate with anticipation on the night of the costume ball. The air was sweetly scented with roses and lilies, freshly picked from the garden. Candle flames glowed and dipped in the warm night breeze that blew through open windows.

Guests moved across the floor in a stately fashion, their movements made slow and graceful by the elaborate costumes they wore. Women were dressed in silk gowns; men wore doublets and plumed hats; and everyone wore jewels that winked in the soft, shimmering light. Waiters in black tie moved through the crowd, offering drinks and food. A group of musicians sat in a secluded corner and played lively music on period musical instruments.

Laughter, conversation, and the expectant murmur of people having a good time rose and fell in the room like waves.

Giacomo leaned against the wall, arms crossed over his chest. Occasionally he exchanged polite nods with one of the guests, but he was careful to keep his face expressionless. In the midst of all this celebration, his mood was black, his heart was broken, and his future empty.

Only the sight of his grandmother cheered him. A foot shorter than anyone in the room, she stalked through the crowd, wearing a funeral black gown and striking the floor at every step with her silver-topped black cane, a small spot of spectral gloom in the middle of the night's fizzing joy.

As she moved out of his sight, Benno rushed up, looking so cheerful that Giacomo could have hit him. "*Ciao*, Giacomo! You know what I've discovered? Parties are fantastic when you don't have to wait on people. I just saw Alessandro and told him to bring me a drink! Ha! Of course, he has no sense of humor so he'll probably spill it on me, but it was worth it to see the look on his face!" He raised himself up on his toes to peer around the room. "Have you seen Lucy?"

"No."

"Oh." Benno's eyes moved around the room. "What about Silvia? Or Tom?"

"No."

"Well, have you seen—"

"*No!*" Giacomo pushed himself away from the wall and glared at his friend, who looked back with an expression of mild surprise.

"What's wrong? You look like you're attending an execution." Benno gave Giacomo a friendly little shove with his shoulder. "Come on, cheer up! This is a party!"

"Yes, I know," Giacomo said, biting off each word. "But I don't happen to feel like—"

He stopped, his attention caught by something across the room. Benno raised his eyebrows, then turned to see what Giacomo was staring at so intently.

It was Kate, descending the grand staircase, her head held high, her eyes sparkling. She was wearing a dress that was a swirl of fuchsia, pink, and gold. Her hair had been cut; a short bob of curls had replaced the long, serious braid.

Benno's eyes widened. "*È bellissima!* She is beautiful."

"Yes," Giacomo said. "She is."

As she reached the floor, one of the older

Shakespeare Scholars—was it Jonathan?—rushed up to greet her. She smiled at him as if she'd been waiting her whole life to see him. Giacomo couldn't believe it. They used to joke about how serious Jonathan was! He saw Jonathan whisper something in Kate's ear. She gave him a laughing glance from under her eyelashes and put her hand on his arm.

Benno flicked a quick glance at his friend. "She flirts very well," he commented.

"Of course she does," Giacomo said bitterly. "I taught her."

Before Benno could respond, a bright fanfare of trumpets sounded, and Professoressa Marchese walked to the top of the grand staircase and held up her hand for silence.

"Dear friends, it is my pleasure to welcome you here tonight. We are celebrating the culmination of our very first Shakespeare Seminar, the first, I hope, of many."

There was polite applause at that. Giacomo didn't hear it; his eyes were fixed on Kate. At that moment, Kate seemed to feel Giacomo's steady gaze. She turned her head, her eyes met his, and she gave him one cool, proud look before turning her attention back to his mother.

"By chance, we have chosen an especially

appropriate evening for this celebration, for this is Midsummer's Eve, the longest day of the year," she continued. "After tonight, our days grow shorter and our nights longer. So let this night remind us to celebrate love, whenever it comes, in whatever form it appears, however enduring or fleeting it may be. For whether we search for love or are surprised by it, it always transforms us in ways we never expect." She lifted her glass. *"Salute!"*

Around the room, guests lifted their glasses and applauded.

Giacomo, his arms crossed, muttered something under his breath. Benno couldn't hear the words but decided it was wiser not to ask him to repeat them. Instead, he said, "We'd better find Tom. It's almost time for our fight scene."

Silvia was pacing up and down the hall outside the ballroom, staring at the floor. She was wearing a long dark jacket, gold brocade vest, dark pants, and knee-high boots. Her hair was pulled back in a neat pigtail. The expression on her face was serious and intent as she muttered a line under her breath, then pulled out her sword and attacked an invisible opponent.

Tom, who was hiding behind a particularly embarrassing statue of a naked goddess, thought

Silvia looked absolutely beautiful and slightly scary. As she did a series of feints down the hall in his direction, he cleared his throat and stepped in front of her.

"Idiot!" Silvia couldn't believe it. What were the odds of having two people in two days step right in front of her and almost die at her hands as a result of their own carelessness? "What are you doing?"

"I just, um, I just wanted to say good lu—"

Before he could finish the last word, she clapped her hand over his mouth. "*Stupido!*" she hissed. "Don't say that, it's bad luck to say that in the theater! Say 'break a leg.'"

"Oh, all right." Tom nodded humbly. "I just wanted to say, 'break a—'"

Once again he was interrupted, this time by Dan. "Come on then, it's your moment," he said. "And this is your cue."

"By my head, here come the Capulets," cried Benno as Benvolio.

"By my heel, I care not," sneered Silvia as Mercutio.

And they were off.

The guests chuckled at first when they saw the four swordsmen appear in the space that had just been cleared by Dan and a few waiters he had recruited to help with stage management. But after the first few lines were spoken, with an intensity that was mainly due to nerves but that was forcefully convincing nonetheless, the partygoers forgot their drinks and were caught up in the drama of the scene unfolding before them.

Tom said his first lines perfectly and, before he knew it, he and Silvia were circling each other, trading macho gibes as Tybalt and Mercutio. When Benno stepped forward to remind his friend Mercutio that it wasn't a great idea to get into a fight in the town square, since "here all eyes gaze on us," Tom actually felt a spurt of real anger that the reasonable Benvolio was getting in the way of a good fight.

Silvia seemed to have the same reaction. She spat out her next two lines: "Men's eyes were meant to look, and let them gaze; I will not budge for no man's pleasure, I."

But then Giacomo entered the scene, playing Romeo, and Tom knew he had to try to provoke this lover boy into a fight. Romeo, however, was not cooperating. Instead, he bleated on and on about how he had never done Tybalt any wrong, and how he really loved Tybalt, and how he thought Tybalt was great simply because his name was Capulet—until Tom felt that Tybalt would be totally justified in running Romeo through without even giving him a chance to draw his sword.

Fortunately, at that moment, Silvia stepped forward as Mercutio. After yelling at Romeo for his "vile submission" (inwardly, Tom cheered), she drew her sword, challenged Tybalt to a fight, and threw in a few other insults just to get things going.

Tom drew his sword. Everyone ignored Romeo, who was still trying to calm things down, and the fight began.

For a few seconds, he could hear small cries or astonished laughs from the audience, but then Tom didn't hear anything except his own breathing, the clang of swords, and the words that Silvia flung at him as they moved rapidly back and forth across the polished floor.

Tom could feel his heart racing the way it did during a close and hard-fought soccer game, and every sense seemed unnaturally keen. And even though he knew he was just acting and he did every move exactly as they rehearsed it, he no longer saw Silvia, only Mercutio.

He swung his sword. Mercutio parried it.

He slipped to the ground. Mercutio lunged forward with a thrust to the heart, and he deflected the blow, scrambling away to safety.

He could hear Romeo shouting something about how the prince had forbidden fighting on the Verona streets, then Romeo was yelling, "Hold, Tybalt! Hold, Mercutio!" and trying to get between them to break up the fight, and this was the moment he had to stab Mercutio. . . .

Tom hesitated.

Silvia made a face at him over Romeo's shoulder. Still Tom didn't move.

"Hurry up, Tom!" Giacomo muttered. "Kill her."

But Silvia was Silvia again, not Mercutio, and Tom couldn't move.

"Imbecile!" Silvia hissed as she slipped around Giacomo and pretended to throw herself on the point of Tom's sword.

And then Tom was running away through the crowd until he reached the hall, where he stopped to watch Silvia saying Mercutio's great last speech — "A plague o' both your houses!" — and, as she had promised, dying beautifully.

The applause was still rippling through the crowd but, as instructed by Professoressa Marchese, none of the actors stayed to acknowledge it.

"The sense that anything can happen at any moment will be completely ruined if we keep stopping for you to take bows," she had said. "Finish your scene and leave the stage quickly. A good motto for the theater as well as everything else in life."

After a hurried congratulations, Giacomo and Benno ran off to get something to eat, and Tom was left alone with Silvia.

"You remembered all your lines," she said as she pulled the rubber band off her pigtail and shook out her hair. "Impressive."

"You were great," he said.

"Of course," she said. "I even saved you there at the end when you froze into a statue. What happened, did you suddenly get stage fright?"

"No, I—" He stopped. He sensed that it would be unwise to say that he could not bear to kill her; he already knew she thought he was foolish, but that could make him look like a complete simpleton. He tried to figure out how to finish that sentence. Nothing came to mind.

Silvia eyed him sarcastically. "Oh, no, it's happening again. Maybe I should call a doctor. Perhaps you have contracted some rare disease that makes you lose the power of speech. Perhaps—"

"I really like you," he blurted out.

It took Silvia three heartbeats to process that statement. Tom knew this because he could feel his heart thudding in his chest and, for lack of anything better to do, started counting. One. Two. Three—

"Rrrreeeaalllly," Silvia said in that mocking way she had, rolling her *R*s and stretching out the word as far as possible.

He took a deep breath. "Yes. Look, I can't write poetry or sing a song to tell you how I feel. I'm not even that good at regular talking. I'm sure you think I'm just a dumb jock, but I know how I feel, even if I would rather play football than give some kind of flowery speech, and I also know that I would always treat you right and I wouldn't flirt with other girls, and if that is the kind of guy you want, then you should have me."

She stared at him, one hand on her hip, her head tilted in disbelief. "I haven't heard you say that many words all month."

"Yeah, well." He looked shy. "I've been practicing."

"Hmmph." She seemed skeptical, but she was still standing there. Tom thought that was a good sign. "So you've told me why I should like you, but you haven't said what you like about me."

"Okay, well." Tom stopped to consider this. "I think that you're sweet." He looked her over: the wild hair, the glinting eyes, the curling lip, and added, "Deep down inside, where no one can see it."

"*Sweet,*" she repeated, spitting out the word as if it tasted like castor oil.

He took a deep breath. "And I like your ears."

A look of surprise flashed across her face. "My *ears*?"

"Yes. They look like little shells." Silvia was looking at him with amazement. "Hasn't anyone ever told you that you have perfect ears?"

In fact, no one ever had. But Silvia had often thought that they should. Secretly, she had always considered her ears one of her undisputed charms.

"Go on," she said.

"And I like your footsteps," he said, encouraged. "They sound so light and happy."

Her *footsteps*? Who noticed something as inconsequential about a person as her footsteps? Tom was an idiot.

"When I heard you run down the stairs," he went on, "I knew that you were really a cheerful person, even though you act like you're not."

Tom thought she was *cheerful*? He was a moron.

She opened her mouth to set him straight, but he had taken her hand in his and was looking earnestly into her eyes and babbling on about something. What was he saying?

"—so, you see, you have to give me a chance."

He met her disbelieving stare and nodded firmly. "You must give me a chance," he said. He said it in a resounding tone, as if he were a four-star general giving her an order. "You *must*."

He was commanding *her*, Silvia! Clearly he was insane.

Still, she felt dizzy. "And why is that?" she asked faintly.

He pulled a letter from his doublet and handed it to her.

She looked down at the envelope, which was covered with her own black scrawl.

"Because Juliet told you to."

Benno frowned with concentration as he counted under his breath.

"Step down, two, three, step up, two, three, then turn, then turn, then step to the right . . ."

The bright sound of trumpets, horns, and drums sounded through the room as the Shakespeare Scholars moved with stately grace through an Elizabethan dance.

So far, Benno had not tripped, stumbled, turned the wrong way or run into anyone. He was, he congratulated himself, finally getting the hang of it.

He risked a quick glance at the others. Giacomo

was staring unhappily at Kate, who was grandly ignoring him. Benno gave a mental shrug. Something had happened there, that was clear, but what had happened was a mystery.

Now Tom — Tom was beaming as happily as if he'd just made the Milan starting lineup. Silvia was looking uncharacteristically bemused and — Benno squinted — yes, she was even smiling slightly. Before he could consider this puzzling sight, they had reached the point where the two lines of dancers faced each other and took a step to the right. He focused and . . . *yes!* Another hurdle overcome.

Now he was stepping forward to clasp hands with Kate and guide her through the next steps.

"You're doing great," she murmured.

"Thank you," he said, gratified.

They did the little step and hop to the side that had so often foxed Benno in the past. This time, he didn't slip or lurch off balance, so, with a great sense of achievement, he did the little skip-hop in the other direction and met Kate again. They turned and, still holding hands, moved together in that tricky one-two-three section. Benno turned his attention back to his feet.

When he looked back up, they were doing that circle thing, and he and Kate were moving clockwise in the outer circle while Giacomo and Lucy moved counterclockwise in the inner circle.

Lucy gave Benno a quick wink, and he grinned. Then it was time to take more of those tricky steps — up, two, three, down, two, three — so all he could do was glance back over his shoulder to see if he could catch her eye again.

But instead, he saw Giacomo, his head turned to keep Kate in sight until the music ended.

Romeo and Juliet's first meeting had already been played three times during the evening by other Shakespeare Scholars. Now that it was Benno and Lucy's turn, Lucy was relieved to see that most of the guests had apparently either already watched this particular scene or had no interest in it to begin with. As she approached the fountain where Professoressa Marchese had placed the scene, she saw that their audience was only a half-dozen people, all of whom seemed more focused on their plates of food than on the acting.

A spray of roses hung down from a trellis near the fountain, where water was splashing quietly. Lanterns hung from the trees, gold against the green darkness. Fireflies flitted through the air. Lucy saw Benno waiting for her, shifting nervously from foot to foot. She managed to smile at him, but her hands were shaking and she felt as if she might faint. He gave her a ghost of a grin in return, then took her hand and said, "If I profane with my unworthiest hand this holy shrine, the gentle sin is this: My lips, two blushing pilgrims, ready stand to smooth that rough touch with a tender kiss."

She just had time to note with surprise that Benno had not only said the words perfectly, but that he sounded as if he actually understood them. And then it was her turn.

She took a deep breath to calm her fluttering nerves. "Good pilgrim, you do wrong your hand too much, which mannerly devotion shows in this, for saints have hands that pilgrims' hands do touch, and palm to palm is holy palmers' kiss."

Benno's stage fright seemed to have vanished. As she finished, he was looking deeply into her eyes and smiling, ever so slightly. For the first time, she noticed that he had a dimple. How had she over-looked that during all those soccer practices?

"Have not saints lips, and holy palmers, too?" he asked. *Don't saints and pilgrims have lips, too?*

And with a little shock, Lucy realized that not only did she understand the words, she was feeling them, too. She said Juliet's next line with just a hint of teasing reproach: "Ay, pilgrim, lips that they must use in prayer."

This was not the answer Romeo wanted. He became a little more insistent. "O, then dear saint, let lips do what hands do. They pray; grant thou, lest faith turn to despair." *Please kiss me, before my faith turns to despair.*

Well, *sure* I'll kiss you, Lucy thought, what a great idea. Just in time, she remembered that, although *she* was completely sold on this notion, Juliet was not yet convinced. "Saints do not move, though grant for prayers' sake." *Even when they're granting prayers, saints don't move.*

How true, Lucy thought, who suddenly felt quite sorry for the saints.

But Romeo had an answer for that. "Then move not," Benno said, with the triumphant air of one winning an argument, "while my prayer's effect I take." *Then don't move while I act out my prayer.*

And he leaned forward and kissed her.

During rehearsals, they had kissed lightly, a peck on the lips to mark the spot; then they had waited to hear Dan's feedback on their acting. They had never really, truly kissed. And now, as Lucy closed her eyes, she thought, What a terrible, terrible waste. . . .

Benno pulled away from her. She opened her eyes

and blinked as he said, "Thus from my lips, by thine, my sin is purged."

Unbelievably, Juliet had enough presence of mind for a witty comeback. "Then have my lips the sin that they have took." *Our kiss might have purged your sin, but now the sin is on my lips.*

Benno grinned. "Sin from lips?" he asked teasingly. "O trespass sweetly urged! Give me my sin again."

This time Lucy leaned forward and they kissed again. And this time Lucy had to pull away to say the last line: "You kiss by th' book." What Juliet meant, Dan had explained, was that Romeo kissed very well, as if he had studied how to do it, and now Lucy had to agree with this interpretation.

Winnie had been assigned the task of standing under the trees all night and saying the nurse's line that would get Juliet offstage and end the scene, a task that she did with a scowling ill grace. As Lucy and Benno stared at each other, she called out in a disgruntled voice, "Madam, your mother craves a word with you," and Lucy ran off.

She stopped after a few feet and heard Winnie slap her script closed and say irritably, "Well, thank goodness that's finally over with! I'm going to get something to eat!" The few onlookers applauded politely and began drifting away. Lucy stayed in the shadows, breathless.

How had she missed Benno? He had been right under her nose for the last four weeks! How had she not noticed his cute grin or his expressive dark eyes or — for heaven's sake! — that dimple in his left cheek? How had she neglected all those chances she had had to kiss him?

"You were wonderful," he whispered in her ear.

She jumped and turned to see Benno standing before her, as if her thoughts had conjured him.

"No," she said slowly. "*We* were wonderful."

His face lit up. "Lucy. When I wrote you that letter —"

"You?" she said, astounded. "You wrote that?"

"Well . . . I mostly wrote it," he said, striving for honesty.

She smiled up at him. "And here we've been hanging out for days and you've been teaching me soccer, which I never in a million, billion years thought I would play, and you've been so patient with me and I've been just going along like a silly goose, never even seeing what's right there in front of me, clear as day and . . . Benno, I'm sorry!" She squeezed his hand even harder, too caught up in what she was saying to notice how he winced. Tears sparkled in her eyes from an excess of emotion. "Oh, that doesn't even make any sense, does it? No, I know I'm kind of giddy and people don't always understand what I say, but—"

"Not to worry, *amore mio*," Benno whispered as he eased his hand out of hers to touch her face. "You have always made perfect sense to me."

"But soft! What light through yonder window breaks? It is the east, and Juliet is the sun."

A short flight of stone steps led up from the terrace to a back door, where there was a small landing with a balustrade. This was Juliet's balcony. Kate leaned forward as Giacomo launched into Romeo's first long speech. She could smell the pink and white flowers that starred the ground, and the spicy scent of the red geraniums that spilled out of pots lining the stone railing. A breeze ruffled her short hair like a benediction, and Kate felt her eyes tear up because this night was so beautiful, and so sad.

Giacomo was nearing the end of his speech. "Oh, that I were a glove upon that hand that I might touch that cheek!" he said, looking up at her with longing.

"Ay, me!" Kate sighed a very Juliet sigh, and then let her thoughts drift as Giacomo started declaiming his next seven lines.

She had let herself believe in him, that was the

problem. She thought that Jerome had cured her, but somehow, somewhere, she had lost her way. She had fallen under his spell, and she had only herself to blame.

Ah, it was her cue.

She leaned over the balcony and said, "O Romeo, Romeo! Wherefore art thou Romeo? Deny thy father and refuse thy name. Or, if thou wilt not, be but sworn my love, and I'll no longer be a Capulet."

Her Romeo seemed stunned by this suggestion. He turned aside and said, "Shall I hear more, or shall I speak at this?"

Kate recited her next lines like a girl newly in love. Then she looked at Giacomo and remembered how he had pretended to be in love with her. A surge of righteous anger gave energy to her words as she looked him in the eye and said, "But farewell compliment! Dost thou love me? I know thou wilt say 'ay,' and I will take thy word. Yet if thou swear'st thou mayst prove false. At lovers' perjuries, they say, Jove laughs. O gentle Romeo, if thou dost love, pronounce it faithfully."

As the scene went on, Kate's emotions made every line ring true. The memory of reading the letter he had sent to Lucy made her watch Romeo even more warily as he swore by the moon that his love was true. It sharpened her voice as she told him not to swear by the moon, since its shape and position were constantly changing. It drove her close to tears as she proclaimed, "Well, do not swear. Although I joy in thee, I have no joy of this contract tonight. It is too rash, too unadvised, too sudden, too like the lightning, which doth cease to be ere one can say 'It lightens.'"

And that, she thought, even as she continued saying her lines, is the real, honest-to-God truth of this love business.

The nurse called to Juliet from inside the bedroom. Kate sighed, disappeared long enough for Romeo to worry a bit about whether she would come back, then returned to deal briskly with a few administrative details about messengers and picking the time and place to be married.

Juliet, Kate reflected, was nothing if not practical. That, at least, she could admire.

The last few lines sped past. The scene had barely started, and it was already coming to a close.

She looked down as Giacomo's face, turned up toward hers. A tear slipped down her cheek as she said her last line.

"A thousand times good night!"

❁ ❁ ❁

She was running down the stairs to the terrace, barely hearing the applause, when a hand caught her wrist and swung her around.

"Kate. Tell me what's wrong."

"It doesn't matter." She tugged at her wrist, but he held tight. "Let me go."

"Not until you tell me why you are so upset."

Kate turned her head so that she didn't have to look at his face. She could see dancers in the ballroom, through the glass doors, and the flickering of candlelight. It was like looking at a stage set, warm and light and welcoming. The doors opened and the sound of music and laughter spilled outside as several people came out onto the terrace. An elderly woman beamed up at Giacomo. "You did marvelously well." She nodded at Kate. "Both of you did."

"*Grazie,*" Giacomo murmured.

"So nice of you to say so," Kate said.

Before Giacomo could draw breath, a young girl poked her head outside. "Your grandmother sent me to find you. She says the caterers have made a mess of her kitchen and she needs nutmeg right now and you must come and help her find it."

He ran his hands through his hair in frustration, but nodded, then turned to Kate. "I have to help her, otherwise she might use the chili peppers and we will be facing a real disaster. And anyway—" Another loud group of revelers interrupted them, this time reeling up to the terrace from the rose garden. "Anyway, we can't talk here. Will you meet me in the maze in fifteen minutes?"

Kate hesitated.

"Please."

The sight of Giacomo pleading was unexpectedly delightful. She nodded. "I'll meet you at Portia's statue. And if you're late, I won't bother waiting."

The sounds of the party gradually faded as Kate made her way through the dark garden, pushing aside an overgrown branch, stopping to pull a bramble that had caught her skirt. The air was cool and sweet with the scent of flowers, of damp earth, of green growing things; it was a night, she reflected bitterly, that some people would say was made for romance.

Some people, but not her. She knew better now. Love was simply a kind of madness, fed on moonbeams, and she had no need of it.

As if the night had heard her thought, a cloud drifted over the moon. Kate hesitated, but she could still see the path and she knew she wasn't far from the maze. It would certainly be easier to go forward than back to the villa. So she walked on more slowly until she stepped out of the trees into a clearing. The moon came out of the clouds and she saw the tall hedges, which now looked black in the night.

Somehow, the maze seemed more mysterious, more frightening than it had in the daylight, as if she could vanish into another world and be lost forever once she entered it.

But this was exactly the kind of moment, she thought, where a clear, rational mind was such an asset. Obviously this was merely an elaborate system of hedges, planted to entertain and amuse. Obviously there was nothing magical about it. Obviously she would not be spirited to another world, because there was just one world, this world, and she was firmly rooted in it.

She gave a brisk little nod of satisfaction as she worked that out in her mind. And then she stepped through the leafy opening and began walking. This time, she kept her right hand on the hedge and let it guide her as she walked, then ran, along the twisting path. Finally she burst into a clearing and stopped; her eyes closed as a wave of dizziness swept over her. After several deep breaths, she opened her eyes to see Shakespeare smiling down at her in the moonlight, and Kate realized that she had finally made it to the center of the maze.

It was an unusual portrayal of Shakespeare. He was young, for one thing, not the pudgy, balding man whose bust sat above his grave. He was caught in the act of taking a step, perhaps the first step of his first journey to London, before he knew what he would become. There was an air of expectation in his posture, a lively and interested expression on his face, a quill stuck jauntily over his ear, and an overall attitude of good humor, as if he found the world and all the people in it completely to his liking.

She made a face at him. "This is all *your* fault, you know," she whispered.

"Well met by moonlight, kind Kate." Giacomo stepped out of the shadows.

Kate turned her head at the sound of his voice, but stood absolutely still. In the darkness, she looked like a statue herself. "That's not the quote."

"Yes, I know, I was just—" He took a deep breath. "So. Here we are. In the center of the maze after all." Giacomo nodded toward the statue, but kept his eyes on her as he added lightly, "How did that happen?"

"I don't know!" Kate snapped. "I hate this maze! Every time I try to get anywhere I end up someplace else!"

Giacomo chuckled. "You sound just like Lucy."

She glared at him. "Well, if you want to be with her so much, why don't you just go back to the party?"

"What?" He frowned. "I *don't* want to be with her. Why in the world would you think that?"

She stopped and turned to face him. "Because you're in love with her."

"With *Lucy*?"

He saw a moment of doubt in her face, then her expression hardened.

"Oh, please," she said. "I saw the letter."

Giacomo shook his head slightly in confusion. "What letter?"

Kate raised one cynical eyebrow. "The one that quoted your favorite sonnet. The one that swore undying love. The one that was written in *your own handwriting*." She stared at him challengingly. "*That* letter."

His brow cleared. Ah, yes, of course, Benno's letter! An understandable mistake, and an easy remedy. "I can explain that."

"I'm sure you can," she said in an acidly sweet voice.

Giacomo felt a flare of resentment, which he quickly tamped down. "As a matter of fact," he said coolly, "I wrote it for Benno. *He's* the one who's fallen for Lucy. Not me."

He crossed his arms and stared back at her, satisfied to see her hesitate.

"You wrote it for Benno," she repeated. "Benno? *He's* in love with Lucy?"

"As I said." He waited, smug in the knowledge that he was, for once, completely in the right.

She eyed him warily. "But you were always paying her compliments—"

"Yes, that's what I do."

"You laughed at everything she said—"

"It's Lucy! How can one help but laugh?"

She gave him a narrow glance. "You couldn't keep your eyes off her!"

He made an exasperated gesture. "Kate! She's pretty, she's sweet, she's adorable, but . . . Lucy? Please! I was just flirting!" He smiled at her, his most charming smile. "It didn't *mean* anything."

She tilted her head to one side and gave him a long, thoughtful look.

"It was just a game, then," she said.

"Exactly," he replied, pleased to have made his point.

She nodded. "So when you were flirting with *me*—"

Too late, he saw his mistake. "A game that you played as well," he pointed out quickly. "And that's not the same thing at all, because—"

"I'm sure." She cut him off. "Well, now that we've

got that cleared up, let's go back to the party. This is my last night in Italy, after all."

As she turned to go, her long skirt swirling around her ankles, Giacomo felt his heartbeat quicken.

She was leaving. Tomorrow.

"Wait." He blocked her way.

He had said good-bye to a lot of girls. It had never made him unhappy.

"Why?" She pulled away.

"Because this is our last night," he began, then stopped when he realized she wasn't listening.

Instead, she was pacing around the grassy enclosure, muttering to herself. "After everything that happened, I can't believe I actually fell—"

She stopped.

"What?" He moved in front of her, his gaze intent.

Kate lifted her chin to meet his eyes, but she didn't answer.

He prompted her. "You can't believe you fell . . ."

"For your act," she snapped.

He felt a wave of anger wash over him. "It wasn't an *act*, it was—"

He stopped.

"What?"

Tell her the truth, Giacomo. He imagined Rosaline's voice, whispering in his ear.

He opened his mouth to speak but, at that moment, someone opened a door at the villa, releasing a swell of laughter and music. Kate turned in the direction of the noise, and there was something about the interested tilt of her head and the sight of her profile, pale against the green darkness, that silenced him.

Then the door closed. The music was snuffed out like a candle. The moment was gone.

She turned her attention back to him. "You were about to say?"

But he had no idea what he would have said; in fact, he didn't have a single useful thought in his head. So he shrugged and fell back on what he knew. "Doubt thou the stars are fire, doubt that the sun doth move, doubt truth to be a liar, but never doubt—"

"Stop it!" she said. "Honestly, Giacomo, do you ever just say what you mean, without *quoting* all the time?"

"Fine," he said, his own voice rising to match hers. "You are the most maddening girl I have ever known. No"—he corrected himself—"you are the most maddening *person*. I'm including everyone, male *and* female, that I have ever met in my entire life! You're irritating and argumentative. And so, of *course,*" he finished with irritation, "*you're* the one I had to fall in love with."

"You . . . what did you say?"

He glared at her. "I said I love you."

An uncertain look flashed across her face and was gone. She curled her lip. "Right. I'm sure you've never said *that* before."

"Well." He considered this. "Well, I've never *meant* it."

For a long moment, Kate stood frozen.

Then she picked up her skirts and spun around, running away from him. He went after her, slipping on the grass and cursing under his breath as he imagined her slipping into the maze, lost to him forever. . . .

At the last moment, he caught her arm and pulled her back.

"Let me *go*." She used the momentum to whirl around and push him, and he stumbled backward. He was still holding on to Kate, though, so she lost her balance and they both fell hard to the ground.

All the breath left his body. She had landed on top of him, her elbow slamming into his stomach.

Giacomo felt the cool grass beneath his head as he gasped for air.

"Are you all right?" Kate's face hovered over his, silhouetted against the starry sky. She pushed herself off him, her hands on the ground on either side of his head. "Giacomo?"

He shook his head. He couldn't speak.

"I'm sorry," she said.

He closed his eyes with relief as air finally rushed into his lungs.

"Giacomo?"

He didn't say anything. He was enjoying the novelty of breathing too much to talk.

She watched him for a moment. Then she asked softly, "Do you mean it now?"

He reached for her hand and put it on his heart.

She could feel it, thudding beneath her fingers.

Giacomo smiled up at her with the same question in his eyes. So Kate answered it with a kiss.

Epilogue

Kate and Giacomo stood hand in hand on the terrace in front of the ballroom windows, which glowed with light and color in the darkness. The music spilled out into the hushed night, a lively tune that had Kate's toes tapping under her silk gown.

Then she caught sight of herself in the window, her short curls shining in the moonlight, her face lit with happiness. She blinked in surprise. She looked so different that she almost didn't recognize herself, and she seemed to hear the echo of Annie's voice, saying, "You will be *transformed*!"

In the reflection, Giacomo's eyes met hers.

"We should go inside," he said, "if we want to dance."

"I know," she said, but still she lingered, watching as the musicians started another song and a new dance began.

First, Tom and Silvia spun by, and Kate raised her eyebrows in surprise. Tom was leading Silvia with the confidence of a prince, while Silvia looked stunned, caught somewhere between delight and disbelief.

Then Lucy and Benno whirled past. Kate smiled to see Lucy shining with happiness and Benno dancing with a grace that seemed to amaze everyone, especially him.

And finally, Giacomo's mother and Kate's father swept grandly into view. Kate gasped at the sight of them, beaming at each other as if there was no one else in the room.

For one long, astonished moment, she simply stared at the scene in front of her. Then she burst out laughing.

"What is the joke?" Giacomo asked.

"I was just remembering something I was once told."

He gave her a questioning look, so she quoted, "Given enough time, even the impossible becomes possible." She nodded toward the dancers, who were circling the room once more. "It's a law of nature, apparently."

"Ah, yes?" Puzzled, he turned to gaze through the windows. Then comprehension dawned on his face, and he smiled down at her.

"Ah," he said, "Yes."

~✥~

Sarah enjoyed wearing her new black suede boots with the silver buckles. She enjoyed it very much indeed.

Author's Note

The Juliet Club (or Il Club di Giulietta, as it's known in Italy) was founded in Verona in 1972. Since then, the club has received thousands of letters every year from people of all ages around the world. The letters, which are all answered by volunteers, usually ask for love advice. Sometimes, however, they simply tell the letter writer's own love story.

To learn more about the Juliet Club, visit the Web site at www.julietclub.com.

If you'd like to write to Juliet, send your letter to:

Club di Giulietta
Via Galilei, 3
1-37133 Verona
Italy